# What Was I Thinking?

## by

## Donna Simonetta

*Rivers Bend Trilogy, Book 3*

**What Was I Thinking?**

Cover Art by *Kristian Norris*

The Wild Rose Press, Inc.
PO Box 708
Adams Basin, NY 14410-0708
Visit us at www.thewildrosepress.com

Publishing History
First Champagne Rose Edition, 2019
Print ISBN 978-1-5092-2905-5
Digital ISBN 978-1-5092-2906-2

*Rivers Bend Trilogy, Book 3*
Published in the United States of America

"I think about a lot of things."

She felt him stiffen up behind her, and Jason's tone of voice was defensive. She hadn't meant to hurt his feelings. "I know you do; I didn't mean anything by it. We poke at each other"—she shrugged—"it's kind of our thing."

His grip on her hand loosened, and then he took control of the dance, by twirling her until her back was pressed to his front, and he began to move sinuously in time to the rhythm. His breath tickled her ear, as he spoke right in it to be heard over the music. "We've got a thing, Moonbeam?"

Jason had ditched the tie and suit jacket after the wedding, and his body heat scorched her through his crisp white dress shirt. And man-oh-Maneschewitz, his lean, hard body felt good. Really good. The Marine might be bulked up, but Jason's body felt like it had been made for hers, which given their mutual antagonism, seemed like proof Fate was enjoying a good laugh at her expense. Against Lily's better judgment, her body melted into his warmth and began to move with his.

"Sure, we've got a thing," she said over her shoulder, and was irritated to hear a trace of breathlessness in her voice. She cleared her throat and continued, "Like that—you calling me Moonbeam, because you know it bugs me."

## Praise for Donna Simonetta and...

*A SWEETER SPOT*: "Do yourself a favor and get a copy. Then settle onto an old chair, get a cup of tea, and feel the warmth and love that flows through this book."

*~Peggy Jaeger, Author (5 Stars)*
~*~

*LOVE IS LOVELIER*: "Well-written, with a touch of humor and an interesting storyline. Love can truly be lovelier the second time around."

*~Iona Morrison, Author (5 Stars)*
~*~

*ANGELS FLY*: "A fun read! Two souls who belong together, with guardian angels working overtime behind the scenes to make sure it happens. By the end of the book, the destined lovers—Kelly and James—felt a bit like family. I was really pulling for their happily ever after. If you enjoy love stories with a supernatural twist, check out *ANGELS FLY*!"

*~Judith Sterling, Author (5 Stars)*

## Dedication

Once again…to Leo,
for everything you are and everything you do.
For AJ…
Ty and Grant's Happy-Ever-After was written
just for you!
Last, but not least, BIG THANKS to my sister Mary.
For all your insight into
being a special education teacher,
and for helping me get the scenes
involving Jason's dyslexia just right.

## Chapter 1

"Do you take this hunka hunka burning love to be your husband?" Elvis asked with an impressive lip curl.

"I do," Heather answered as she gazed into Mick's eyes.

Lily smiled at her friends. The happy couple may have chosen to elope to Vegas to be married by an aging Elvis impersonator, but they both approached the ceremony as solemnly as if the Archbishop of Canterbury were marrying them.

Elvis tossed his white, studded cape over his shoulders with a flourish, and pronounced them husband and wife, before launching into a heartfelt version of "Can't Help Falling in Love." Yeah, Lily definitely didn't remember the Archbishop doing that at Harry and Meghan's wedding.

As Mick and Heather shared a passionate first kiss, she felt her heart catch the tiniest bit. She didn't regret her decision to move to Rivers Bend, Virginia to take care of her niece, but sometimes she got a little lonely. And she couldn't deny she was a little envious of what the newly married Mr. and Mrs. Evans shared.

A light touch on her arm broke her out of her pity party, and she turned her head to see the beaming face of Mrs. Presley, who was a matronly woman of a certain age dressed most incongruously in a white leather mini dress, with a huge, bouffant brunette wig

1

perched on top of her head. Her white patent leather go-go boots reflected the twinkling fairy lights around them.

"We have another happy couple waiting, and we need to finish up Mr. and Mrs. Evans' paperwork. Do you think you could hurry them along?" she whispered, as she gestured toward the still kissing couple.

"Sure we can," Jason piped up and aimed one of his huge smiles at Grandma Priscilla Presley, who appeared to melt a little under its high voltage brightness. She blinked owlishly, and Lily worried the lady was going to pull off her underpants and throw them at Jason, the way she had probably done during Elvis's show back in the day. Jason Braden hadn't gotten his reputation as the heartbreaker of Rivers Bend, Virginia for nothing.

Jason tapped Mick on the shoulder and asked in a light, breezy tone, "Hey man, do you think you can stop mauling my sister long enough to sign the marriage certificate and make this thing legal?"

"Right...yeah...sorry," Mick said completely without remorse, and never taking his attention off his bride, who looked retro-fabulous in her fifties style white lace cocktail dress.

Heather blushed and spoke to Mrs. Presley. "Sorry about that—we'll get out of your way."

"Don't worry, dearie, I like to see happy couples in love. I wouldn't run a wedding chapel if I didn't, but we do have a schedule to keep, so if we could go into the other room and sign your paperwork..."

Heather reached for her bouquet, which Lily had been holding as part of her Maid of Honor duties. Lily took one last whiff of the purple and white blossoms, which smelled like spring, before she handed off the bouquet to the bride.

"I don't know how you managed to find lilacs in November," Lily said to Mick.

The groom shrugged. "It took a little doing, but they're Heather's favorite flower. Nothing is too much for my bride."

Mick placed his hand on the small of Heather's back and guided her as they followed Mrs. Elvis into the smaller chamber off the chapel. It was such a gentlemanly gesture; some might find it old-fashioned, but Lily liked Mick's solicitude for his new wife. No one could doubt for a minute that strong-as-steel Heather Braden was perfectly capable of taking care of herself, but now Mick and she were a team—looking out for each other.

Jason followed them without even a glance in her direction. Lily followed the rest of their little bridal party. She blinked against the blinding whiteness of the room, and swiped at the fake roses that bounced back in her face after Jason had shoved them out of his way.

"No, really, don't worry about me. Jerkwad!" she muttered under her breath.

Mick and Heather signed the legal documents on the ornate podium provided for the task, and then Mrs. Elvis hustled them to a trellised arch at the front of the room, which was also covered in fake red roses, like everything else in the room.

Mrs. Elvis reached up to position Mick's shoulders toward the camera on a tripod positioned in front of the trellis. She stepped back to look through the camera at the new pose. "There! That's better." She called to Jason and Lily without looking back at them, "You two need to sign as witnesses, and then we can get some shots of all four of you together."

Jason picked up the white pen, wrinkled his nose, and swiped at his face, where he was tickled by the huge white feather on the top of the pen. He frowned as he studied the paper. His usual sunny expression vanished, his blue-gray eyes clouded over, as his gaze darted around the document.

Lily cocked her head as she watched. A special education teacher, she'd often seen students with reading issues look at a test in just that way; it seemed as if Jason had no idea where he was supposed to sign his name. But Rivers Bend was the most gossip-happy place on earth, and free-spirited ladies-man Jason Braden was a favorite source of gossip. If he was dyslexic there's no way Lily wouldn't have heard about it. At length. And from multiple sources.

Jason looked up at her, and when he saw her looking at him, he fixed his huge, bright smile firmly in place, even if it didn't reach all the way to his eyes. The feather bobbed, as he held the pen out to her. "Ladies first."

Confused by his mood swing, and a little stunned by being on the receiving end of a Jason Braden charm offensive for the first time, she frowned and said, "Okay."

She stepped up to the podium, and the full skirt of the vintage 1950s red dress she'd bought at a funky consignment shop, back when she lived in Baltimore, brushed against Jason, as he stayed close to the podium rather than stepping away to make room for her. She took the pen, and found the spot where she was supposed to sign, and did so. She felt his body heat burn against her back, as Jason leaned in even closer and peered intently at where she was signing.

Not sure if he wanted, or even needed, her help, she tapped the pen on the line where he needed to sign, and felt the tension release from his body, where it was pressed against hers.

"Your turn," she said as she passed him the pen.

"Hurry it up, y'all! We need you for pictures!" Heather's happy voice called from under the arch.

Jason scrawled his name on the paper with a flourish, and answered his sister in true brotherly fashion, "Hold your horses, Heather! We're coming—jeez!"

Lily craned her neck to look up at the much taller man beside her. Any clouds that had marred his sunny expression lifted as he looked up from the marriage certificate to glance at his sister. This time he did place his hand on her back, where the fitted bodice gave way to the flared skirt of her dress, for the short walk to join the happy couple. His touch burned her skin through the silk. Oh no. She was not going to fall victim to Jason's charms. He'd been a jerk to her since he met her, but her traitorous body seemed willing to forget all of that after one smile and a little touch. Stupid, fickle body.

"Maid of honor next to the bride, best man next to the groom," Mrs. Elvis commanded.

They assumed their positions, and Heather turned her head to grin at Lily. "This place is all I hoped for and more!"

Mrs. Elvis adjusted her bouffant wig, which had slipped to lean precariously off to the left side, and said, "Happy to hear it, dearie, tell all your friends about us. Now everyone look this way and say 'Blue Hawaii'."

"Blue Hawaii," the four of them called out in unison, as she clicked the camera.

"Lovely! Now bride and groom, stay where you are. Best man, move next to the maid of honor."

Jason moved over beside her, as Mrs. Elvis looked through the camera mounted on a tripod. "Get in nice and close, so I can get all of you in the picture."

And just like that, Jason snaked his arm around her waist, and used his huge hand to pull her close and tuck her into his side. He felt so warm and hard-muscled, and she fit perfectly. She couldn't help but sink into him the tiniest bit. He smelled like soap and sunshine, and Lily could see why the female population of Rivers Bend all swooned before his charms.

"Perfect!" Mrs. Elvis trilled. "You're every bit as handsome a couple as the bride and groom! Remember us when you're ready to tie the knot."

Quick as lightning, they jerked apart at those words. If Mrs. Elvis thought they were a couple, she'd loosened her guard a little too much. Although, she missed the warmth and strength of his body next to her, and frowned in disgust at the feeling.

"Oh no, we're not a couple," Lily said.

"No, no, no, no." Jason spoke firmly at the same time.

"As enjoyable as it is watching these two squirm over your assumption they're a couple, are we done here, ma'am?" Mick asked Mrs. Elvis with a grin. "I've arranged a wedding dinner for us back at the Venetian, and the car will be here to pick us up in a couple of minutes."

\*\*\*\*

They stepped out of the wedding chapel and into

the neon glare that was night in Las Vegas.

Mick walked to the curb and looked in both directions. "I don't see our limo; it should've been here by now. Sorry." He pulled out his phone. "Let me call and check on it."

Lily shivered in the unexpected chill of the night air. Heather's dress had long, lace sleeves, so she didn't look cold, but her own dress had tiny cap sleeves, and there was a definite nip in the air.

"Don't you have a coat, or one of those shawl things women always seem to have with them?" Jason asked as she wrapped her bare arms around her waist in an attempt to keep warm.

"No. I didn't expect it be this cold. I mean, Las Vegas is in the desert, right? And deserts are hot."

Jason shrugged out of his dark sports coat. "Not at night. The temperatures can really drop after dark at this time of year." He draped his jacket over her shoulders. "Haven't you ever been out west before?"

Given his past rudeness to her, Lily was suspicious of his sudden kindness, but was really chilly, and the coat retained a lot of his lovely body heat. She slid her arms into the silky-lined sleeves, and enjoyed both the warmth and the way the jacket smelled like Jason.

*Huh.*

Where was this interest in his scent coming from? Normally she had no use for Jason. He was so rude to her but a player with every other woman in his orbit. She'd always assumed he was shallow and not the brightest of the Braden clan. So why did she suddenly feel like a shy bookworm who'd been given the popular boy's letterman jacket?

Jason stood behind her and rubbed the top of her

arms to help warm her up, and Lily admitted to herself she wasn't that cold. She was from Connecticut after all, and had grown up in a much colder climate than even a November night in Vegas had to offer, but she liked the little flutter in her belly Jason's touch stirred. She smiled over her shoulder at him.

A bright flash of light jerked her attention back forward, where the bride lowered her smartphone from her face to reveal a cheeky grin. "You two look so cute together! This picture is so going online."

"Won't it give away where we are, and what you're doing?" Jason asked.

Maybe he wasn't as dumb as she thought he was. Heather and Mick had opted to elope, and were probably going to be up to their necks in hot water with their respective families when they got back east. It was the one argument that might actually stop Heather from posting this very couple-like picture of Jason and Lily.

Heather snapped her fingers. "Dang! You're right. Well, after we tell the families, I'm posting it. It's a great picture of you both."

Mick disconnected his call and walked toward them as he slipped his phone into the interior pocket of his suit jacket. He was impeccably dressed, as always. In some ways Heather and Mick seemed like an unlikely couple, but they went together like peanut butter and jelly; although her normally tomboyish friend stepped up her game and looked beautiful and chic tonight.

"Our ride is stuck in traffic. The driver said he's a couple of minutes away."

Anxious to get Heather away from any misguided matchmaking efforts she might have, Lily held out her hands and launched into a subject sure to distract any bride. "Give me your phone; I'll get some pictures of you two by the wedding chapel sign while we wait for the car."

"Oh! Great idea!" Heather handed over her phone and dropped the subject of Jason and her making a cute couple. Jason Braden and her a couple? Pfft—not bloody likely.

Chapter 2

"To Mrs. Evans," Lily lifted her Manhattan in a toast.

Heather clinked her Martini glass to Lily's cocktail and grinned from ear to ear.

They were waiting for the guys, who were checking into the hotel rooms and getting their stuff situated. Mick and Heather would spend the night in the bridal suite Lily had shared with Heather the night before, while Lily's stuff needed to be moved to a new room for the night.

"This worked out so well. I can't believe we pulled it off without anyone in Rivers Bend knowing. Thanks again for being my maid of honor; I couldn't have done any of this without you."

Lily took a sip of her cocktail, and waved her other hand dismissively. "Thank you for asking me. I know I had to be like your fourth choice, after Bethanne, your sister, and Magda, but I'm having a blast!"

"Bethanne went to her parents' on Hilton Head for Thanksgiving. She would've been able to keep a secret, which could be why we've been friends since we were kids. But, my sister Deirdre?" Heather shook her head and took a sip. "No way could she keep a secret, and since she owns the only café in town, the news would have been all over in no time. They give away the latest gossip for free with every purchase of a latte and a muffin at the Nosh Pit. If my sister or Magda had come with us, there is no way this wedding could have been a black op. My whole family would've known in no time, and then it would've turned into the type of huge wedding I didn't want. Not to mention, it would suck attention away from Jeff and Magda's wedding, which I really didn't want to do."

"But your brother can keep a secret?"

"Jason can. I'm not sure about Jeff, which is why I ruled out Magda. Now they're engaged, I couldn't ask her to take off for Vegas Thanksgiving weekend without telling Jeff where she was going. It was such a relief when you said 'yes'. I was afraid you wouldn't be able to come, because of Hadley."

Lily relocated to Rivers Bend to be guardian to her niece, when Hadley's mom, Lily's half-sister, Gloria, married for the umpteenth time, and moved to an unstable country, where her latest husband was ambassador. It wasn't a safe place for Hadley to live, so Lily agreed to move to the Bend to take care of the girl. She loved her niece to pieces, but she still missed her previous home, job, and friends in Baltimore.

Lily reached for a bowl of peanuts on the bar, and popped a couple in her mouth. They hadn't gotten to the wedding dinner yet, and she was hungry. She savored their crunchy salty goodness before answering, "Hadley is going to spend the weekend with her father in Richmond, so I would've either had to hit I-95 traffic, with everyone else on the east coast, to drive to see my folks in Connecticut, or come to Vegas for your wedding. Hmm…let me think…bumper-to-bumper traffic versus partying in Vegas and first-class seats on the plane, courtesy of your amazing groom? It was a no-brainer."

Heather's eyes grew soft at the mention of Mick. "Mmm…First class was heavenly."

Okay. Maybe it was memories of extra legroom and free champagne in first class that had her looking so dreamy.

Lily gulped down her second handful of peanuts and said, "Here come the guys."

Heather grinned. "Oh, do you mean my husband?"

Lily rolled her eyes. "When do you think you might get over saying 'my husband' in that goofy tone of voice?"

Heather smiled as she took a sip of her martini. "I'm not sure, maybe by our fiftieth anniversary."

"Hello, Wife," Mick said as he approached.

Heather turned, and Mick kissed her as if it had been years since they'd seen each other, and he'd been at war the whole time.

"Yeah, this 'husband' and 'wife' crap isn't getting old at all," Jason grimaced at Lily.

Heather reached around Mick to smack her brother's arm. "Lily just said something very similar. Back off, both of you cynics! You knew you were signing on for a romantic elopement when you agreed to come with us. Sappy talk is part of the bargain."

Mick raised a finger to get the bartender's attention. "I'd like to settle up the tab for these ladies, we have a dinner reservation to make."

"Yes sir," the young man replied, and slid a slip of paper across the bar to Mick.

As he signed the check to his suite, and pulled out his wallet to leave a cash tip, Mick said, "Something came up that wasn't part of the bargain with tonight's room situation."

The warning tone in his voice made Heather sit up straight on her barstool and frown. "What's wrong?"

"The bridal suite is all set," Mick said with a reassuring squeeze to Heather's hand.

"But the hotel can't find the reservation for one of the other rooms, and it's full to the rafters between the holiday weekend and some convention. Bottom line, it looks like you're gonna be bunking with me tonight, Moonbeam," Jason said.

Caught mid-sip by his words, Lily felt bourbon burn her sinuses, as she coughed and sputtered.

Jason pounded her on the back. "Easy there, Moonbeam."

"Stop calling me that, and quit whaling on my back! I'm fine."

Hmm…might have been a more convincing statement if her voice wasn't still raspy from choking on her cocktail.

"But I got a confirmation number when I made the reservation," Heather said with a frown.

"I know you did, oh-organized-one, but it doesn't change the fact there's no room at the inn," Jason said. "It's only one night, and there are two queen-sized beds in my room. It's not like Moonbeam is going to be sleeping on the street."

The two women picked up their drinks, and Mick herded their group toward the exit. "Our table is ready, has been for a while now; arguing with the front desk has made us late. Let's get moving, and we can discuss it over dinner."

Lily saw Heather's furrowed brow and the mulish set to her friend's mouth. The bride was going to delay her own wedding dinner, and by extension, her wedding night with her smokin' hot new husband, all to do battle with the hotel over her room. Lily couldn't let it happen—no Maid of Honor worth her salt could.

"It's fine, Heather, there are two beds, and it's only one night."

Jason rubbed his jawline. "Gee, I thought I heard someone say the very same thing a couple of minutes ago."

Heather still frowned, and Mick steered her through the lobby, with a hand placed on the small of her back, away from the reception desk and toward the restaurant. "You heard Lily—she's fine with it."

He leaned down and whispered something in Heather's ear, which set her to blushing, and she smiled and nodded. "We do need to get to bed...er...um...I mean to dinner, so if you're sure, Lily?"

Lily forced a smile to her unwilling lips. "Of course I'm sure. I want to hit a club after dinner anyway, so I won't even be in the room for more than a few hours before we have to leave for the airport in the morning."

\*\*\*\*

Lily had gone ahead to the club, while Jason dealt with the concierge about their present for Heather and Mick. He scanned the bar area for her as he entered. Lights flashed, and loud techno pop music blared as he looked around, but Lily was nowhere in sight. He hopped on a stool at the bar, and pulled out his phone to check for a text from her. Maybe she'd given up on him and gone back to the room. Nope. No message. Jason signaled for the bartender and ordered a bottle of beer.

He swung around on the stool to face into the club.

Maybe she'd gone to the ladies' room. He didn't know why he was so eager to find her. There were plenty of other women here who were more his type—stacked, breezy, and easy. Lily might be sorta stacked, and with other people she did seem breezy, but nothing about the damn woman was easy. At least with him, she was always pricklier than a porcupine.

And there was the matter of what she did for a living. No, Lily was definitely not for him, but he didn't want to abandon her in Vegas either. Yeah. That's why his eyes still searched the room for her red dress, short black hair, and funky tortoise shell, cat-eye glasses.

Three guys with buzz cuts momentarily blocked his view, as they squeezed in next to him at the bar, and ordered four beers.

"I don't know why you ordered one for Jimbo. We won't see him again until our leave is over."

The men all laughed knowingly, and one of them replied, "He spotted that little hottie as soon as we walked through the door. She's exactly his type, with that retro, hipster chick thing going on, I hope she's got her own room, because I'm sharing a room with Jim this weekend, and I don't want to listen to him banging her until we have to go back to Pendleton."

Jason grinned as he took a swig of his beer. Camp Pendleton. These guys must be Marines on leave for the weekend, and it looked like their buddy's hipster chick was in for a helluva ride this weekend. He stopped looking for Lily, and started looking for another man with a buzz cut, because he had to admit he was curious to see the hottie dancing with these guys' friend. He spotted broad shoulders and buzzed blond hair on the dance floor, and craned his neck to look around the big guy to see…a red dress?

Dammit, the Marine was dancing with Lily! And she was laughing, and gazing up at him like there was nowhere she'd rather be.

He felt an unfamiliar burn in his gut. He didn't feel protective of her, the way he would for his sisters. Nooo…it definitely wasn't a brotherly feeling.

If he didn't know any better, he'd swear it was jealousy burning in his gut. Lily never looked at him the way she was looking at the Marine, but he didn't want her to—wouldn't want her to if she was the last woman on Earth, and he had a lifetime supply of Viagra. So why did the thought of this stupid Jarhead thinking he was going to be 'banging' Lily all weekend stick in his craw?

He pushed to his feet and shoved his way across the crowded dance floor to Lily. He tapped the Marine on the shoulder. Damn the dude was big! Working on the family horse farm meant Jason was no slouch in the muscle department himself, but this guy was built like a tank. Tattoos peeked out from under both too-tight sleeves of his polo shirt.

The guy had a smirk on his face as he said to Lily, "C'mon babe, I'll show you my tats if you show me yours."

Tats? Lily had tats? He'd never seen them, which meant they were on a place on her body which was normally covered by clothing. Why did that thought have all his blood rushing south?

"I can already see yours, so that's not a fair deal," she touched the Marine's bicep, although she wasn't so much touching him as stroking him, Jason observed with another rush of jealousy. And they both seemed completely unaware he was standing right next to them.

"Hellooo…Lily!" Jason waved the hand not holding his beer to get her attention.

She started, as if she had seriously not known he was there. Could she really be interested in this douche?

"Oh, hey Jason. This is Jim. Jim, this is Jason. He's the best man from the wedding I was in tonight," Lily said.

Jim nodded at him once, with the universal 'hit the pavement, dude, you're in the way' glare men had, as Lily asked, "What's up, Jason?"

Good question. What *was* up with him? Why did he feel the need to interrupt their dance? He shouldn't care what, or who, Lily did.

"I wanted to let you know I got everything straightened out with the champagne we're sending to Mick and Heather's suite."

She cocked her head and smiled quizzically. "Okaaay. Thanks for letting me know, but you really didn't need to come out on the dance floor to tell me."

"You really didn't." Jim crossed his arms against his chest and scowled at Jason.

Jason eased around the man mountain, and slung a possessive arm around Lily's shoulders. "I know we were both worried after the mess the hotel made with our room reservation that they would mess up our present for the bride and groom. But, it's actually not the only reason I came over, I wanted to see if you were ready to go back to our room, Moonbeam?"

Chapter 3

Lily's white-hot rage was so evident in the way she glared at him over her glass Jason was amazed her cocktail wasn't boiling.

She swung back and forth on her barstool, in a deceptively slow, mellow manner, and her voice was calm, even if her eyes told a different, more violent, story. "Tell me again why you felt the need to scare off Lance Corporal Hottie McHotterson, USMC?"

"I heard his friends talking about you, Moonbeam, trust me, that guy was only after one thing."

She stopped her stool so abruptly, the amber liquid sloshed out on her hand, and Jason must be way drunker than he thought, because he had the sudden urge to lean over and lick it off her skin.

"News flash, Einstein, I was only after one thing! And you blew it for me!"

The sarcastic way she called him Einstein was like a kick in the 'nads to a guy who'd spent most of his life being told how stupid he was. And not just by the other kids growing up—some of the teachers, like Lily, who ought to have known better. A learning difference didn't make him stupid. Just different. At least that's what his mom and older brother Jeff had always told him. Deep down, Jason knew they were right, but it was hard to get past a lifetime of other people telling him he was dumber than dirt.

He knew his next words had their roots in that dark place, but he couldn't stop them from coming out if he tried. Here Moonbeam was, ready for a little Vegas action, and she still couldn't be bothered to consider a roll in the hay with the stupid horse farmer she was sharing a room with—she'd rather go with some douche, who didn't give two shits about her? Did she really think he was a worse option than that?

"Where were you planning to let your inner slut loose, Moonbeam? Last time I checked, you and me were sharing a room, and for the record, the room is the only thing I want to share. I'm not into sharing when it comes to women."

She sat up ramrod straight on her stool and raised one eyebrow. How did people do that? Jason never could. Maybe it was a genetic ability, like being able to roll your tongue; he'd have to look it up online sometime.

"Are you so insecure in your performance, Romeo? Or is it you don't want another man seeing your..." her eyes drifted to his crotch, before she continued, "...inadequacies?"

He'd take Romeo as a nickname over Einstein any old day, and Jason's insecurities didn't run to his bedroom skills or equipment, so the insults ran off him like water off a duck's back. Plus, the way her pink tongue darted out to lick her lips when her gaze finished its downward journey told him Lily knew there was nothing inadequate there, and she wasn't nearly as immune to him as she tried to act.

He took a long draw of his beer and swallowed, without ever taking his eyes off hers. "No, Moonbeam, I just don't want the other guy to feel bad."

\*\*\*\*

Hoo boy, Lily didn't doubt for a second the other guy in a threesome with Jason would be a blubbering mass of insecurities before things even got started.

The look in his blue-gray eyes was so full of sensual promise Lily was ready to toss aside their mutual animosity and drag him back to their room right now to have her way with him, and that was a bad idea. Very bad.

Okay, since going all Barbarella on him was not an option, she'd settle for second best. She sighed and grabbed his hand. "Since your glare is scaring away any other potential partners for me, you're leaving me no choice—let's go, Braden."

Jason let her pull him to his feet, but his dropped jaw, wide-eyed expression, as he stood as if his cowboy boots were bolted to the ground, made her smile a little. He was always so confident; it felt good to throw him off his game.

"What do you mean, Moonbeam? Because I was just yanking your chain about the Vegas fling."

She held onto his hand, turned her back, and tugged him to the dance floor. "Dance partners, Romeo. Jeez Louise, do you ever think about anything but sex?"

"I think about a lot of things."

She felt him stiffen up behind her, and Jason's tone of voice was defensive. She hadn't meant to hurt his feelings. "I know you do; I didn't mean anything by it. We poke at each other"—she shrugged—"it's kind of our thing."

His grip on her hand loosened, and then he took control of the dance, by twirling her until her back was pressed to his front, and he began to move sinuously in time to the rhythm. His breath tickled her ear, as he spoke right in it to be heard over the music. "We've got a thing, Moonbeam?"

Jason had ditched the tie and suit jacket after the wedding, and his body heat scorched her through his crisp white dress shirt. And man-oh-Maneschewitz, his lean, hard body felt good. Really good. The Marine might be bulked up, but Jason's body felt like it had been made for hers, which given their mutual antagonism, seemed like proof Fate was enjoying a good laugh at her expense. Against Lily's better judgment, her body melted into his warmth and began to move with his.

"Sure, we've got a thing," she said over her shoulder, and was irritated to hear a trace of breathlessness in her voice. She cleared her throat and continued, "Like that—you calling me Moonbeam, because you know it bugs me."

She felt his body tighten up again in his grip on her hips. "You mean like when you called me Einstein, to point out what a dumb yokel I am?"

She stopped moving. "No. I didn't do that...at least I didn't mean to. I don't think you're a dumb yokel. I would've called Neil deGrasse Tyson Einstein at that moment. I was pointing out the obvious."

He hesitated, and then once again moved his hips in time to the sensual rhythm of the music, so she assumed everything was okay, and began to dance again too.

She couldn't see his face, but could hear the smile in his voice when he said, "You think Neil deGrasse Tyson would've tried to cockblock you with the Marine?"

She chuckled. "It sounds like it would make a good episode for a sitcom, but he probably wouldn't. Although you never know!"

The slow music segued into a more pounding techno beat, and Jason raised his voice to be heard over the louder music. "Want to head back to the bar for another drink?"

\*\*\*\*

Jason tossed back his shot. "C'mon, Moonbeam, you're falling behind!"

"We can't let that happen." She scrunched up her elfin face and tossed back the shot like it was an especially vile tasting cough medicine. She shuddered and then laughed. "How have I never done shots of Jäger before?"

*And how did I ever think you were plain looking?* With her short, dark brown hair all tousled and sexy, and her intelligent hazel eyes glittering in the neon lights of the bar, she looked like some sort of pixie come out of the forest to party with him. He shook his head once. When he started thinking shit like that, maybe it was time to ease up on the shots.

"Barkeep, two more please!" Lily yelled to the bartender, but the last word sounded more like "pleash." She frowned and tried again, "Pleash."

Jason erupted in laughter, and she smacked him on the arm.

The bartender poured two more shots for them, but held the small glasses in his hands, rather than put them down in front of them. "You guys aren't driving anywhere, are you?"

"No, sir," Lily said, and she still sounded a little slushy, albeit really earnest. "We've got a room right upstairs, in this very hotel."

"Then, here you go," the bartender put down their shots on the bar.

Jason felt heat spread through his body, and it had nothing to do with the Jäger. He'd forgotten they'd be sharing a room tonight. All of a sudden, the notion of staying on his side of the room all alone didn't seem nearly as appealing as it had a little while ago. He was having fun with Lily. She was cute, funny, and sexy in her own quirky way. He just never appreciated it before.

When a little voice in his head suggested the champagne, beers, and shots of Jäger he'd downed tonight might have something to do with his change of heart, Jason calmly told the little voice to go to hell.

"I'm getting ahead of you!" Lily called out with glee, before she tossed the shot down, with her now patented Jäger shudder.

He did his shot without fanfare, and never once took his eyes off Lily. "The bartender seems ready to cut us off…"

Lily swayed on the barstool, as she held up a finger to interrupt. "And he might have a point."

Jason reached out to steady her. He swore that was his intention, but he ended up smoothing down her short hair, which had gotten pretty disheveled with the dancing and the drinking. Her eyes fluttered shut, she leaned into his touch just the slightest bit, and all his good sense and intentions flew out the window. "What do you say we settle up the tab and head up to our room?"

\*\*\*\*

Lily heard the electronic beep of the key card, took

her left arm from around Jason's neck, reached to turn the handle, and kicked the door all the way open with her foot. She twined her arm back around his neck, and said, "I think Mick has to carry Heather over the threshold. The best man does not have to carry the maid of honor," Lily said through her laughter. "And even the groom doesn't have to carry the bride all the way from the elevator."

Jason hip-checked the door shut, and man, the combination of the broad shoulders she currently had her arms wrapped around, and those narrow hips, made her heart go pitter-pat.

She was drunk, yeah, no doubt about it, but once Jason had stopped being a douche to her, he was a great guy. He was fun and funny, not to mention he was sexy as hell. It would take a tougher woman than Lily was, evidently, to resist his charm when he set out to be charming. The question of the moment was, which one is the real Jason Braden—the douche or the charmer?

Maybe it was the shots talking, but Lily hoped this Jason was the real deal, because she liked him, and she really wanted to kiss him.

She turned her face toward his, and as if he'd read her mind, Jason closed the tiny distance between their faces, and murmured, "Moonbeam," before capturing her lips in a surprisingly tender kiss.

The tenderness did her in, and Lily didn't care any longer which one was the real Jason, or what would happen when they got back to Rivers Bend. She wanted this man.

Right.

Freaking.

Now.

She kissed him back, and upped the intensity a notch.

Jason released his hold under her bottom, so she slid down his body to stand on her own feet. Her little tour of his body left no doubt Jason was as up for this as she was. Very up, as a matter of fact.

When he cupped her face in his hands, and deepened the kiss, the room spun, and Lily hoped it was her new best friend, Jägermeister, causing it, because she didn't want Jason's kiss to have so much power over her.

He pulled back, still holding her face, and looked searchingly into her eyes. "Are you sure you want to do this, Moonbeam?"

Even the annoying nickname sounded like an endearment now, and drunk or not, Lily didn't want this opportunity to pass her by—damn the consequences, full speed ahead!

She licked her lips, and unbuttoned the top button on his shirt. "I'm sure."

Jason's smile was blinding, and she realized for the first time he had a dimple on the left side of his mouth.

"Oh yeah, gotta like a woman who's sure about what she wants."

She kept unbuttoning until she got to his belt, and then tugged his shirt out of his pants. His shirt fell open, and she got her first look at his bare chest. There was just the right amount of golden-brown hair, which she appreciated, she hated when guys waxed, and a little happy trail led down his abs into his pants.

He had a small tattoo of a harp and wings over his heart. She reached out, and traced it with her fingertip. "This looks like a meaningful tattoo."

"It is. I got it to honor my dad. It's the Irish harp, to recognize his heritage, and the wings, because, well...you know."

She did know. Rivers Bend residents liked to talk, and one of their favorite topics was the Braden family, so she knew his dad had passed away when Jason was a young boy.

"It's really beautiful."

His lips curled up, and his eyes flashed. "I just remembered something—you told that Marine that you had a tattoo. Do you really, or were you playing with him?"

She smiled, turned her back to him, and peeked over her shoulder. "Unzip me, and find out."

Okay, that was totally the shots talking. Lily wasn't normally so bold.

She heard the rasp of her zipper being lowered, and felt the tight bodice of her dress loosen.

"A tramp stamp?" Jason asked as he unzipped, "That doesn't seem like your style."

She glanced back over her shoulder, and saw him looking at her unmarked lower back. He frowned. "And I was right, you don't have a tramp stamp. Where is it?"

She reached up to pull the dress off her shoulders. As it pooled at her waist, she felt shy in just her strapless red bra.

Then Jason reached out to touch the tattoo on her right shoulder, and her shyness vanished into a fireball of lust at the sensation.

"A little owl in red eyeglasses, sitting on top of a pile of books—that is so frigging cute and nerdy."

She noticed an ice bucket in the room, and asked, "Did you order champagne?"

"No," Jason stepped around her to read the card with the bottle. "It's from the hotel, to thank us for being gracious about the room mix-up."

She snorted. "They didn't really leave us much choice. Our options were share this room, or sleep on the street."

Jason grinned, as he pulled the dripping bottle out of the melting ice, and opened the cork like a pro, with the tiniest of pops, and no bubbling loss of champagne. Clearly, he was a man of hidden depths.

"Can't honestly say I'm sorry." He poured two glasses, and handed her one. She took it, and laughed as she sipped it.

"What's so funny?"

"Us—all topless, drinking champagne."

He undid his belt buckle. "You're right, Moonbeam, we're only topless. We are way overdressed."

As he pushed his pants down, she stepped out of her dress. The man looked fine in a pair of boxer briefs, and the appreciative look in his eyes as he stalked toward her, made her think he felt the same way about her matching red bra and lacy boy shorts. She didn't know if it was the champagne, or the lusty expression on Jason's face, but she didn't feel like an average-looking schoolteacher—right now—she felt like a sex goddess.

Jason put down his glass on the nightstand, and picked her up again, and they tumbled together onto the bed, spilling their champagne in the process. He stretched to reach for his pants on the floor, pulled a little foil packet out of the pocket, and in an instant she ceased to worry over the spilled champagne.

He tugged off his boxer briefs and sprang free and mouth-wateringly erect. Lily reached for the condom in his hands, as he reached behind her to unhook her strapless bra.

Then everything was a blur of limbs, of flesh, of touching and licking, and sliding, and kissing. Frenzied, frantic, and exactly what she needed tonight.

## Chapter 4

A shrill ringing sound pierced through Lily's pounding head. She groaned, as she fumbled for the phone on the nightstand. Her eyes burned, her throat felt like the Sahara in dry season, and her pulse throbbed in her temples.

"'lo," she mumbled; it was as much of 'hello' as her cottonmouth would allow.

"Good morning! Mick and I are ready to check out, and the car will be here to take us to the airport in half an hour. Are y'all ready to roll?"

Heather sounded way too chipper, but then again, she'd gone to bed with her hot new husband right after dinner, and hadn't stayed up most of the night learning the wonders of Jäger shots, the way Lily had.

"Sure." Her voice croaked. "We'll be down in a bit."

"Great, see you soon!" Heather said in way too cheerful a tone of voice for Lily's current physical state.

Lily put the receiver back on its cradle, and realized she was in a pool of dried champagne on the bed. She wrinkled her nose, lifted the sticky sheet, peeked underneath, and saw she was naked. Like not a stitch on her—totally, bare-assed naked. *No, no, no, no, no.*

She took a deep breath, as all the events of the previous night rushed back to her.

The bed shifted, and she realized she wasn't alone in it. She opened one eye to see an equally buck-naked Jason sit up, and wipe his hands across his grimacing face.

"What the hell was that racket?"

His voice sounded as rough as hers felt, and his gaze dropped, making her all too aware of her undressed state. She pulled the champagne-soaked sheet up to cover her breasts.

She cleared her throat, but it still sounded like she'd gargled with razor blades when she said, "It was your sister on the phone. The car will be here in half an hour."

He rubbed the back of his neck. "We've got to hustle then. Do you want first crack at the bathroom?" He grinned wolfishly. "Or do you want to save time and shower together?"

"I don't think that's a very good idea."

He shrugged and waggled his eyebrows. "You're probably right. We'd never get out of here if we lathered up together."

This conversation was making her head hurt even more than it had before. She rolled her eyes. "That is so not what I meant. This whole thing was a bad idea of epic proportions. Like Napoleon invading Russia in the middle of winter bad...or Bay of Pigs bad."

Jason threw back the covers and stretched. He was as buck nekkid as she was, and whoo boy, did he look good. Maybe there had been a tiny upside to sleeping with Jason.

"I don't know, Moonbeam. From what I can remember, we had a damn good time together."

He winked at her, and her heart went pitter-pat, and

she felt giddy. Good God. What was the power this man had over women? See…this…this feeling was why it had been a bad idea to sleep with Jason Braden—an experience never to be repeated. Everyone in Rivers Bend knew he ran through women the way most men ran through tissue, and there was no way in hell she could afford to make herself vulnerable to that type of playboy.

"Maybe we did. But we can never do it again. Ever. Never ever."

Jason squinted at her. "I'm pretty hungover, so I'm not firing on all cylinders this morning, but that seems insulting. Look, I'm going to run into the bathroom for a minute, and then it's all yours. We don't have time to hammer all this out right now—the newlyweds are waiting for us—but we will be revisiting this topic. Because I am not accepting 'never ever' as a possibility. We were good together, Moonbeam. You know it as well as I do."

He pointed at her before he turned to go into the bathroom. The door clicked closed behind him, and Lily fanned herself. Riding horses for a living had given Jason one very fine behind. She shook her head briskly, and regretted it instantly, as it made the room swim before her eyes. She fought back a surge of nausea, and realized Jason was right. Neither of them was at their best this morning, and they needed to get cleaned up, dressed, and out of here in record time.

She looked down at her nakedness. Dressed. Definitely dressed. It would be easier to deal with Jason if they both were covered up. She stood and wrapped the sheet around her, wrinkling her nose at the stale champagne odor on it. Lots of bad ideas were acted on last night, starting with the shots at the bar, moving on to the bottle of champagne in their room, and climaxing with having sex with Jason freaking Braden—the manwhore of Rivers Bend.

There was a flushing sound from the bathroom, and water running, before Jason opened the door and emerged, still wondrously, gloriously nude. He frowned when he looked at her. "All covered up? No need to be shy, Moonbeam, I've seen it all. Been up close and personal with it all, as a matter of fact."

She gathered the sheet around, lifted her chin, and swept past him to get into the bathroom. She turned to face him and said, "Which you never will be again. We will never speak of last night, Jason. I mean it."

She closed the door to his wide-eyed gaze and dropped jaw. Once it was shut, she slumped against it and shook her head. She had a bad feeling forgetting last night was going to be easier said than done.

\*\*\*\*

Lily put on sunglasses before they left the room, and they were still on her face while she slept on the plane.

"What the hell did you to her last night?"

Jason snapped in response to his new brother-in-law's question. "Do to her? I didn't do anything to her!"

Mick held up his hands, and settled into his seat across the aisle. "Man, you two must have gotten seriously toasted after Heather and I left, but you know what they say, what happens in Vegas…"

Heather came back from the bathroom, looking fresh as a daisy, and decidedly not hungover.

"Don't get up, there's plenty of room. You've

spoiled me, Mick, I'll never be happy flying in coach class again. First Class all the way for me from now on!" She settled into her seat, and asked, "What are we talking about—the Hangover Twins? I'm sorry we missed all the fun."

Mick grinned, and waggled his eyebrows. "We missed all the fun, huh, Mrs. Evans?"

His sister grinned coquettishly at her husband. "Well...not all the fun."

"Enough!" Jason barked the words out, even though it hurt his own head to do it. "You are my sister, and I'm nauseated enough without hearing the rest of that sentence."

The flight attendant stepped up between their seats. "May I get you anything? Champagne?"

"Not champagne." Lily groaned. "Definitely not champagne. May I have a ginger ale, please?"

Huh. Moonbeam was awake. Jason thought she was asleep, but she must've been playing possum.

"Well, I want champagne!" Heather said with a huge grin on her face.

Jason winced. He'd never noticed how flipping loud his sister was before. "I'll have a ginger ale too, please, darlin'."

\*\*\*\*

Lily cracked her eyes open and everything around her looked dark since she was wearing her shades. Las Vegas was a freakishly bright city. She hadn't noticed when they arrived yesterday, but today it was unbearable. Did the flight attendant stick out her chest when Jason spoke to her just now? What a floozy...for all the woman knew, Jason and she were a couple. They were sitting together and obviously hungover together.

Who licks their lips that way at a man who was clearly with another woman?

Her head pounded, and she checked to make sure the airsick bag was front and center in the seatback in front of her, because her stomach was still rocky— whether it was because of the excessive drinking last night, or the fact she was feeling possessive about Jason with the pretty flight attendant, she didn't know. "Could you put a rush on the ginger ale, please? I'm not feeling very well."

"Of course, ma'am. I'll be right back."

The bitch winked at Jason. What the actual hell?

Heather leaned forward to peer across the aisle at her. "You look like crap, Lily."

"Thank you very much," Lily said. "Now, would you lower your voice, please? There is no need to yell."

"I was thinking I never noticed how loud Heather was before." Jason nodded. Then he stopped abruptly, and rubbed his temples. "Okay. Nodding is a bad idea. No more sudden head movements."

"What did you two do last night after dinner? It must've been off the hook, because I've never seen either of you look this lousy before," Heather asked.

"We went to the nightclub in the hotel," Lily said.

Jason leaned back against the headrest and closed his eyes. "Seriously, Heather, could you whisper or something?"

Mick chuckled, as he flipped through the in-flight magazine. "I hope you two survive the flight home."

Heather laughed, and Jason groaned. She then said in a stage whisper, "And what happened at the nightclub, to leave you both looking like you've both been dragged behind a horse for twenty miles?"

Lily managed to shake her head and shrug, but then closed her eyes again, when the world swam at the motion.

"I introduced Moonbeam to Jäger shots—no biggie. Oh, and the hotel sent us champagne to apologize for the mix-up with the room," Jason said.

Lily sighed in relief he wasn't going to spill to Heather and Mick about what had happened between them between the sheets last night.

"The champagne was a mistake." She groaned.

"True that," Jason agreed.

"Here we go—two ginger ales, and two glasses of champagne."

Lily opened her eyes at the sound of the flight attendant's voice, and reached for her soda. "Thank you."

She guzzled down most of the little glass in one sip, and felt the bubbles tickle her nose.

She glanced over to see Heather squinting at her as she sipped her own glass of champagne. She fought against nausea at the sight of the golden, bubbly liquid. The bottle of champagne last night had been a serious error in judgement, and Lily wasn't sure when she'd be able to face it again. "What?"

"Defensive, on top of being hungover, I sense a mystery here, Mr. Evans."

Mick looked up from his magazine, and turned his head to stare at Jason and Lily. "Really, Mrs. Evans? You are probably right, but I think we should cut them a break. It looks like they're suffering enough."

Bless Mick Evans. Lily had liked him well enough before, but they were more acquaintances than good friends. However, right now if the thought of moving didn't make her want to toss her cookies, she would go over there and kiss him. She really wanted Heather to back off about last night. As far as she was concerned, last night never happened. And even if it had, she would take what happened to her grave.

****

Lily curled up on the overstuffed sofa in the family room. This was the only room in her half-sister's ridiculously huge Georgian-style mansion where she felt comfortable. Even the guest room she was staying in while she lived here with her niece, made her feel like she was a lady-in-waiting at the court of Marie Antoinette at Versailles. But this room had comfortable furniture and a big-screen TV mounted on the wall over the stone fireplace. It was cozy and welcoming, and clearly designed with someone other than her sister Gloria in mind. Lily had asked Hadley about it once, and her niece said Gloria's husband between the Argentinian polo player and the investment broker had requested this room specifically. Hadley's father was Gloria's first husband, but there were four men who followed him to the altar with Gloria. Number five...five...was Lily's current brother-in-law. An elderly diplomat, his current assignment in a dangerous part of the world brought Lily to Rivers Bend to live with her niece.

She shook her head, which felt world's better after a hot shower and some dry toast, than it had a few hours ago, and wondered how she and Gloria Davis Diemer Vazquez Peterson Carr Endicott could even be half-sisters. They were such different people.

Her phone vibrated on the sofa next to her, and she picked up to see who was calling. Hadley wasn't due

36

back from her father's house until tomorrow. It was a video call from Veronica Bailey. She tapped to answer, and her best friend from Baltimore's pretty face popped up on the screen.

Roni waved at her. "Hi! How was Vegas?"

Lily groaned, and Roni grinned and asked, "That good, huh?"

"Have you ever done something so colossally stupid, you never even told me about it?"

Her friend shook her head so hard she had to push her sun-kissed blonde hair off her face. "No. I tell you everything."

Lily pulled the phone closer to her face and then back out again, while she studied Roni's image on the screen. "Not everything. When did you get the pink streaks in your hair?"

"Yesterday. I was bored with my look, and did it on a whim. What do you think?"

With her big blue eyes, and tall, playmate body, Roni could shave her head and still be a knockout. Lily never understood how her friend could ever be insecure about her appearance. "You look gorgeous, as always."

Roni blushed and smiled. "Thanks. I was worried it might be a little too out there."

"No, I love it. Will it be okay at your new job?"

With a shrug, Roni replied, "I hope so. This private school gig is much more conservative than the public school where you and I worked. I can't even wear jeans, except on days designated to dress down."

"Do you like working there though?"

"I do. It's just different, and I'm still getting used to it. But the budget cutbacks eliminated my program, so I needed to find a job fast. I was lucky there was an opening here." She narrowed her eyes and said, "But you're not going to distract me so easily, Lily. What did you do in Vegas?"

"Do we really have to talk about Vegas? I want to hear more about you...your hair...your job...your mailman...anything but my trip to Vegas."

"We have a new mailman, actually. Reggie—I met him the other day, and he seems like he's going to be better than the last guy. But I will not be deterred...what in God's name happened in Vegas? It was only a quick trip, and you had your friend's wedding taking up most of the time. How much trouble could you get into?"

Lily laughed humorlessly. "You'd be surprised."

"So, surprise me. What did you do?" Veronica gasped. "Oh! Maybe I'm asking the wrong question...who did you do?"

"It's bad, Roni, really bad."

Lily knew she'd vowed to take her fling with Jason to her grave, but Roni wouldn't let up until she had the whole sordid story. Besides, she needed to talk to someone, and this was one topic she couldn't discuss with her friends in Rivers Bend, as all of them were connected to Jason one way or another. Damned small town living.

"If I tell you, you have to swear not to tell anyone. Ever. Even under torture."

Roni held up her hand. "I swear."

Lily swallowed hard. "Okay...here goes. Remember I told you how I wished the best man was anyone other than the guy it was?"

"Sure. He's the guy who's been such a jerk to you since you moved to Rivers Bend. Jason, right? It's too bad Mick's brother couldn't get off work to go. Did you end up killing this Jason guy? Do I need to alibi you? Because you know I will."

The corners of Lily's mouth turned up and she said, "I know you would. BFF code. You would even help me bury the body."

"Damn straight, I would. Do I have to?"

Lily shook her head. "I wish. It's even worse. I slept with him."

"Did you want to? He didn't…"

"No!" Lily interrupted. "He most definitely didn't. I wanted to. Oh, man, how I wanted to."

Tension released visibly from Roni's shoulders, so much so Lily could even see it on the little screen. "So, was he bad? Is that the problem?"

"No, he was good. Best ever, as a matter of fact."

"Was he a jerk this morning?"

"If either of us was a jerk this morning, it was me. But in all fairness, I was seriously hung over. Jason was really nice."

Roni scrunched up her nose. "I don't understand. He was nice to you for a change, it was the best sex ever—what's wrong? Does he not want to see you again?"

"Nooo…he made it pretty clear, he wants a repeat performance. It's that he's Jason Braden! He's been rude to me since the first time I met him. Which, by the way, was at a party at his brother's house, and he was on the dance floor surrounded by women."

"He's a player?"

"He's the reigning world-champion player. Seriously, aside from his family members, I think I was the only woman in town he hadn't slept with before this weekend."

"That's not good."

"No."

"But even players settle down sometimes. Y'know, once they sow their wild oats. Maybe he's ready for a relationship."

"Well, I don't want one right now. I have my hands full taking care of Hadley. I am so over my head, suddenly being the sole guardian of a tween, I have this massive house and property to take care of, and a new job to adapt to—I don't have time for a relationship with anyone. Least of all with Jason Braden. Talk about complications I don't need."

"Do you think he's going to be a nuisance? Is that why you're so flipped?"

"No. I said I didn't want Heather and Mick to know what happened, and he didn't like it, but he was cool about it on the trip home." She hesitated, and Roni flapped her hand impatiently to continue. "I guess the problem is I ended up liking him too much for my peace of mind. And I don't want to like him. He might be nice to me now, but can I trust it? How do I know he's not going to go back to being a douche to me? Or if he has any intention of curbing his man-whore ways? He might just want me to be one of his harem, and I'm not down with that. There are too many complications with him."

"Okay, then. So, you had a fling. It's over now, and you can go your separate ways. No harm, no foul."

"Right," Lily responded with false cheer. "Thanks for listening, Roni, but I have to get going."

Roni pressed her lips together. "Don't think I don't realize I'm being rushed off the phone, so you can avoid talking. Know we will revisit this topic, but I'll let you go for now. Have a good night, sweetie."

"Thanks, Roni. G'night."

Lily pressed the button to end the video call, sank back into the sofa, and shut her eyes. There would be no harm, no foul, if she could stop thinking about Jason, and how much fun they had together both in bed and out of it.

She could not be falling for Jason freaking Braden. Full stop. End of story. She wouldn't allow herself to go down that road. She just needed to put him out of her mind, and get on with her already too complicated and busy life.

So why was it when she shut eyes, all she could see was naked Jason, tangled sheets, and the cute little dimple on his face when he smiled at her?

Chapter 5

Lily's ears crackled as she tried to smother a yawn. She held the cocktail glass, which contained her Manhattan, in front of her mouth. Seriously, why did she agree to go on this date? She had even forgotten she'd told Heather she would go out with Ted. He had been the assistant professor for one of Heather's classes, and on paper he was a good match for her. But in reality…Snoozeville USA.

"I'm sorry, you must be bored with all this work talk. The research I've been doing is fascinating, and I wanted to share it with you, but obviously you are not interested, " Ted said with a disapproving frown,

Okay—maybe she hadn't hidden the yawn as well as she'd thought.

"I'm sorry, it has nothing to do with your work. Going to Las Vegas for Heather's wedding was such a whirlwind trip; now my niece is home, and I'm back to work. I'm a little tired." A little white lie, as Lily was beyond bored with his research talk.

Ted frowned. "Yes. Your niece."

Lily didn't like the way he said the words, like he was saying 'your infectious disease,' instead of 'your niece.' "What about my niece?"

"I was wondering how long you're committed to living with her."

"Until." Lily knew her answer was curt, but she was one more snide comment about Hadley away from tossing her drink in his face.

"Until when?"

Lily put down her drink a little too hard, and some amber liquid sloshed over her hand. She swiped at it with her napkin, and said, "Until my half-sister comes back to the States, or at least her husband is re-assigned to a more stable country."

"And now I'm sorry, because I seem to have irritated you. I only asked because I don't want to be involved with a woman with a child."

The patronizing way he'd behaved with Hadley when he picked her up at the house before dinner made it crystal clear Ted was not fond of children, and clueless how to behave around them. It had gotten the evening off on a bad foot, when he was such a jerk to her beloved niece.

"Then it's a good thing we're not involved."

"Not yet," he said with an ingratiating smile, and reached across the table for her hand.

Lily pretended she didn't see it, and used that hand to pick up her glass as a way to avoid his touch. "Not ever."

His face fell. Man, was this guy clueless. He'd really thought they were having a good date?

"But...but...it doesn't sound like you'll have to be with your niece forever..."

"I don't have to be with my niece now," Lily interrupted. "I chose to become her guardian, because I love her. And I will continue to be her guardian for as long as necessary...even if it's forever."

Ted furrowed his brow, leaned back in his chair, and took a sip of his Scotch on the rocks. "That's very big of you—she's at a difficult age, and if you don't mind me saying so, she is extremely rude."

She slammed her drink down, took the napkin of her lap, and tossed it on the table. Reaching for her purse, which hung on the back of her chair, she said, "I do mind you saying so, Ted. But I'll do you the same courtesy of being just as honest with you—I think you are rude. You were rude to my niece when you met her tonight, and you were rude to me right now. I don't think you need to concern yourself overmuch about my guardianship of Hadley, though, because you and I won't being seeing each other again."

She pulled her wallet out of her purse, and put some bills on the table. "This should cover my share of dinner. Good bye, Ted."

"This is all very dramatic, but I drove. How do you propose to get home?"

"Uber."

His jaw dropped as she stood and walked away, and she had the unflattering thought Ted looked a little like a fish. It wasn't fair though; he was an attractive enough man. Just not as handsome as Jason...

Oh, damn. Did her date with Ted go awry because she had feelings for Jason? She shook her head. No, Ted was a jerk, and she didn't...wouldn't...have feelings for Jason. That wasn't quite true. She felt some emotions regarding Jason. She felt disdain, and a little disgust with herself over last weekend's events, but romantic feelings for Jason Braden were out of the question.

On the other hand, she had a lot more fun with Jason, even before their misguided fling in Vegas. He liked her niece, got her jokes, was a good dancer—he was fun. Ted was not.

She pulled out her phone, and called up the app to get a ride home. What a night this had turned out to be. She had no idea what she was going to tell Heather. She didn't want to hurt her friend's feelings, but Ted and she were clearly not a good match.

\*\*\*\*

"What time is your dad picking y'all up today, Sam?" Jason asked his niece, guessing it would be his brother picking up her and Lily's niece Hadley from their riding lesson today, as Lily had managed to avoid doing it since they got back from Vegas. They drove home from the airport with Heather and Mick, but Lily had been dodging him ever since, in order to avoid acknowledging what happened between them in Vegas. He wasn't sure he wanted to acknowledge what happened, so much as have a repeat performance of it, because it had been rock-'em sock-'em good.

"Dad's busy," Sam said.

"Aunt Lily is getting us today, but she's running late; she should've been here by now," Hadley said.

The girls had already taken care of their own horses and tack, and were helping Jason muck out the stalls.

"I can give y'all rides home," Jason offered.

"Thanks, but she'll be here. She said she has a lot of paperwork she needs to get done by the end of the quarter, and she meant to get in early this morning, but she was wiped out after her date with Professor Snoozy McBore."

Jason froze mid-shovel.

Date.

She had a date.

He hadn't even been out since they got back, and

45

his family was forever teasing him about being a serial dater. He'd never seen what the problem was—women liked him, he liked women, it was a win-win.

But back to Lily…it was not just a date, it was a date with a professor, someone smart like Lily, not a man whose life was spent outdoors in physical activity like him. He would not ask. He would not put a child in the middle of whatever the hell was going on with Lily and him.

He would not ask.

"Snoozy McBore, huh? Of the Charlottesville McBores?" he asked. Huh. Look at that—he did ask.

The girls giggled, and Hadley said, "You sound like my mother, although she would've been serious, when she wondered about his social position."

True statement. Hadley's mom's picture was in the encyclopedia next to 'Social Climber.' The woman was a total snob, and when she had to move for her new husband's job, her plan for Hadley had been to ship the kid off to boarding school in Switzerland. Hadley had been worried sick over having to leave her home, friends, and school. That was why Lily, Gloria's half-sister, stepped up, quit her teaching job in Baltimore, and moved to Rivers Bend to take care of her niece. Since Gloria never cared for much except herself, it was actually a huge improvement in Hadley's life, as far as Jason could tell.

"He teaches at Aunt Heather's old college," Sam said. "She hooked them up."

Thanks, sis. Good job. Hook Lily up with some brilliant professor guy. What a perfect way to make him look like a big dumbass by comparison.

Before he embarrassed himself by probing further,

Jason was saved by the appearance of the woman in question, who stood in the door to the barn, with her hands on her hips.

"Why is it you can shovel manure here at the barn, but your bedroom at home always looks like a horse stall?" Lily said.

\*\*\*\*

Instead of her niece answering her, Lily heard a deep chuckle come from one of the stalls, and Jason's voice said, "I resent that—our horse stalls are always clean as a whistle; they are much tidier than a teen's bedroom."

She looked around, and had to admit the barns at Braden Farms were always spotless. She'd never done much riding; her hippie parents didn't approve of domesticating animals. Therefore, she'd never set foot in a barn before she came to Rivers Bend. She always pictured them as smelly, dirty places, but the barns where her niece boarded her horse were nothing like her imagination.

"I'm sorry; I didn't mean to cast aspersions on your farm. It's lovely."

Her voice sounded stilted and too polite, even to her own ears, so she could only imagine what it sounded like to everyone else. Maybe she shouldn't have been avoiding seeing Jason after their Vegas fling. She'd thought a little time away from him would create distance, and make everything less awkward between them, but it seemed like it made things even worse. At least the girls were here to ease the way.

"We left our school stuff in Grandma's house," Sam said.

"Y'all run up and get it, I can finish up here.

Thanks for your help," Jason said.

"You're welcome!" the girls called as they scrambled out of the barn.

Lily ducked her head and turned to follow them to the house.

"Wait a minute, Moonbeam. I'd like to talk to you."

Jason's words stopped her in her tracks. His tone was slow and easy, but there was a hint of iron beneath it, much like the man himself was between the sheets. And that unwanted thought only served to make her heart rate kick into high gear.

"Okay." Great, now her voice squeaked. She cleared her throat, and continued in a more normal tone, "What's up?"

"How was your date with Professor Snoozy McBore?"

His question was casual, but his eyes narrowed and flashed with what, in another man she would think was jealousy.

Huh.

Interesting, even if her date with Snoozy McBore…um…Ted McGivens, was just to get Heather off her back about dating, without forcing her to admit to her friend she'd slept with her brother in Vegas, and wasn't interested in dating anyone else now. Because how pathetic was that? Jason had no interest in her; they'd been drunk and in Las Vegas, the land of bad judgment. Their ill-advised fling didn't count.

Except, to her, it did. She wasn't a one-night stand kind of woman. As a matter of fact, her one night with Jason was her first, and she didn't know how you were supposed to behave afterward, but wasn't the best defense supposed to be a good offense?

"That's not his name."

"It's what Hadley called him. He sounds nice."

She shrugged. "I guess he was okay. He isn't super comfortable with kids, and didn't really know how to talk to Hadley." No reason to let Jason know she didn't have nearly as much fun with Ted as she'd had in Las Vegas with him.

And Ted's hatred of children had been a real turn-off to Lily. Jason was always so at ease with kids. He taught most of the riding lessons here at the farm, and maybe she'd watched him once or twice...or every time she picked up her niece, and she liked his fun, but authoritative, manner with the kids. He was in charge, but kind and gentle, to both the children and the animals, and even before she'd seen him naked, it made her heart melt a little bit.

"How long have you been seeing Snoozy McStick-up-the-ass? Were you dating him before we went to Vegas?"

Her jaw dropped, not at the new, ruder, nickname for Professor Snoozy—since it totally suited him, but at the idea she could've been seeing someone when they'd spent the night together in Vegas.

"It was our first date! Do you honestly think I would have...you know...with you in Vegas if I was dating Snoozy—damn it—Ted?"

"I don't really know enough about you to know if you'd...you know...with someone else. I mean you've got that whole hippie thing going on, Moonbeam. I thought maybe you were into free love." He grinned and flashed a peace sign with his fingers.

"My parents are hippies. I'm not. And I would

49

never have…you know…with you, if I had a boyfriend."

"Gloria's father is a hippie?" Gloria was the ultimate high-maintenance socialite, and he found it very hard to believe her father was a hippie.

Lily laughed. "No. Gloria and my father are most decidedly not hippies, and neither was Gloria's mother. She was his first wife. My mom was his third, and she was totally a hippie. I don't really understand what they saw in each other; they had nothing in common. After she realized that and left Gloria's father, she met my stepdad, also a hippie, and they lived happily ever after. My stepdad really raised me, so I think of them as my parents."

He leaned on the pitchfork. "Interesting. Hippies in Connecticut?"

She rolled her eyes. "Trust fund hippies."

He cocked his head. "I don't know what that means."

"It means their ample trust funds provided them with the means to follow a life driven by their ideals, and in my stepdad's case, to pursue his artistic endeavors."

He was learning more about Lily in this brief convo than he had their whole night together. Not much talking was done then, unless you counted things like "harder," "faster," and "oh yeah, baby."

"Your stepdad's an artist?"

"A good one." She nodded and then blushed. "He designed my tattoo."

Remembering discovering her tattoo, and then tracing each other's tats with their tongues, had him ready to drop the pitchfork, and take a step for her, but he was stopped by Hadley's voice from outside: "Aunt Lily! We're ready to roll—c'mon!"

Her pupils dilated, and she licked her lips. It was like she'd read his mind and was on the same page, but she cleared her throat and called out, "Coming, Hadley!"

Chapter 6

Heather slid into the seat across from Lily at Vinnie's Pizzeria. "Okay, order placed. Thanks for getting our sodas." She pulled the pebbled plastic glass of Dr. Pepper toward her, and pounded the straw on the table to get it out of the paper wrapper.

Lily took a sip of her diet cola. "How do you stay so skinny drinking regular soda? You might as well be free-basing sugar."

"I'm active, I work out, and I help at the farm when they need me. Plus, I've got good genes. Have you seen my mother?"

Lily had, and Joyce Braden could still pass as Heather's sister rather than her mother. She sighed and looked down at her own body. She wasn't fat, but she had curves, and even the kindliest description of her mother's build was 'plump,' and that wasn't easy for a vegan like her mom. Nope. You can't beat your genes.

Heather barreled on to another topic—the one Lily suspected she was lured here with the promise of Vinnie's eggplant pizza to discuss.

"How was your date with Ted? He's a nice guy, isn't he?"

She shrugged. "It didn't work out between us."

Heather slumped in her seat. "Oh, no! Why not?"

"He wasn't very nice to Hadley when he picked me up, and was downright rude when he mentioned her at dinner. He made it very clear he didn't want to be involved with a woman with guardianship of a child."

"I didn't know Ted was so down on children—I'm so sorry, Lily! I'll have to think it over, and come up with someone else for you."

"It's okay…" Lily began, but was interrupted by the arrival of Vinnie with their pizza.

"Ladies, your eggplant pie! And for two such lovely customers, I brought over two free breadsticks."

The man looked surprisingly like the beaming, rotund cartoon man on his pizza delivery boxes, and he was a welcome interruption for Lily. It bought her some time, so she wouldn't blurt out something insane like: *Your brother rocked my world in Vegas, y'know, on your wedding trip? The one your husband paid for?* Yeah. That would go over like a lead balloon.

And while Lily's mind knew there was no future with a playboy like Jason, let alone with a playboy who didn't seem to like her very much when they weren't in bed, her body didn't seem to be on board with the plan. No. Her traitorous body was all too willing to jump into something with Jason, and that route would guarantee heartbreak.

As Vinnie walked away, she fiddled with her straw paper, while Heather took a huge bite of her warm, soft breadstick, and gestured with her free hand for Lily to continue.

"I was going to say you don't need to fix me up with anyone else," she said with more certainty. "I have so much going on in my life right now, and"—here her voice faltered, but she carried on—"I'm just kind of, sort of, interested in someone else."

Heather swallowed her bite, and shoved the other

breadstick at her. "Yum! You've got to try this, it's bread heaven!"

Lily sighed, she really had intended to try to get in better shape starting this week, but who could resist a warm, chewy, homemade breadstick? The aroma from the garlic salt and Italian seasoning coating the top, reached her nose, and all resolve was lost. Oh hell, if she couldn't beat her genes, she might as well enjoy the ride to plump. She took a bite, and closed her eyes in bliss.

While she chewed, Heather got to work, putting a slice of gooey, cheesy pizza, covered with fried eggplant pieces on each of their plates. "Someone else, hmm…intriguing. Who is it?" She bounced in her seat, "Oh, I know! It's the new swim coach at the high school. I saw him at the grocery store the other night, and that swimmer's body is amazing! The broad shoulders and the narrow waist…"

Since Heather's new husband was a former NFL player, who was so handsome he could pass for a GQ model, Lily knew Heather's admiration of the new coach was all talk.

"He is hot, but it's not him."

Heather wrinkled her nose, and munched her pizza. She thought so hard, Lily was amazed she couldn't hear her thoughts out loud—like the voiceover in a movie. Heather bobbed her head to the Louis Prima music blasting from the speakers, and swallowed before adding with speculation clear in her narrowed eyes. "Who else? Rivers Bend doesn't have much to choose from, man-wise. Let's see…Mick's brother is new in town. Is it Billy? He's a little younger than you, but he is a sweetie."

Before Lily could tell Heather no, her friend had gone on to the next likely prospect. "Is it that guy who recently moved up here from Roanoke? Who opened the little gift and florist shop? 'Cause I've got to tell you, I'm pretty sure he's gay."

"No. It's not him, and before you can ask, yes, I know Ty Harris is gay too, and it's not him either."

"Sheriff Monroe? He's a nice guy, but he started seeing someone this Fall."

Lily sighed. "It's not Dan Monroe. Look, it's not serious, and it's not something I even want to feel, so could we please drop the whole thing?"

"There aren't that many other single guys in town..." Heather's voice trailed off, and she slowly lowered her slice of pizza. Her eyes grew wide, like she was watching a real-life horror story unfold right before her. "No, no, no, no, *no!* Please tell me it's not my dumbass brother, Jason!"

Lily cheeks burned, as she took a cheesy, saucy bite of pizza. Normally, it was her favorite—it tasted like eggplant parmigiana on a pizza crust. Today it tasted like cardboard. This was not a conversation she wanted to have with Heather.

"Mebbe," she mumbled around the mouthful of pizza that felt like it was getting bigger and bigger as she chewed it.

"Have you lost your ever-lovin' mind? Jason? He's my little brother, and I love him, but he is not boyfriend material. I know you started getting along better in Las Vegas, but..." Her jaw clamped shut. "Oh...my...God. What did you do in Vegas?"

Lily gave up trying to eat her pizza and washed down this never-ending bite with a gulp of her diet soda. "Mistakes were made in Vegas," Lily admitted after swallowing hard.

"Mistakes? Plural? Oh man, I don't even know whose ass to kick. I mean, he's my brother, but you're my friend, and when it comes to 'mistakes, Jason has a long and storied history."

"It wasn't all his fault. It was both of us."

"Oh, merciful heaven! She's defending him." Heather smacked the table and rolled her eyes.

"Not defending him, exactly, it's just not fair for him to take all the blame for what happened. As a matter of fact, you can't talk to him about it at all, because then he'll know I told you."

Heather leaned back in her little café chair, narrowed her eyes, and crossed her arms across her chest. "Technically, you didn't tell me anything."

Saved by a technicality! Lily would take it.

Heather cocked her head to the right, and continued to study her through narrowed eyes, which Lily just noticed were the same shade of grayish-blue as Jason's.

"Are you dating him now? Because, I'm sorry to tell you, but Jason doesn't date. He boinks and runs. I don't mean to be cruel, but you're still new in town, and you might not know..."

Suddenly very aware of the public location of their talk, Lily looked around nervously, and leaned forward. "Not so new I don't know we shouldn't be having this conversation in public! It's nobody's business but Jason's and mine, and if we keep this up, it will be all over town before morning."

Heather took a deep breath and released it. She leaned forward, and picked up her slice. "Fine. Good point. In the meantime, I think maybe I need to arrange a girls' night, to get your mind off my idiot brother. Maybe Jeff, Cisco, and Mick can watch the kids while we go out for some fun. I'll look into it for this Friday night and let you know. And I won't bring anything up in front of everyone else, but this conversation is not over, missy! Not by a long shot."

Lily took another bite too, grateful for the reprieve, but like this discussion, she knew things with Jason weren't over either, and she didn't know whether to be happy or sad.

\*\*\*\*

"To girls' night!" Heather toasted.

Lily, Magda, Bethanne, and Deidre surrounded the high-top table in the bar, and all clinked glasses with her, before replying in unison, "Girls' night!"

There was no bar in Rivers Bend, so Jeff arranged a car and driver for them, and they'd gone down the road to Leesburg for their party night, and it seemed to Lily that meant all bets were off for the night.

Deidre, the oldest of them, and mother to twins who were currently in their freshman year of college, pounded the table and yelled, "Shots! We need shots."

Lily shuddered.

"Oh, no." Bethanne pointed at her. "You are not going to be a party pooper. We are getting shots."

"I had a bad experience with shots in Vegas," Lily explained.

Heather narrowed her eyes and frowned. "Too many shots can lead to remarkably bad decisions."

"Ooo…that sounds interesting," Magda said.

"It does," Bethanne agreed. "Bad decisions in Vegas, this is a story I've got to hear."

Lily tried to burn Heather to a pile of ashes with

her gaze, while still attempting to look innocent and casual to everyone else. Not an easy tightrope to walk.

Heather must've gotten the message, because she flapped her hands in dismissal and said, "No story. I was merely making an observation."

Magda put down her Cosmo so hard, a little of the pink liquid sloshed onto her hand. "Jeff went to all the trouble and expense of arranging for a car and driver for us tonight, and I'm not letting him have done it for nothing! Someone come to the bar with me to help me carry the shots."

Lily jumped at the chance to get away from the table before someone pressed to discuss her Las Vegas mistakes. "I'll do it!"

The bar Heather selected had a little of everything. They had opted to sit on tall stools around a table, but there was also an area for shooting pool, throwing darts, and a small dance floor. An old song came across the sound system, and Magda bopped to it on the way to the bar.

"What can I get for you ladies?" the bartender shouted to be heard.

Magda looked at Lily and laughed. "We forgot to ask everyone."

"Anything but Jäger shots."

The bartender wiped the bar in front of them. "Do y'all want me to come back?"

The bar was hopping on a Friday night, so Lily was relieved when Magda yelled their order to him, "We want shots—five Cake Balls, please."

"You got it." He turned his back to pull a couple of bottles from the wall behind him.

"What's in a Cake Ball, dare I ask?" Lily grinned.

Magda continued to dance in place to the music. She took Lily's hand and twirled her. Lily seriously loved her new friends in the Bend, and wished Roni could be here tonight—she would fit right in and have a blast with them.

"It's Fireball whisky and cake vodka."

This time, Lily twirled Magda and laughed. "Cake vodka is a thing? Those are two of my favorite things in one; how did I not know it existed?"

Loud shrieks of feminine excitement could be heard from the dance floor.

"Wonder what's happening?" Magda asked.

Lily stood on tiptoes to try to see over the crowd. "I don't know."

"We should have brought one of the Braden women over with us, they would've been tall enough to see. We're both shrimps." Magda jumped up a little to try to see what was causing the female catcalls, rising in volume and excitement.

The bartender put the shots on the bar, just as a tall guy stepped out of the way, clearing the view to the small dance floor.

"Finally! We can see," Magda said, and then burst out laughing. "We should've known."

The floor felt like it dropped beneath Lily's feet, as she saw Jason on the dance floor, surrounded by an admiring throng of women while he danced. And as she'd learned in Las Vegas, he could do things to a woman on a dance floor that were illegal in several states, and if they weren't...they should be. One of the women sidled up close to him, and Lily feared she was going to mount him like an over-excited Chihuahua.

It seemed as though Jason was over what happened

between them in Vegas, and on to the next woman. Or twenty women—honestly, was there no other man in the bar? It seemed like all the females in the place were vying for his attention, except for the four women she was with—and that was only because one was his soon-to-be sister-in-law, and two of them were his sisters. She bit her bottom lip as she watched the Jason Show on the dance floor, and was forced to admit based on the shit-eating grin on his face, Jason loved every minute of it.

It stung. Lily didn't know why, she had no claim over him, and had even gone on a date last week herself, but it still stung.

She grabbed one of the Cake Balls from the bar and downed it in one.

Magda's pretty blue eyes bugged out of her head. "What brought that on?"

The whisky burned on its way down, and Lily coughed a little. She shook her head. "Nothing I shouldn't have expected. Bartender—" she peered across the bar to read his nametag—"Jim. I'd like another Cake Ball, if you please."

He laughed. "Sure thing, darlin'."

"We'll be right back for our drinks, Jim," Magda called across the bar. She grabbed Lily's hand and dragged her to the dance floor. "Let's show these women how it's done!"

Lily tried to dig in her heels, but Magda was a freakishly strong little thing, and resistance was futile. Her friend tugged her straight to the center of the floor, and threw her hands in the air and moved in time to the music. Lily joined in, and felt a tap at her shoulder. Expecting it to be Jason, her heart raced a little, and she was furious with the stupid organ for doing it. He wasn't worth a heart pitter-pat, let alone a race.

She turned, and was surprised to see Bethanne's brother, Ty, and Mick's brother, Billy. "Can we join you ladies?" Ty asked with a grin.

Magda squealed and grabbed his hand to pull him into the dance. "It's Ty and Billy—yay!"

Since Ty and Magda began to dance together, Billy smiled shyly at Lily. She grinned back and turned to dance facing him. "I seem to have lost my partner, Billy. Care to dance?"

The young man grinned and swayed his hips in time to the music. He had rhythm, but his blush and downcast eyes gave away his self-consciousness. "You're a good dancer," Lily leaned in to shout near his ear.

His face brightened. "Thanks, Ms. Davis."

Good God. She felt like she was one hundred years old. "Lily. Please, call me Lily."

A tingle of awareness tickled at the back of her neck, and she instinctively knew Jason watched them. She shot a glance over her shoulder, and saw him frozen in place, scowling at her, while his harem danced around him.

\*\*\*\*

What the actual fuck?

Billy Evans was a good kid, but didn't Lily realize he was too young for her? And...c'mon...in the past week, she'd been on a date with Professor Snoozy and now she was cozying up to Billy on the dance floor? Jason didn't think he was an especially egotistical man, but it was a blow to his vanity she'd moved on from him so fast.

61

One of the women dancing with him grabbed his ass, and he jumped. What was he doing, standing here frozen in place, staring at Lily like some kind of lovelorn goober? He was Jason freaking Braden, and there were plenty of fillies in the paddock—he didn't need Lily. He shook his head once. He was not lovelorn. Love? No way in hell was he going to fall victim to that particular ailment, even if all the other men in town were falling like ninepins.

He smiled at the woman who grabbed his ass and moved his hips in time to the music. She beamed back at him, and ground against him. Okay. It was more than he was looking for with her. The last time he'd danced like that it was with Lily in Las Vegas, and...dammit! He was doing it again—being an idiot over Lily. Maybe he needed a break, a few minutes to regroup and get his head back in the game.

"I'm going to head to the bar, sweetheart," he said to his dance partner, whose name escaped him. "I think I need a drink."

She stuck out her bottom lip, and looked at him with wide eyes. He winked. "Sorry, but you ladies have worn me out dancing."

He turned and maneuvered his way through the crowd to the bar, forcing his head not to swivel in Lily's direction, so he could see what was happening between Billy and her.

He held up a finger to call the bartender over, "Hey, Jim. Could you get me another beer?"

"You got it, Jase."

The upbeat dance music gave way to a slow song, and he lost his mental fight against looking at Lily. He leaned back against the bar, and squinted out to the dance floor, but couldn't see her.

"Looking for us?" He heard Ty ask.

He looked to his left and saw Lily, Magda, Billy, and Ty. He clenched his fist, which itched with the urge to wipe the knowing smirk off his friend's face.

"Hiya, Jason!" Magda stood on tiptoes and kissed his cheek. "I didn't know you guys were going to be here tonight."

"That was quite a show you were putting on out there, Einstein. Or maybe I should start calling you Twinkletoes...or Chippendale...since you looked like a male stripper at a bachelorette party on the dance floor just now." Snarkiness dripped from Lily's words.

Her arms folded across her chest, and the icy glare she sent his way, was enough put down a coat of frost in a jungle. Why was Lily so pissed off—she was the one cozying up to Billy on the dance floor, for Pete's sake.

"Your friends took your shots back to the table," the bartender said to Magda and Lily, as he slid Jason's beer across to him.

"We'll take two more then," Lily said.

"Jäger?" Jason asked with a chuckle.

Magda's head pivoted toward Lily, and she stared at her friend with her jaw hanging down somewhere around her knees.

"No," Lily's reply was curt. "Never again."

"Too bad, you're mighty fun with a little Jäger in you." Jason winked at her.

Magda looked back and forth between them like she was at the Finals at Wimbledon.

Ty still had an annoying grin on his face. "Do tell."

They were spared having to answer, by the arrival

of his sister, Deidre, who bounced up next to him. "We've got a table over there." She jerked her thumb toward the seating area by the window. "Do y'all want to join us on our Girls Night? We're willing to bend the no-men-allowed rule for you."

\*\*\*\*

He just wanted to go out and have a little fun with Ty and Billy tonight. Maybe hook-up with a little cutie to help him scrub the memory of his night with Lily out of his head. Especially since Lily had clearly moved on and was dating other guys. But here he was, clustered around the same little table with Lily and the rest of the Girls' Night crew. He sighed and took a swig of his beer.

Someone tugged on his sleeve, and he looked down to see the woman he'd been dancing with when he'd spotted Lily. Well…technically, one of the women he'd been dancing with, as there had been quite a few women on the floor with them.

"Remember me?" she asked with a coquettish grin, as if fully aware he would, in fact, remember her.

Problem was, he didn't. Sure, he remembered dancing with her, but he couldn't remember her name to save his soul.

"Of course I do, sweetheart. We were dancing with each other a little while ago." He smiled down at her, and saw her face fall at his response. Uh oh. Did he know her before tonight?

"I know it's been a while since we went out, but I can't believe you'd forget." She pouted in an exaggerated manner, but he saw hurt in her eyes.

What was her name? And when had they gone out together? Stall for time, Braden.

She made it easy for him, as she bounced in place and squealed, "Ooo, they're playing our song! Let's dance."

Their song? How many freaking times had he gone out with this woman?

He glanced over at Lily, as the woman slid her hand down his arm to grasp his hand and pull him toward the dance floor. Lily scowled at him and pushed her glasses up on her nose. He was mighty grateful for those glasses right about now—they were the only thing protecting him from the daggers she was shooting out of her eyes.

He smiled at the woman and said, "Slow down, sweetheart. We've got all night."

\*\*\*\*

All night? They had all night? What the hell was that supposed to mean? Lily grabbed some peanuts from the bowl on the table and crunched them vigorously. She knew exactly what it meant, maybe better than most. Okay, not most, it was Jason Braden in question...he had been with more than his fair share of the female population of the greater Rivers Bend area. And they weren't a couple, in spite of their fling in Vegas, so she had no claim on him. He could dance with whatever trashy slut he wanted to. She mentally slapped her own wrist—she didn't know this woman. She probably wasn't a trashy slut, Lily was jealous and lashing out...and, oh, how upsetting was that idea? Jealousy over Jason was one emotion she most certainly did not want to feel.

The slow, romantic song the DJ was playing segued into a fast-paced country song, and Billy leaned across the table, pointed to the dance floor, and asked,

"Want to dance again?"

"Sure? Why not?"

\*\*\*\*

"Good night! The Retreat is my stop too, Cisco is waiting for me here," Bethanne called as she got out of the giant SUV Jeff had hired for them to use tonight.

"This was so much fun!" Magda blew Heather and Lily a kiss before she followed Bethanne out of the car. She giggled as she slid out of the car; being a petite woman, it was a lot bigger drop for her than it had been for Bethanne.

"I'll pick up Hadley tomorrow morning at ten. Thanks for letting her sleep over tonight," Lily called after Magda, who turned and flashed her a thumbs-up sign.

The driver closed the door behind them, and got in behind the wheel. He turned to look at them in the farthest back row of seats. "One of you lives on Main Street, and the other out on River Road, right?"

They replied in the affirmative, and he nodded. "I'll stop at Main Street first, since it's closer, and then bring you to River Road."

Lily nodded, but Heather leaned forward in the seat and said, "I don't mean to be a pain, but could you go to River Road first, and then bring me back to Main Street? I'm sorry, I know it's taking you out of your way."

He winked at her. "For what your brother is paying me, I could drive her to Canada before taking you to Main Street, and I'd still be making a profit. It's nice to see a big-time sports hero who's such a generous down-to-earth guy."

"Thank you. I'm really proud of my brother, but if

you tell him I said so, I'll deny it," Heather replied with a grin.

The driver turned around and started the SUV. As he pulled around the circular drive in front of the Retreat at Rivers Bend to wend his way down the long road through the woods, Lily turned in her seat to look at Heather.

"Why do you want him to take the long way home? I'd have figured you'd be in a hurry to get home to your new husband."

Keeping her voice low, so the driver couldn't hear, Heather said, "Trust me, I am. But I wanted the chance to talk to you alone."

Lily flopped back against the seat and faced forward. She exhaled loudly. "If this is about Jason again, I don't want to discuss it."

"My brother is a doofus."

Lily nodded. "No argument here, maybe I'll enjoy this conversation after all."

Heather laughed and swatted at her arm in a teasing manner. "Hey! He *is* still my brother."

"Sorry."

"You don't sound especially sorry, but I'll let it slide, because he was a jerk tonight." She shook her head. "Knowing you two had been together in Vegas, I couldn't believe he spent all night dancing with that bimbo in front of you. Are you okay?"

"Sure," Lily lied. "There's nothing between us; Jason can dance with whoever he wants to, but she was a bimbo, wasn't she? I thought maybe I was being hard on her, but…"

"You weren't. She's a total floozy, which is just Jason's type. It's why I didn't want you to have feelings for him—"

"I told you, I don't have feelings for him," Lily interrupted.

"We haven't known each other long, but I think I've gotten to know you well enough to call bullshit on that statement."

Lily shrugged, but didn't answer. What could she say? She did have feelings for Jason, even if she really didn't want to.

"He always picks that type of woman for a reason. He may seem all light and breezy, but he doesn't trust people easily. If he only goes out with superficial women, he doesn't need to worry about them wanting to get too deep. And he doesn't do deep."

Lily was silent for a bit, as they drove past Heather and Mick's apartment over the Nosh Pit on Main Street. The car turned right at the end of Main Street, at the one streetlight in Rivers Bend, which was currently set to blinking because the small town had no traffic at this time of night.

"Why would he have trust issues? No offense, Heather, but your family is like the frigging Waltons."

"All families have their problems, but we are lucky we're close and always have each other's backs. That's why it's hard for me to admit to you my brother is a doofus, but I didn't like the way he treated you tonight."

"Thank you, I don't want to cause problems in your family, though. I understand your loyalty is to Jason."

"To a point. His issues are his to discuss, so I don't want to go into any more detail, but I did want to try to explain why he was being the kind of guy I would normally want to punch in the nose."

The driver pulled up to the big gate at Lily's temporary home, and looked in the rearview mirror. "Is there a code to the gate?"

Lily told him, although she wasn't sure of the protocol with the gate code. Should she have not told him? If she hadn't, how else would they have gotten onto the property? She sighed, Gloria and she were such different people, and led such different lives; it was amazing they were half-sisters.

"I get it. Sometimes I want to deck Gloria too, but she's my sister, so what can I do?" Lily glanced at Heather and shrugged.

The driveway up to the Georgian-style mansion was lined with tall trees, currently bare of leaves and their branches stood out in stark silhouette against the night sky.

"Jason is a good guy, and I really like you too. I think you'd be good for him, if he could get his head out of his ass. But I have to warn you, I don't know if he ever will, so I don't want you to get too attached to him and end up hurt."

The exterior motion sensor floodlights came on as the SUV pulled up to the front door of Gloria's mansion and bathed the driveway in a bright light. Lily turned to give Heather a quick hug. "Don't worry about me—I'm tougher than I look, and I also have no intention of getting involved with Jason. What happened in Vegas was a mistake, and he's clearly back into his regular dating ways now we're back in Rivers Bend. Plus, taking care of Hadley is a full-time job, on top of my actual full-time job…I don't have time to get involved with anyone right now."

Heather hugged her back, but Lily could see her clearly in the glow of the floodlights, and her smile didn't reach her eyes. Lily knew she wasn't fooling herself, but it seemed like she wasn't fooling Heather either.

Chapter 7

"Thanks for fitting in my mom's car for an oil change today, Billy. Normally, I'd do it myself, but it's been crazy busy on the farm." Jason said, as he got out of his mom's small SUV at Miller's Garage in town.

Billy pulled a rag out of the pocket of his coveralls, and wiped his hands. "No problem, man. I'm happy to do it. What's got you so busy at the farm? I always picture it as such a peaceful place."

Jason laughed. "It can be, but we've seen a real increase in the number of riding lessons we're giving, and our breeding program really seems to be taking off like a rocket."

A blessing and a curse, as far as Jason was concerned, as his dyslexia made it hard to keep up with forms and correspondence, and other written work involved in that undertaking.

He tossed the keys to Billy, who caught them one-handed, and then walked over to the red cooler next to the garage bay doors. "Do you want one, Billy? I can never resist the ice-cold Coke here, even on a day as chilly as today." He shivered, in spite of his fleece-lined denim jacket. You could never tell what the weather would be like in November in Rivers Bend…sometimes it would be fairly warm and pleasant, but today there was a definite nip in the air.

"No thanks, I might get a coffee. It's too cold for

me to want a soda today. Want to head inside?"

"Sounds good." The smell of oil reached his nose as Jason followed Billy past the service bays and into the small office area.

Billy went straight for the coffee maker, and poured a cup, which he held between his hands for warmth. He leaned back against the counter next to the coffee pot and blew on his steamy mug before taking a sip.

Jason popped the top of his bottle of soda, and cocked his head to look at Billy. He really looked at him for the first time. He was good looking, like all the Evans men were. Mick could be a frigging fashion model, if he wanted to be, and Billy was almost as handsome as his oldest brother. Jason could see what Lily might see in him, but it frosted his ass, nonetheless.

He gestured at Billy with the bottle, "So…you and Lily, huh?"

Billy scrunched up his face and squinted at him. "Me and Lily, what?"

Jason shrugged and tried to look casual, which he was far from feeling. If he didn't know better, he'd swear the churning in his gut was jealousy. But he couldn't be jealous. He didn't care about Lily one way or the other. No sir, not him.

"You two seemed to be hitting it off Friday night."

Billy smiled, but wrinkled his forehead and blinked a few times. "We danced, but that was it. She's a good dancer, and a lot of fun, but we're not a thing, if that's what you're thinking."

"Why not? Are you saying she's not good enough for you?" Jason clenched the fist of the hand that wasn't holding his soda, and he had that bottle in a death grip. What was with him today?

Billy seemed to be wondering the same thing as he held up his hands. "I didn't mean to insult her. Like I said, she's great, just not for me. Not that way. I didn't mean to step on your turf, dude, but you were with that other girl all night. I didn't know you and Lily had anything going."

"What? Lily and I don't have anything going. I didn't understand what you had against her and wanted to get to the bottom of it."

"Riiight," Billy drew out the word. "I've got nothing against her. I like to dance, and so does she, so we had fun the other night, but, she's like ten years older than me."

Tension drained from Jason's body, and he unclenched his fist. He grinned at Billy. "I don't think it's quite ten years, and you better not let her hear you say she's old."

"What do you care, anyway? You're love 'em and leave 'em Jason Braden. You never go out with any girl more than once or twice; you're a legend in these parts. Does Lily have you considering settling down with one woman?"

Jason snorted. "Me? No way."

Except, maybe he was. And with the one woman in town, he really didn't want to like or trust.

"Hellooo! Billy, are you here?"

"I'm in the back, Lily," the mechanic responded.

He heard Lily's heels click across the concrete floor of the service bays. Jason shook his head and chuckled, although he wasn't feeling the slightest bit amused. "Nothing between you and Lily, huh? Then what's she doing here looking for you?"

Before Billy could respond, Lily breezed into the office; she had on dark green jeans tucked into brown boots, and a short red pea coat. She stopped in her tracks and stared at Jason, her mouth forming an 'O.' "Sorry to interrupt. I thought Joyce was here. Isn't that her car out front?"

"It is, Moonbeam. I'm dropping it off for her."

"Oh, that's too bad." She frowned.

Jason thought his eyebrows were trying to make a break for it, they shot up so far on his forehead. "Well, I'm terribly sorry to be such a disappointment to you."

She sighed, as if he really was a disappointment to her, and Jason felt his heart drop to the vicinity of his knees. Why did he care if Lily was disappointed in him?

"You can't help it."

Billy looked between them with confusion apparent in his gaze, and asked, "What did you need, Lily? Something the matter with your car?"

She shook her head and leaned around Billy to knock on the paneled wall behind him. "No, knock on wood, my car is fine. I had a check for Joyce for Hadley's riding lessons and boarding fees; I was hoping I could give it to her."

"She's tied up back at the Farm, but I could take the check to her." He frowned and squinted at Lily. "Unless you don't trust me with it?"

"Of course I trust you with it." Lily rolled her eyes. "I just didn't think of it, because it's usually Joyce who handles the financial stuff. And I always enjoy having a chat with her."

"I have an idea," Billy said with a slow smile. "I

was going to give Jason a ride back to the Farm, why don't you take him? That way, I can keep working and you can see Joyce—kill two birds with one stone."

Lily's eyes grew round behind her tortoise shell glasses, and her jaw dropped. "Um...well...."

Was the idea of giving him a lift so off-putting to her that she was unable to form a sentence?

Jason shook his head. "Doesn't seem like Moonbeam wants to do it, Billy. Can you give me a ride? If not, I'll kill time in town until Mom's car is ready."

Billy frowned and shook his head once. "It could be a while, I have two cars in front of Joyce, since I'm fitting her in last minute."

Lily took a deep breath, squared her shoulders, and found her voice. "I can give you a ride."

"Are you sure?" Billy asked.

She nodded a couple of times briskly. "Yes, I'm sure. Can you go right now, Jason? I have some time before I have to pick Hadley up from field hockey practice."

He straightened up and took the last swig of his soda. "I'm ready."

****

The interior of her classic VW Bug felt way too small, with Jason jammed into the passenger seat next to her. Her hand brushed his denim-clad thigh when she shifted gears, and the warmth and muscular firmness of said thigh, brought her straight back to their night together in Vegas. Damn her excellent memory, sometimes it could be a curse.

She felt her cheeks grow warm. "It's hot in here, sorry. The heater can be temperamental, and sometimes

75

it doesn't want to shut off."

Jason turned his head to look at her, and she wanted to wipe the sly smile off his face. "I don't think the heat's on, Moonbeam. Maybe it's the company?"

The heat in her cheeks went from slightly warm to thermonuclear in a flash, and she hated her body's reaction to this man. "Your ego really is the size of Texas, isn't it? I guess it's no surprise, given the way women throw themselves at you. You had quite a mob following you around on Friday night; although, you ignored most of them, except for that one girl...what was her name?"

Jason shrugged. "I can't remember."

She gripped the steering wheel with both hands, and stared at the road straight ahead. "You really are a prince, aren't you? You sleep with a woman on Friday night, and can't remember her name by Monday afternoon."

"I did what? You think I slept with her Friday night?"

"Didn't you?" She snuck a peek over at Jason, who seemed honestly shocked at the idea.

"No! But even if I had, you and Billy seemed awfully cozy at the bar Friday night too. People in glass houses, Moonbeam, shouldn't throw stones."

She saw the sign for Braden Farm and put on her turn signal. She reached for the gearshift and again brushed Jason's leg. "Billy and I were only dancing. He's like ten years younger than me!"

She turned into the drive, and followed the road past white fences and green fields, toward the house and barns.

Jason visibly relaxed and sank back against the

seat, which caused his legs to spread a little further, and now her hand brushed his thigh when she shifted. Such a simple touch shouldn't cause her pulse to pound, and her breath to quicken, so why was it?

He smiled at her, and when she saw his dimple, she fought the urge to lean over and kiss it. "Not into the whole cougar scene?"

She returned his smile. "No. He's a nice kid, but he's still a kid. What about the no-named woman from Friday...is she not your type?"

He frowned and squinted his eyes as he stared straight ahead. "She's exactly my type."

"So what was the problem?"

"Damned if I know."

They approached the back of the house, and she shifted to a lower gear. "Do you want me to drop you here, or at the barn?"

"Here is good. I could use the walk to the barn to clear my head. If you want to give the check to me, I can take it with me, and drop it off in the office on my way."

"Thanks. I would love to visit with your mom, but I'm running late to get Hadley, and this will save me some time."

She stopped the car, and he hopped out, only to rest his hands on the roof and lean back in to say, "Thanks for the ride, Moonbeam."

"No problem. Oh, wait! Let me get you the check." She reached for her bag in the backseat and dug around in it. She pulled out the check and waved it in triumph. "Here it is! I couldn't find it for a second there. Maybe I need to get a smaller bag."

Their fingers brushed when he reached in to take

the check, and Lily shivered. Jason pulled his hand back like he'd received an electric shock, so she didn't feel too bad about the shiver. Whatever she felt for Jason, his reaction made it clear she wasn't alone in her feelings. It seemed like neither of them knew exactly what those feelings for each other were…neither was the other's type, but they were pulled to each other like a natural force.

Chapter 8

Jason pulled up the sweeping drive to his brother Jeff's home and business, the Retreat at Rivers Bend. The big plantation style house was divided in two, with the corporate retreat facilities and guest lodging on one side, and his brother's home on the other.

Last Spring, Jeff proposed to a great woman. Magda was a Connecticut Yankee like Lily and had moved to the Bend to escape a controlling grandmother and a certifiable ex-fiancé. At which time, his brother had promptly fallen ass over teakettle for her. Tonight, Jeff was in Jason's personal idea of Hell—the happy couple were meeting with their wedding planner in D.C., so Jason offered to hang out with Jeff's daughter Sam tonight.

No skin off his nose, his niece was a great kid, whose company he enjoyed, and it's not like he had anything else to do. Yesterday he thumbed through the contacts on his phone and didn't see anyone he felt like going out with tonight. Of course, he didn't have Lily's info on his phone, and a replay of Vegas sounded pretty damned good to him, so good, in fact, he couldn't imagine being with anyone else this weekend. He liked Moonbeam way more than he wanted to, and it baffled him.

He pulled his pick-up around to the back of the house so he could go in through the kitchen door, which was the usual way the family entered the house. As he hopped out of his truck, a classic VW Bug pulled around the corner, and parked next to him.

Moonbeam.

He grinned when he saw her emerge from her old car. She might claim her parents were the hippies and not her, but she did have a little hippie chick thing going on, and damned if he didn't think it was cute. Since when did he feel that way? Usually he went for girls with big hair and tiny shorts. Not teachers with short hair and eyeglasses, who wore coats that looked like they were made from Grandma's old sofa—brocade, he thought his sisters called the fabric—over flowy skirts and tops.

His niece, Sam, and Lily's niece, Hadley, jumped out of the car and ran toward the house. Lily followed at a more sedate pace.

"Sorry we're late, Uncle Jason!" Sam called out as she darted by him, "I'm just gonna dump my school books, change my clothes, and then we'll be ready to go." She ran up two steps, stopped short, and turned around to ask, "Is it okay if Hadley comes to the movie with us tonight? Her Aunt Lily said it's okay with her, if it's okay with you."

"Fine by me," Jason said.

The two girls squealed and thundered into the house.

As the screen door slammed behind them, Lily said, "I'll pick her up here after the movie, so you don't have to drive out to River Road, just let me know what time. I'm really sorry we're late; I hope it hasn't messed up your plans for the night. I got held up at work, and the poor kids were stuck waiting for me."

"No problem. We still have plenty of time before the movie starts, as long as they don't take forever changing their clothes."

She smiled, but he noticed faint circles under her eyes, and her shoulders seemed as if they drooped under the weight of the world. "Two twelve-year-old girls? Good luck with that notion. You'll be lucky if you make the late show."

"You look beat, Moonbeam. Tough day?"

She walked to the back steps, her skirt blowing around what he now knew were a very fine pair of legs. He remembered what those legs felt like wrapped around him, and he felt a stirring of desire.

She stopped on the top step and shook her head once. "You have no idea. It was the worst."

Jason realized she didn't need a horn dog right now, she needed a friend, so he squelched his lust and said, "Why don't we head inside, where it's warm?" Jason held the door open for her and put his hand on her back as he followed her into the cozy kitchen. Feeling the warmth of her body where his hand touched her, made it a little trickier to send the horn dog packing, but he tried. Which was not him. He never tried with women. They chased him, and he let them worry about what he needed, and not the other way around. He removed his hand from her back and shut the door behind them to keep the chill outside where it belonged.

He gestured to the kitchen table, and Lily walked to the nearest chair, took off her coat, tossed it on the ladder-back, and slumped on the seat. She stretched out her legs, rolled her head on her neck, and he heard an audible crack, as the tension released.

"I didn't realize teachers had to work late. I always

figured y'all ran out of the building at the last bell, shoving kids out of your way to hop in your cars and get out of Dodge."

The corners of her mouth tilted up a bit. "Unfortunately, no. And as a special education teacher I have all kinds of extra reports that need to be written and filed, additional meetings, and today I had the joy of dealing with an especially stubborn parent and my esteemed predecessor.

"Ms. Wentworth," Jason said through clenched teeth, amazed the mere mention of the woman could still make him want to put his fist through a wall, all these years later.

Lily's lips tightened. "That's her."

"Want to talk about it?"

She glanced over her shoulder at the kitchen door. "I shouldn't. There are confidentiality issues."

He shrugged. "You said it yourself—the girls aren't coming back anytime soon, and sometimes you need to get stuff off your chest, otherwise it sits there and eats away at your peace of mind. I won't tell anyone, and you don't have to give me names. Think of this kitchen as a Confessional."

The idea drew a chuckle from her, and he felt inordinately pleased he was able to make her laugh.

"Father Jason? I don't see that happening anytime soon. The whole celibacy thing would put a serious crimp in your lifestyle."

He nodded in agreement. "You got me there. Plus, I'm not Catholic. But I am one of the few people in Rivers Bend who can keep a secret. Why do you think Mick asked me to be his best man at the super-stealth wedding?"

She grasped her right hand in the left and lifted her arms over her head to stretch, and leaned back as she considered his offer. The position caused the tank top under her flowy blouse to pull across her breasts. They weren't overly large, but he knew from experience they were mouthwateringly perfect, and he felt his body stir as he remembered how responsive they were. He sincerely hoped there was no celibacy in his future—at least as far as Lily was concerned.

"Okay. If you swear what I tell you doesn't leave this room…"

He crossed his heart over the waffle knit Henley he wore under his unbuttoned plaid flannel shirt.

She bit her bottom lip, and spoke in a low voice, so the girls couldn't hear her. "There's this student at school, his teacher approached me because she suspects he has dyslexia. It's a learning difference…"

"I know what it is," Jason interrupted through gritted teeth.

She looked at him with a question in her eyes, which he had no intention of answering. When it became clear he wasn't going to say any more on the subject, she lifted one shoulder and continued, "All right, then. I met with the student, and I agreed with the teacher's assessment. I recommended further testing, and said I would begin pre-referral interventional services, which basically means I would start working with him while we wait for the special education eligibility evaluation."

"That's good, right? It means he'll get the help he needs?"

"Normally…yes, but in this case…no. Because when I spoke to his parents this afternoon, they refused their permission for us to go forward."

Jason whistled low between his teeth. "So you're willing to help the kid and his parents are saying no go?"

Her eyes flashed at the suggestion in his tone that she might not be willing to help. "Of course I'm willing, I'm more than willing—I'm eager to help him. It's my job."

"Not all teachers feel that way."

Lily screwed up her mouth. "No. I learned that lesson today, when I spoke to Ms. Wentworth."

Jason bit back a growl at the name of the woman who'd made his school life a living hell on Earth as a kid.

Lily looked at him quizzically. Guess he didn't do as good a job as he thought at suppressing his noise of rage. She didn't press him though, which he appreciated. No way they had the kind of time they needed to discuss his issues, and he really didn't want to anyway.

"I asked her why, when his teacher last year had voiced the same concerns, nothing was done to help the boy. Do you know what she said?"

Lily probably thought it was a rhetorical question, but Jason scowled and replied, "I have a pretty good idea, but why don't you go ahead and tell me."

"She said, after emphasizing it was all off the record, he didn't seem that bad to her, and she was so swamped with work she didn't see the point in putting in all the time to help a boy with such a chip on his shoulder." Lily punched the kitchen table, and this time he could swear she growled. "Of course he has a chip on his shoulder! He's a kid, and he's been struggling with his schoolwork with no help from any adult. His parents feel like working with me would be too much of a stigma." She snorted in derision. "A stigma for him or for them is what I'd like to know. He's completely on his own."

"Poor kid," Jason said quietly, but with feeling.

"His father actually said to me not everyone is cut out to be book smart." She made air quotes with her fingers. "And his boy was not one of God's brighter creatures. But here's the thing, from my limited interactions with his son, I can tell he's smart as a whip. He's trying to figure out ways to cope with his schoolwork on his own, which is a Herculean task, and his father is calling him stupid—when he's not! So he's getting frustrated and acting out, but he's a bright kid, and I know I could help him."

"The kids are lucky to have an advocate like you in their corner. Someone who really gets them, and wants to help."

"You sound like you're speaking from experience."

Before he could figure out how to respond to her very loaded statement, their nieces ran into the kitchen, in clothes that didn't look all that different to Jason than the ones they'd worn to school. He didn't understand why it had been so all-fired important to them to change.

"We're ready!" Sam said.

"Aunt Lily, do you want to come with us to the movies?" Hadley asked.

"I don't know, sweetie, it's been a long day for me."

Jason stopped and patted her shoulder on his way to the door. He offered her a hand as she rose from the chair. "Now see, I think it's the best possible reason to come out with us. A little popcorn, some Milk Duds, and a post-apocalyptic teen love story is a time-tested remedy for a bad day."

She smiled and didn't release his hand, even though she stood next to him now. He felt a zap at the small contact, like there was one of those practical joke buzzers in the palm of her hand. One of the reasons for his animosity toward Lily was her profession, but she seemed totally different from the Special Ed teacher he'd had as a kid, the very same Ms. Wentworth from Lily's story, who'd shunted him aside, and left him floundering on his own like the boy Lily wanted to help. What he wouldn't have given for a teacher who cared for her students like Lily seemed to do. He couldn't help but wonder if she was for real, since she was so different from his experience. He wanted to believe she was, because the attraction between them was strong, and the sex in Vegas had been insanely good, but he wasn't sure he did.

"Okay, you sold me. I'll go with you guys."

"Y'all," Jason corrected with a grin, "You are such a Yankee, Moonbeam. Tell me what did the trick. It was the Milk Duds, wasn't it? No one can resist a Dud."

She winked. "Yep. It's the Milk Duds that have lured me out with you tonight; nothing else." She leaned closer and whispered, so the girls wouldn't hear, although the storm door slammed behind them as they ran out to the truck, while chattering away to each other. "So don't think it's your charms, or anything, Braden."

Hmm…the lady protested a little too much. Maybe

he wasn't the only one feeling conflicted.

****

Jason trotted down the steps on the side of the barn, which led from his apartment on the second story. At the bottom, he paused to stamp his feet on the ground, in an effort to get his jeans to fall better over his boots.

"Here you are."

He started at his brother Jeff's voice.

"Hey man," Jason replied. "How come you're not at the house for family brunch?"

Family brunch was a Sunday tradition in the Braden household, which no one ever missed if they were in Rivers Bend. Back when Jeff played football for the Portland Pintos, the family would gather around the TV to watch his game after gathering for brunch.

"I was looking for you."

Jason narrowed his eyes and peered at Jeff. "I took a quick shower after my morning chores. I'm not that late, why are you hunting me down?"

"Heard you went on a date with Lily Davis Friday night."

His brother's tone was casual, but didn't fool Jason, who pursed his lips and clenched his fists at his side. "It wasn't a date. She came to the movies with Sam, Hadley, and me while I was babysitting for you. But, even if it was a date, I don't see what business it is of yours."

Jeff scratched his head, which made his perpetually messy hair even messier. Jason rolled his eyes—he worked on a horse farm, and always managed to present a tidier appearance than his older brother, who ran the corporate retreat facility now that his football playing days were over.

"Maybe it's not any of my business, but Lily is Hadley's guardian, and Hadley is my daughter's best friend. Our families spend a lot of time coordinating with each other as a result, and I don't want you to play your usual games with Lily, and make it hard for the kids to keep on being friends." He shrugged and continued, "Plus, I like the woman. She's friends with Maggie, and a good teacher at the school—I don't want you breaking her heart and driving her away from Rivers Bend."

The wind went out of Jason's lungs, as sure as if Jeff had punched him in the gut. "Wow, man, I had no idea you had such a low opinion of me."

Jeff held up his hands. "Not fair, Jase. You know how much I think of you. Even if you weren't my brother, I'd respect the hell out of your work here on the farm, your loyalty to your friends and family—"

"But I'm not good enough for Lily," Jason interrupted with a frown.

"What the hell? I never said any such thing! It's been your pattern with women to get some and get gone. You can't deny it…and you've never even tried to deny it before."

Jason took a deep breath and released it. "Maybe you have a point."

Silence hung in the air between them, and then Jeff's eyes opened wide. "Oh my God. I figured it out—you like this woman. Really like her." He laughed and shook his head. "Holy hell…the mighty ladies' man, Jason Braden is being taken down by a little hippie gal. A teacher, no less. This is rich!"

"Back off, brother," Jason said.

His warning made Jeff laugh even harder,

sometime being the little brother really sucked eggs.

"I'm sorry"—Jeff held his stomach and wheezed—"It's just too good."

"Give me a freaking break; I'm not even going out with the woman."

Jeff stopped laughing and glared at him. "Does she know it? Because if you're leading her on…"

His warning went unspoken, and Jason glared right back at him for several beats before he said, "I am not leading Lily on—we're on the same page, not that it's any of your business. And that page is cautious friendship."

Jeff screwed up his mouth, and studied Jason's face. He shook his head once. "I don't think so…I think you really like this woman and it's freaked you the fuck out, and you don't know what to do. Am I right?"

Jason kicked a clump of dirt and couldn't look his brother in the eye. "Mebbe."

"Why don't you try to date her? Y'know, like a normal man would. She's really nice, and cute if you go for her type."

"Oh yeah…the dyslexic guy and the special education teacher. It's like an after-school special waiting to happen."

He snuck a peek at his brother, and saw light dawn in his eyes. "That's what this is about? Your dyslexia? C'mon man, who is better to understand it than Lily?"

"Yeah, right…so she can look at me like I'm one of her students? No thank you. That's not the kind of relationship I want."

"What kind? You mean the kind where you know all about each other, including the challenges, and support each other through them?"

"Easy for you to say. You're not the one being pitied all the time."

"Lily doesn't pity her students, and she wouldn't pity you. But you'll never know it if you never give her a chance, and knowing you, you won't. And y'know what, bro? That makes me sad."

\*\*\*\*

"Thanks for driving out here to spend the day with me, Roni, I really appreciate it."

Her best friend smiled and shrugged. "No problem. It's a nice Sunday drive, and it's pretty here." She looked out the window of the country inn, where they were having brunch. "A little bucolic for my taste, as you know I'm more of a city girl, but it's nice. Peaceful."

Lily snorted, and picked up her coffee cup to take a sip. Mmm…strong to the point of bitter, exactly the way she liked it. "It may look that way, but Rivers Bend is a hotbed of gossip and intrigue."

Roni raised her eyebrows, "Intrigue? I find that hard to believe."

"Okay, maybe not intrigue, but there's a lot going on under the surface here."

Roni's crystal blue eyes looked over the rim of her coffee cup as she drank. She put the cup down, and asked, "How about with your farmer? Is there a lot going on under the surface with him? Or should I say…under the sheets with him?"

"He's not a farmer, per se. His family runs a horse farm, and a very successful breeding program. He also gives riding lessons. Hadley is taking lessons to improve her jumping right now."

"Is that where she is today?"

"She's at the Braden's house, but not for lessons today. She's having brunch with her friends Sam and Madison at Sam's grandmother's place."

"You'll notice I'm choosing not to tease you about your professional defense of Lover Boy, a few moments ago."

"Really? Because it seemed a lot like teasing to me."

"I couldn't resist." Roni grinned.

"And he's not my lover boy."

"Not since your Vegas fling, but he could be."

Lily shook her head so emphatically; she had to push her glasses up on her nose. "No, he couldn't be. We've reached a sort of détente between us, but we're not going to take it any further. Not again."

Roni scrunched up her nose, "Why not?"

Lily unfolded the napkin from the basket of pastries in the middle of the table, and selected a mini-muffin. "Cinnamon crunch. These are the best."

"I will not be deterred by a yummy basket of carbs"—Roni peered in the basket and pulled out a miniature croissant—"Not for long, anyway."

Lily closed her eyes in bliss as she took a bite. The crunchy topping, combined with the tender muffin underneath was pastry heaven. She swallowed, and shrugged. "Fine. We'll go there, because you're more relentless than a bloodhound once you get going. There are tons of reasons not to get involved romantically with Jason. I'm busy learning a new job, finding my way in a new town, figuring out how to take care of an almost-teenager—but most importantly, Jason is a player. On a level, I've never seen before, and I don't want to get involved with a guy like that."

"Fair enough." Roni shrugged. "But aside from the player thing, he seems like a pretty good guy. And even players settle down eventually."

Lily tsked her tongue and rolled her eyes. "Oh yeah, name one."

"George Clooney," Roni pointed what was left of her croissant at Lily. "He's married with twin babies now, and he used to swear he would never do any such thing."

"He also must be, like, thirty years older than Jason. I don't really feel like waiting until I'm in my fifties for him to decide to settle down."

The waitress approached with their plates, and Lily put her finger up in front of her lips to shush her friend, while the girl put down their dishes in front of them. She'd opted for the French toast, and her mouth watered as the aroma of warm bread, cinnamon, and nutmeg drifted up to her nose. She looked over at Roni's Egg Benedict on a biscuit, and briefly had food envy. "That looks amazing!"

"So does yours. Want to share?"

"Good idea."

As the two women busied themselves dividing their entrees, Roni leaned forward and whispered, "Why did you shush me just then?"

"The waitress is friends with Jason's older niece and nephew. I didn't want her to hear us discussing him. It would be all over his family—and town—in no time."

"I'm starting to see what you mean about it being a hotbed of gossip here."

\*\*\*\*

Roni whistled softly as they pulled up to Joyce

Braden's house to pick up Hadley.

"It's an impressive spread, isn't it? I don't know much about horses, but they look so beautiful in the fields."

"I didn't mean the horses. Now that's what I call some fine-looking scenery." Roni jerked her head in the direction of a pick-up football game between the Braden brothers, Mick, Billy, Ty, and Cisco.

Lily laughed and smacked her friend on the arm. "You are so bad!"

They got out of the car and met at the hood, Roni still had her gaze riveted on the game. "Which one is yours?"

"He's not mine. How many times do I have to tell you?"

Roni grinned and waggled her eyebrows. "No need to tell me. I can guess which one is Jason."

Lily turned her head to look at the guys, just in time to see Jeff throw the ball to Jason, only to have it bounce off his chest, because Jason was too busy staring at Lily to catch it.

"C'mon, man! You're not even trying." Jeff yelled at his brother. "What are you staring at…oh, crap…"

Lily felt a blush start at her neck and spread to her hairline, and was grateful when her niece and her friends spotted her. "Hi, Aunt Lily! Hi, Ms. Roni!"

Joyce Braden called from the back door, "Why don't you two c'mon inside. We have mulled cider, coffee, or tea. It's too cold to stand around outside watching the boys play ball, the rest of us are in here."

Lily glanced at Roni and asked, "Do you have time?"

"To meet your new boyfriend and his family?"

Roni murmured under her breath. "I'll make the time."

She narrowed her eyes at Roni, but called up to Joyce, "We'd love to—thanks!"

"Y'know, Mom is right about the cold. Do y'all want to head inside too?" Lily heard Jason ask, as they stepped through the back door and into the Braden's cozy kitchen. A chorus of greetings met them, and she smiled at all her new friends, and felt a frisson of happiness Roni was going to meet everyone. It was nice having her friends all together in one place.

"Hi! This is my friend, Veronica Bailey from Baltimore. Roni, this is Joyce, Magda, Heather, Deidre, and Bethanne."

"Hi everyone." Roni waved to the room.

"What can I get for you?"

"The mulled cider sounds delicious," Roni answered with a smile.

"For me too, thanks," Lily said.

Heavy footsteps thundered up the steps to the back porch, as the guys abandoned their game for the warmth of the kitchen.

\*\*\*\*

Lily introduced her friend to all the guys. She was pretty, in the way that usually appealed to him—tall, built, and blonde...although her wavy blonde hair did have some pink streaks in it. Jason smiled to himself. It made sense a friend of Lily's would also exhibit the same free-spirited individualism she did.

He leaned forward to shake Veronica's hands and noticed her blue eyes sparkled as she checked him out from head to toe. Either, she was interested in him, or she knew about Lily and his Vegas fling. His money was on Roni knowing about the fling.

His mother handed Lily and Roni steaming mugs of aromatic mulled cider, and both women squeezed into seats around the kitchen table.

"How do you know Lily?" Joyce asked with a smile, as she sat back down at the head of the table.

"We taught at the same school in Baltimore. We started the same school year, and were both new in town, so we ended up being roommates. I know she's happy here with y'all, but I can't pretend I don't miss her a lot."

Magda squeezed Bethanne's hand. "We were long-distance besties for a long time. It's not easy—although texting, video calls, and social media make it a little easier."

As Lily's friend continued to chatter away with everyone, Jason cocked his head to stare at her. Seriously, Roni was everything he loved in one beautiful package. So, why didn't he even fill a flicker of attraction to her? A sort of tingle on the back of his neck gave him the nagging feeling someone was looking at him. His gaze drifted to Moonbeam, and found her glaring at him. What crawled up her butt and died?

Jeff knocked him on the back of his head and whispered, "You'll find it kinda pisses off women you're involved with when you check out their best friend in front of them."

"I wasn't checking Roni out that way, and I'm not involved with Lily." He hissed the words back at his brother.

"Keep telling yourself that." Jeff laughed.

\*\*\*\*

"I can't believe the way Jason was staring at you!"

Hadley had gone upstairs to finish her homework, and Lily and Roni were alone for the first time since they'd gotten home from the Braden's house.

Roni laughed. "Please, Lily. I don't know when you thought he was staring at me, because every time I looked his way, he was devouring you with his eyes."

Lily leaned against the marble counter on the other side of the gigantic kitchen island from where Roni sat on one of the stools. Her heart fluttered at the thought Jason had been watching her, but she shook her head. "Right after I introduced you, he was totally checking you out."

"Studying me like a bug under a microscope, is more like it. I've had plenty of men interested in me, I know the signs, and Jason wasn't giving me any of them. He likes you, Lily. Better get used to the idea."

Lily sputtered, and Roni laughed and dug through her handbag for her car keys. She pulled them and rattled them. "Found them! I better head back to Baltimore. I hate to leave—I really miss you, Lily."

Lily walked around the island and they hugged. "I miss you too, Roni."

Her friend pulled back and winked at her, eyes twinkling. "You'll have to occupy your time with a certain hot farmer."

"Roni—" Lily shook her head and drew out the name in a warning tone.

"I know, I know, you're not interested in Jason. See—that's how you can keep yourself busy...pretending you don't luvvv him." Roni made kissing noises.

Lily rolled her eyes. "Remind me again why I miss you?"

"Because you know I always have your back, and you can count on me to tell you the truth, even when you don't want to hear it. Like now, when you're working so hard to pretend you don't care for Jason, when you really luvvvv him."

Roni dodged Lily's swat at her arm and ducked in to kiss her soundly on the cheek. Lily pulled her in for a hug.

"Text me when you get home, so I know you arrived safely."

After Roni left, Lily stood in the middle of the kitchen. She had a million things to do to prepare for the upcoming week, but she couldn't seem to move. Roni did know her better than anyone, and she seemed so certain Lily had feelings for Jason. And not feelings of disdain either—friendly feelings. Loving feelings.

She heaved a sigh and shook her head, before walking to the huge stainless-steel refrigerator, and pulling out the fixings for Hadley's and her lunches tomorrow. Even if Jason wasn't the playboy of Rivers Bend, she didn't have time to get involved with anyone right now.

## Chapter 9

Each day this week had been busier than the last, so there hadn't been time for Lily to do anything but rush from one task to the next. Now it was Saturday morning, and she was back in the laundry room...again.

Lily exhaled with a huff and her bangs fluttered against her forehead. She shoved the hair off her face and was fairly certain it was now standing straight up. Lovely. She hoisted a pair of Hadley's jeans from the pile of dirty clothes she stood in the middle of, like a human volcanic island in the South Pacific of laundry. She knew she had to hop in the shower, but first she needed to get a load of laundry in the washer if there was any hope of finishing it by the time they went back to school on Monday. She seriously had no idea how one tween girl created so many dirty clothes.

Hadley was into sports, which Lily had never been, and it created a lot of grass-stained clothes to be pre-treated and washed. Like every stinking day.

She looked up at the clock and sighed before yelling, "Hadley! Get your tushy in gear! We're running late for your riding lesson."

She tried in vain to finger-style her hair, before she pushed the button to turn on the huge high-efficiency washer, and it began its series of beeps and clicks and sensing. She'd done her laundry in ancient machines in the laundromat in her neighborhood in Baltimore, and these high-tech jobbies took some getting used to.

"No need to bellow, Aunt Lily, I'm ready to go."

She turned from the washer to see Hadley at the door of the cavernous laundry room, decked out in her equestrian gear. The kid was an excellent rider, even Lily who knew nothing about it, loved to watch her ride—she moved as one with her horse. Jason was teaching her about jumping or something, and they were going to be super-late for today's session, so Lily's shower would have to wait until she got home. There was no time to change into something halfway decent either, she thought ruefully, as she tugged her Baltimore Orioles jersey down to cover her yoga-pant clad butt. She really hoped she didn't see Jason when she dropped Hadley off at the Braden's farm.

Her niece raised an eyebrow as she gave Lily the once-over and said, "Especially since you're the one who's not ready to go."

Lily replied through gritted teeth, "There would've been time for me to get cleaned up if you had gotten up when you were supposed to. It's Saturday, you remember, the day we both pitch in to do the household chores. Since you chose to sleep in, I've been cleaning the kitchen, getting the laundry together, and cleaning up the mess you and your friends left in the family room last night, so spare me the attitude, Had."

Hadley's face grew red, but not with embarrassment, she clenched her little fists at her side. "I never had to do anything like that when Mother lived here. We had people to do it for us! You're the genius who said we could do it all ourselves, so why should I be punished for your bad decision?"

Lily stumbled back, in part because she was

standing knee-deep in laundry, but mostly because Hadley's angry words hit her like a physical blow. "I thought we were doing good here, Had. That we were happy together?"

Hadley averted her eyes, and toed the ground with a booted toe. She shrugged and replied with studied disinterest, "I guess. Can we leave now? I'm going to be late, and I don't want my lesson to be cut short."

Lily sighed as she picked her way through the dirty clothes, to follow her niece out of the laundry room, and into the kitchen. She picked up her keys and her oversized orange hobo bag—it was quite a look, but at least the bag matched her Orioles jersey. "Sure, we can go, but we need to discuss what's happening here, sweetie."

Hadley was already out the door, but called over her shoulder, "If we must, but can we do it in the car?"

By the time she shrugged into an oversized black cardigan, to complete her charming outfit, Hadley was waiting at the car, her arms crossed, and tapping her foot on the driveway.

Lily fumbled her keys as she rushed to lock the back door, and jogged to her classic Bug. She got in, and reached over to unlock Hadley's door.

Once they were on the road, Lily broke the uncomfortable silence, and asked, "Are you missing your mom?"

Gloria's calls were infrequent at best, and while Lily was secretly relieved not to have to talk to her sister too often, she imagined Hadley felt differently.

Hadley shrugged again. It seemed to be her default response this morning. "Not really, but I don't like cleaning the bathroom, making my bed, doing the dishes—I feel like I'm a slave! I've got a lot going on in my life, and I don't have time for all these menial tasks."

Lily rolled her eyes. Oh yeah, like she was a lady of leisure, with no other time obligations or things to do, but clean the vast mansion they were living in to keep things more stable for Hadley. But she wanted to ratchet back the tension in the car, and lighten the mood with her niece, so she forced a smile. "I'm sorry, Had, but if we don't do the household chores, we'd be buried under a mountain of dirty laundry and dishes within a week, and that's not how I want to go out."

The mulish set to Hadley's mouth made Lily think her lame attempt at humor had been an epic fail.

"I'm not suggesting we live in filth, just that we re-hire the staff."

Lily bit her bottom lip, as she rolled up to a stop sign. Hadley was not completely wrong. Working full-time, looking after Hadley, and maintaining her sister's grand Georgian style mansion, was a tremendous undertaking. If she was going to be honest with herself, Lily sometimes felt like she'd bitten off more than she could chew.

Before she could make that admission, Hadley heaved a long-suffering sigh. "And could this old piece of junk go any faster? I'm late!"

"Hey—back off my ride, kiddo! She's a beautifully restored classic car."

"But we have new cars, ones from this century even, in the garage. Why do we always have to take this one?"

Lily took a right turn at the low sign that heralded the entrance to the Braden's farm, and drove up the long driveway that meandered along next to the white fences, which outlined the lush fields dotted with hay bales. It would be a beautiful view if she weren't in the middle of a super-tense conversation.

"Because it's mine, and I love it. I thought you liked it too." Lily tried to keep the hurt from her voice, but she felt blindsided by Hadley's anger and disdain.

Hadley stared out the side window and—surprise—shrugged again.

The Braden homestead was on their right, and straight ahead Lily saw Jason waiting at the entrance to the largest of the Braden's barns, the one which held the ring where Hadley's lesson would take place.

"Just drop me here. I can run there faster than your car can drive."

Hadley's face was flushed, and she had tears in her eyes—from anger or from sadness, Lily didn't know. Hadley hopped out when the car was barely stopped, and slammed the door behind her without even saying goodbye. She ran across the yard to Jason without a backward glance.

What the hell happened? Lily's head fell back, and she fought against the tears stinging her eyes. She jumped at the tap on her window, and saw Joyce Braden, Jason's mom, standing next to her car, with sympathy and kindness in her eyes.

"Hello, Lily, no offense, but you look like a woman who could use a cup of tea and some cookies. C'mon into the house, and we'll solve all the problems of the world."

\*\*\*\*

Jason frowned as he pushed off where he leaned against the barn. Hadley rushed toward him, looking flushed and flustered.

"Sorry I'm late, Jason!"

"Slow down, Hadley. It's no problem."

"But I don't want to cut my riding time short today, and now I have to…because of her!"

Jason followed Hadley into the ring, where their horses waited.

"You saddled Flash for me, thanks!" Hadley said.

Jason swung effortlessly into his saddle as Hadley greeted Flash, and then mounted her pride and joy.

"No problem, when it looked like you were running late, I thought it would speed things along, but you peeled in here so fast, I can see you've got the speed part covered. Did you even wait for the car to stop before you tucked and rolled out of it?"

A grudging grin split Hadley's previously sullen face. "Barely. I just wanted to get away from her and start our lesson."

"Her? Do you mean your Aunt Lily?" Jason asked as they trotted the horses around the ring as a warm-up to their lesson.

"Yep."

"Did y'all have a fight or something? You were getting along just fine last Sunday."

"That was ages ago," Hadley said in the world-weary way she used to talk in all the time. Since her selfish socialite mother moved out and her Aunt Lily moved in, Hadley had been sounding more like a regular kid, but today it seemed like she'd taken ten steps backward.

"It was last weekend, Had, not fifty years ago, so tell me what happened to change things."

"We're having a little disagreement about whether

I'm her niece, or a servant in my own home."

Jason raised his eyebrows. "What do you mean?"

"When Aunt Lily moved in, she let all the help go, and now she expects me to do all the housework, but I have school and riding and field hockey! I don't have time to be her own personal Cinderella."

"If you're Cinderella, does that make Lily the wicked stepmother? Harsh. Is she mean to you?"

Jason had never seen any sign of it, but living in a small town taught him you never really know what goes on behind closed doors in other people's homes.

"Noooo." Hadley pressed her lips together. "But she expects me to help her do the laundry, and dishes— even clean my bathroom."

"But she pitches in too?"

"Yes. We were late today, because she was doing laundry and cleaning and stuff."

"And what were you doing, Cinderella?"

She scowled. "I thought you were different from other grown-ups, but you're going to take her side, aren't you?"

Jason refused to rise to the bait, and silently waited for her to answer his question, which she finally, reluctantly, did.

"I slept in—Sam and Madison came over last night, and I was tired. It was a very busy week."

"I reckon it was for your aunt too. Her job seems really stressful, and you live in a big house to keep clean and running, but I heard Lily wanted to stay in your house, instead of moving somewhere smaller and more manageable, so you wouldn't be uprooted."

Jason couldn't imagine jumping right from a carefree single life to being solely responsible for his twelve-year old niece and a huge property in another state, with very little warning or time to prepare, which was exactly what Lily had done.

"See—you are taking her side! It's because you like her. I saw you making moon eyes at her at the movies."

"I was not making moon eyes at her!" Jason Braden never in his life made moon eyes at any woman—they made eyes at him, dammit!

Hadley rolled her eyes in an exaggerated manner. "Denial—it's not just a river in Egypt. Can we move on to my lesson now, please?"

****

As Hadley and Jason walked from the barn to the house after her lesson, Jason mulled over their conversation from earlier. He hadn't wanted to preach to Hadley, and he wasn't altogether sure why he felt the need to defend Lily, but he thought he'd gotten through to the kid. Lily gave up her whole life to come take care of her niece when the girl's own mother couldn't be bothered to do so, and in his book that had to be worth cutting Lily some slack. However, it was clear Hadley didn't feel the same way.

Hadley stopped dead as soon as they came through his mother's kitchen door. He put his hands on her shoulders to stop himself from bumping into her back.

"Aunt Lily!" Hadley exclaimed.

He looked over Hadley's head in time to see Lily sitting at the kitchen table with his mom, and swiping at her eyes, which looked as pink as a bunny's. She grabbed her eyeglasses off the table, and shoved them back on her face. He'd teased his brother Jeff and friend Cisco about their naughty librarian fetish, since their women were, in fact, the town's librarians, but he'd never seen the appeal before. But right now, with Moonbeam and her total adorkability, he was starting to get it.

"Hi, Had. Ready to head home?" Lily sniffed, and her voice sounded thick, like she'd been crying. Jason fought the sudden urge to shove past Hadley and take Lily into his arms to console her.

Huh.

He'd never had that particular instinct with a woman who wasn't a part of his family before.

"Sure," Hadley nodded, but concern clouded her eyes. "Do you want to go grocery shopping on the way home? I know we have to, and my sleeping in totes messed up your day…"

"You have your sleepover at Madison's tonight—I don't think we'll have time to get to the store."

"I'm sorry—we can go grocery shopping now, and I'll stay home tonight."

Maybe he'd gotten through to Hadley after all, it certainly seemed like the kid was trying to make amends with her aunt.

Lily smiled gently at her niece's desperate offer. "No need to do that, sweetie, we can go tomorrow." She glanced at Jason's mom before continuing, "And you didn't mess up my day—totes or otherwise. C'mon, let's go home. I have some stuff I want us to talk over before you go to Madison's house."

"Thanks for the tea and company." Lily hugged Joyce, before turning back to her niece. She started when she locked eyes with him, as if she hadn't noticed he was even in the room before that moment.

Flattering.

Actually, he kind of liked it. From the time he reached puberty, girls had gone out of their way to get his attention. He knew it was just because of his looks, so it never meant much to him, but Lily was a woman who required a little chasing on his part, and when he did get her attention, it felt deeper. Her glance meant more to him, than all the fawning on him other women did.

She pulled her bulky sweater on, and wrapped it around herself like protection against something more than the nip in the early December air. "Hi Jason, sorry we were late for Hadley's lesson today."

"No problem, Moonbeam."

She flashed him a brief smile, before she put her arm around Hadley to shepherd her out of the house. She called over her shoulder, "Thanks again for the advice, Mrs. Braden."

"Joyce," his mother corrected with a smile. "Don't be a stranger, honey. I'm always around here somewhere."

"You'll be sorry you said that." Lily chuckled on her way out the back door.

"She's darling." His mother beamed at him after the door slammed shut. "I know you'd never look twice at her, but she's the kind of girl I hope you'll settle down with someday."

"Mom, what the hell?"

"Language..." she warned as she carried the teacups to the sink, and began to wash them.

His mother frowned at him over her shoulder, and he grabbed a towel to dry the cups. "Sorry, I meant to say 'what the heck?' Better?"

She handed him one cup, and washed the second

under the steamy water. "Better."

"But seriously Mom, it's not like I'm going out with bimbos…"

"It's not?" She interrupted, and handed him the second cup.

"No," he muttered, as he dried the dainty cup with the linen towel.

She turned to him, folded her arms, and raised her eyebrows.

"Okay. Maybe I do have a type…"

"And Lily is not it," his mother interrupted again—not that he had much of a defense anyway, Moonbeam was different from the girls he dated, but he was beginning to appreciate her unique charm.

"How was Lily doing? Hadley was really upset when she got here, but I think I convinced her she needs to appreciate her aunt a little bit more."

His mom took the cups to put them away in the china hutch. She gestured with her head to the big table at the center of her cozy, country kitchen. "Snickerdoodles on the table. Help yourself."

"My favorite!"

"I know." She smiled as she put the cups away, and pulled out a glass. She walked to the fridge, and took out the milk carton to pour a glass. She put the cold, frosty glass of milk in front of him to drink with his cookies. "I convinced Lily to ease up and get a little help around the house. She thought the two of them could do it all, except the landscaping, and she's drowning in housework."

"It's a big house," he said around a mouthful of gingery Snickerdoodle.

"Mansion," his mom corrected. "It's way too big

for the two of them, but she wanted to minimize the changes in Hadley's life, so she stayed there."

"That's what I told Hadley. But it's not like Gloria Peterson can't afford help. She's rolling in dough, and it would be cheaper than the ritzy Swiss boarding school she was ready to shuttle Hadley off to, before Lily stepped up to the plate."

"Gloria is providing funds, but Lily's been putting that money into an investment account for Hadley. Sweet and smart—I do like that girl."

He inhaled another cookie, and rolled his eyes as he took a gulp of milk. "We've already established how much you like Lily, Mom, and how superior she is to every other girl I've ever dated."

****

Lily looked around the granite and stainless steel temple that was her half-sister's kitchen, and wished Hadley and she were having this conversation back in the Braden's very cozy, albeit more old-fashioned, kitchen. Her niece, on the other hand, looked perfectly at ease and happy, although it could have more to do with the news she'd just imparted, rather than their location.

"Really? We can hire some help?"

Lily grinned at the enthusiastic disbelief in Hadley's voice.

"Yes. I still don't believe we need a full-time, live-in housekeeper, cook, and chauffeur like you had before..."

"We didn't have the chauffeur all the time," Hadley interrupted.

"You do realize most people don't even have a chauffeur some of the time, right?"

Hadley rolled her eyes. Now things were on a more even keel between them, Lily was able to smile at the gesture, rather than feel hurt or angry.

"As I was saying, Mrs. Braden convinced me there's no shame in getting a little help when you need it, and this is a huge house. I work full-time, and you have a boatload of activities, so we can get someone in once or twice a week to help with cleaning, laundry, and some cooking. Mrs. Braden gave me the name of a lady she thinks would suit our needs, and is trustworthy.

Joyce had actually given her an earful about how she would've hired help in a New York minute when her four kids were younger, but she couldn't afford it. And, while she agreed Hadley needed to learn some responsibility, and glimpse how the rest of the world lived, she could assign some chores to her niece without both of them getting overwhelmed and fighting as a result.

"Cool! Thanks, Aunt Lily." Hadley scrunched up her mouth and inspected her fingernails. "And, um, Jason reminded me you gave up a lot to be here for me, so I'm going to help you out more too."

Lily's eyes widened. The man never ceased to amaze her. There was a lot more to Jason Braden than the carefree playboy image he showed to the world. Why on earth would he keep the stand-up guy he really was hidden? "He did?"

"Uh huh." Hadley nodded and looked up from her nails to say earnestly, "And even if we have someone cleaning, I can still help with the day-to-day stuff."

"Thanks, Had. Maybe we can do the dishes together, and you could make your bed, and keep your room tidy?"

"Sure!" Hadley blushed. "I didn't mean to be such a spoiled brat."

Lily frowned. "Did Jason call you a spoiled brat?"

"No! But he kinda made me see I was being one, and I so don't want to be that girl. I might not say it enough—or y'know, ever—but it means a lot to me you moved here for me."

Her niece's eyes filled with tears, and Lily blinked away a few of her own. She walked around the black granite island and pulled Hadley into her arms. "I love you, Hadley; you know that, right? I'd do anything for you."

Hadley sniffed. "Me too, Aunt Lily. I'll even clean the bathroom, if you really want me to."

Lily gave a watery laugh. "While I appreciate the offer, I don't think we need to go crazy, Had. Let's start with the dishes and your room."

Chapter 10

Lily's shower had to wait until she'd gotten Hadley ready and delivered to Madison's house for the slumber party. By the time she got home and enjoyed her long-delayed, steaming hot shower, Lily was beat and decided to get straight into her pajamas. She was going to be home alone all night anyway, might as well be comfy while she plugged away at the never-ending laundry, and tried to scrape up something up to eat. Since they hadn't gotten to the grocery store this afternoon, it was going to be slim pickings for dinner.

Lily tossed the last sock into the dryer, slammed the door shut, and pushed the button to get it tumbling again. She sighed as she bent over to pull the whites out of the pile of dirty clothes on the floor to get the next load going. She didn't regret leaving Baltimore to come to Rivers Bend to take care of Hadley, but this was the kind of night she seriously missed the multitude of take-out options available in a city, which were completely lacking here in the Bend.

She jumped at a loud knock on the back door, and she dropped the white blouse she'd been holding. Who could possibly be here? She wasn't expecting anyone, and there was a gate with a code someone would have to get through to come up to the house.

She chuckled as she picked her way through the laundry on the floor. Maybe she'd been wishing so hard for Indian food her thoughts summoned a deliveryman to miraculously appear at her kitchen door with a container of biryani.

In the brightly lit kitchen, she peered out the windows to see who was there, but only saw her own reflection, in the flannel pjs with the pink flamingos on them her friend Roni had given her as a farewell present when she left Baltimore. She hadn't bothered to style her hair after her shower, she'd just shoved it back with a stretchy headband, and she wore fuzzy, pink socks on her feet. At best, her look could be described as eccentric, and she hoped it was Heather, Bethanne or Magda at the door—it would be too mortifying to be caught by a stranger in this ensemble.

She flipped the switch to turn on the porchlight, and her stomach plummeted to her pink socks at the sight of the person it illuminated.

Jason freakin' Braden.

At her back door, with a pizza in his hands and a wicked grin on his handsome face. She licked her lips—he was one unbelievably fine-looking man, and if that wasn't enough, he held a pizza box. Her stomach rumbled at the sight. She hadn't eaten anything since the cookies at Joyce's house earlier today, and that had been hours ago now.

She opened the door, and willed herself not to feel self-conscious in her silly pajamas. After all, Jason had seen her in nothing at all, and he had seemed to like the view just fine.

****

Jason smiled at her through the door—it was taking her long enough to open it. He was starting to wonder if she was going to leave him standing in the cold, holding this pizza like a loser. The last girl he'd gone out with B.V—Before Vegas—would have squealed, thrown open the door, and then thrown open her legs. Moonbeam made him work for her, and damned if he didn't like it.

She finally opened the door.

He lifted the steaming pizza box. "Hiya, Moonbeam. My mom told me you were on your own tonight, so I thought you might like a little company and some dinner." He paused, but she didn't answer right away, and it occurred to him maybe what happened in Vegas was a one-time thing for Lily, and she didn't want him here. Her stomach growled, and the thought flashed through his mind she might snatch the pizza box and slam the door in his face. This unfamiliar fear of rejection made him set to babbling. "I heard you tell Hadley you'd go shopping tomorrow, so I thought you might need something to eat for dinner. Do you not like pizza? There aren't many choices for food in Rivers Bend on Saturday night—it's pretty much pizza from Vinnie's, or a hot dog from the gas station, so I went with pizza. Mr. Mancini told me eggplant is your favorite, so I got half eggplant and half sausage. I hope it's okay."

*Oh, God, Braden, stop talking.*

She patted her hair in a self-conscious manner. It was damp, pulled back, and sticking up all over the place. She wore those clunky eyeglasses, no make-up, and ridiculous pajamas, but she looked so good to him he went half-hard at the sight of her and the memory of what was hidden underneath all that flannel.

Her cheeks flushed, and she smiled up at him shyly, which given their wild, naked night together in

Las Vegas, amazed him.

"Pizza sounds great, and it smells delish! I was wondering what I was going to have for dinner, and thinking since I didn't go to the store it would have to be cheese and crackers or popcorn, so you're a lifesaver. C'mon in."

She stepped back and waved him into the kitchen, which had so much gleaming stainless steel, he felt like he was on the set of a sci-fi movie. He brushed by her as he entered, and caught a whiff of her vanilla body lotion. Since when had vanilla become so arousing?

He put the pizza on the kitchen island, and as Lily scuffed over to the cupboard, he noticed the goofy socks she wore. He'd never seen a woman other than his sisters in this kind of get-up. Usually when he saw a woman at bedtime, she was in sexy lingerie, or better yet, nothing at all. Based on his body's reaction to Lily, it seemed he had a thing for flannel. Who knew?

She put two plates next to the pizza box, and pushed her eyeglasses up on her nose and cocked her head. "How did you get through the gate?"

Great. Now she seemed worried he was a stalker. Was he a stalker? Since he'd always been the pursued and never the pursuer, he didn't know the rules. Had he crossed a line here? He could've called first, but he was afraid she'd say no, so he decided to pop in instead.

Jesus. He *was* a stalker.

"I know the code from bringing Sam over to visit Hadley. I'm sorry to surprise you. I should've called…"

She turned around from the open fridge with a smile on her face and two longneck bottles of beer in her hands. "Jason, chill. I'm glad you came by—and even gladder you brought food. I was just curious, and afraid maybe something was wrong with the gate. In a big place like this, it seems like there's always something needing repair. Beer okay?"

He nodded and felt like a thousand pound weight had been lifted from his shoulders. She was happy he was here. Not freaked out. Not pissed. Happy.

She popped the tops, and handed him a frosty bottle. She didn't meet his gaze, and her cheeks grew even pinker. "Sorry I'm not looking more presentable."

He shook his head once and grinned at her. "Moonbeam, I think you look beautiful."

The pink turned to lobster-red. "That's laying it on a little too thick, Jason. I mean, seriously, even a supermodel couldn't carry this look off."

She opened the lid of the pizza box, closed her eyes, and moaned in ecstasy, as the aroma wafted out and filled the air with its oregano-y goodness. The moan reached straight to his already semi-aroused body—man, she was killing him here.

He reached across the island to tilt her chin up with his index finger. When her hazel eyes locked with his, he said slowly and with absolute certainty, "Maybe not. But you can. And I love how you look tonight, Moonbeam."

She blinked. Once. Twice. Three times. Then cleared her throat. "Okay then. Can I get you a slice of a sausage pizza?"

Jason released his gentle touch on her chin with reluctance, and leaned away from her. This was more like it! She was off-balance too, which placed Jason firmly back in his comfort-zone. He hooked one of the stools with his boot, and pulled it toward him. He grinned as he sat down. "Pizza me, Moonbeam."

As she pulled a slice out of the box, his mouth watered at the sight of the gooey, stretchy cheese.

She said in an off-handed manner, as she handed him his plate, "We know why I'm alone on a Saturday night…"

Lily wasn't the only one who could pretend to be casual, while fishing for information. "Actually, I don't know. I was surprised when my mom mentioned you were staying in to do laundry. I thought you'd be out with the professor dude."

She glanced at him, and when he returned her gaze, she quickly shifted her attention to the pizza, as she dished up a slice of eggplant for herself. "Um…he asked, but I turned him down."

"Why?"

She took a sip of beer before she answered. "I wasn't feeling it for him. I didn't think it was fair to him to keep seeing each other."

He felt a flash of elation at her response. He might be a dumb, hick farmer, and not some hotshot professor, but maybe he still had a chance with his Yankee city girl. He took a long draw on his beer, and loved how she drank straight from her bottle too. No crystal glass or pink wine for his Moonbeam.

"Sounds good."

She looked at him, and scrunched up her cute little nose, as if she didn't understand his answer. "Okaaay…to get back to my original question…why is the legendary playboy, Jason Braden, free on Saturday night? I imagine you normally have hot and cold running blondes on the weekend."

He laughed. "That's an old joke—my dad used to say something like it."

The corners of her mouth tilted up. "I love old movies. I must've gotten it from one of them. Now stop evading my question."

He could always count on Moonbeam to see through him, and to call him on his bullshit.

"Truth?"

"Always," she said, before tilting her beer bottle to her lips. Lips he sincerely hoped to kiss again, and before too much more time had passed.

"I haven't been out with another woman since Vegas."

At his announcement, Moonbeam choked on her beer.

\* \* \* \*

What a humiliating way to die—choking on beer, while wearing flamingo pajamas. Jason jumped up so fast, his stool fell over with a clatter on the Italian tile floor, and he ran around the kitchen island to pound her on the back.

"Moonbeam! Are you okay? God! Please be okay."

Her throat burned, her eyes watered, and she knew her face was red as a beet, but she managed to get her thumb and forefinger in the 'okay' position.

"Do you want a glass of water?" Jason gingerly held her shoulders, which given the pounding he'd given her a minute ago when he thought she was choking to death, made her giggle through her coughing, which brought a frown to Jason's mouth. "Seriously, Moonbeam, do you need CPR?"

She managed to rasp out, "Beer CPR? God, Jase, please stop making me laugh! You're killing me!"

He chuckled, but didn't release his hold on her shoulders. "It's good to hear your voice, I would've felt really bad if the news of my lack of a sex life was so shocking it killed you." His smile faded, and he dropped his hands, and looked down at his boots, as he scuffed his toes on the kitchen floor. "Is it really so amazing to you, to find out I haven't been with anyone since Vegas?"

An insecure Jason Braden was not something she'd ever expected to see, and it floored her. Her mouth opened and shut a couple of times, as she thought about a way to answer him that wouldn't insult him, or hurt his feelings.

A loud series of beeps from the laundry room saved the day. "That's the washer. I need to put the clothes in the dryer."

Laundry as a lifeline was odd, but appreciated by Lily, until she heard the thump of Jason's boots behind her, as he followed her into the cavernous laundry room

He whistled between his teeth. "This house is something else again! This laundry room is almost as big as my whole apartment."

Lily glanced over her shoulder, as she tossed the clothes from the dryer into a wicker laundry basket. "Apartment? I thought you lived with Joyce?"

He laughed and took the laundry basket from her and carried it to the counter that ran along the back wall of the room. "I'll fold. And, no. I don't live with my mom in my childhood bedroom." He winked at her. "Although I'm not far—I live in quarters attached to the barn."

She tossed the damp clothes into the dryer, and felt her cheeks heat up for the fiftieth time since he arrived, as she realized the load included her undies. "That must be handy for your work."

He nodded as he neatly folded one of her niece's shirts. "It is. Especially when we have a sick horse or a mare ready to give birth. It's good to be close by, and since my day on the farm starts at Zero Dark-thirty, you can't beat the commute."

More beeps sounded as she pushed the buttons to the dryer and blurted out, "Have you really not been with anyone since Vegas?"

He folded a pair of Hadley's gym shorts, and shrugged. "Well, one night I went out with three girls…"

She turned the dryer on and the drum thumped in time with her pounding heart. "Three? Jason!"

He shook out a long-sleeved T-shirt with a snap. "Three real cuties too."

Her heart sank. Had she seriously been considering a possible relationship with the playboy king of Virginia? "Oh. Well. Good for you."

He placed the T-shirt on the pile of folded clothes, and then turned to face her. He leaned his backside against the counter, and mirth danced in his eyes. "Best time I've had in a while. Their names were Lily, Hadley, and Sam."

She looked up from the black-and-white checkerboard tiled floor. "You meant us? The night we went to the movies? It was a fun night. I'm sorry I thought you meant…" Her voice trailed off, and he smirked.

"I'm not sure if I should be flattered or insulted you thought I'd been part of a foursome."

She rolled her eyes. "You *are* legendary with the ladies."

He shrugged. "I guess. I mean, I know how stories

spread around this town, but, y'know, it's never really bothered me before."

Lily busied herself gathering the clothes to put in the washer. "It does now?"

"Knowing you think I'm some sort of man-whore? Hell yeah, it bugs me."

"But you've been out with lots of women, no? You've been a hot topic in the faculty lounge ever since I got back from Las Vegas. Heather posted those pictures of us online, and everyone wants to know if something happened between us, and everyone has some sort of story about you."

"Sometimes living in a small town really sucks."

Lily poured liquid detergent into the little dispenser tray, slid it shut, and slammed the lid of the washer. "There are good parts to small-town living too."

He inclined his head in agreement. "I can't see myself living anywhere but the Bend, to tell you the truth. But you have to admit, everyone is always in everybody else's business, and no one ever forgets anything!" He studied his boots. "What stories did you add to the Jason Edward Braden canon?"

She kicked the toe of his boot with her fuzzy pink sock. "As if. I haven't said anything to anyone. Except…well…your sister guessed."

"Which one? Not Deidre. Please not Deidre. She'll tell everyone."

"No, not Deidre. It was Heather."

He exhaled a whoosh of air. "Good. Good. Heather can keep a secret."

"So, I'm your dirty, little secret?"

His eyes bugged out, and Lily would've thought it looked comical, if her feelings weren't so hurt.

"What the hell, Moonbeam? Is that what you think I meant? No! I meant Deidre owns the Nosh Pit, gossip central here in town, and I don't want the whole town to know, and jump to conclusions about us. Because, this…" he gestured between them with two fingers of his left hand. "Between us? It's different for me. I don't want people talking about you like you're every other girl I've been out with, because you're not."

The air in the laundry room felt steamy, and not just because of the hot-water load of whites she'd just started. Lily took a step closer to Jason. "I'm not?"

He closed the distance between them, until they were standing almost, but not quite, touching. "No, Moonbeam, you're not like any woman I've ever met before."

She gulped. "What does that mean?"

He put his big, work-roughened hands on her waist, and lifted her as if she weighed no more than the laundry basket. He turned, placed her on the folding counter, and stepped between her legs. "Damned if I know, Moonbeam."

He placed his hands on the table next to her thighs, and lowered his head to whisper against her lips, "But I want to try to figure it out together. Whaddya think?"

Her answer was to reach up, twine her fingers in his soft, brown hair, and pull his face down to hers to plant a kiss on him.

She felt his smile against her lips. "Good answer, Moonbeam. I like the way you think."

Then he took control of the kiss. He wrapped one arm around her waist and jerked her forward on the counter until their fun bits were pressed against each other. Soft flannel made contact with rough denim and all his masculine hardness.

She sighed and he took her slightly opened mouth as an opportunity to tangle his tongue with hers. Lily couldn't get close enough to this man. She wrapped her legs around his narrow waist to increase the delicious friction where their bodies were pressed together.

Now it was Jason's turn to groan. He ratcheted the kiss back from passionate to gentle. He pressed his lips against hers with a tenderness that might be her undoing where Jason was concerned.

He sighed, and rested his forehead against hers. "I didn't come over here tonight with this in mind."

"No?"

"Nope." He chuckled. "I wanted things to be different with you. I thought we'd hang out, eat some pizza, get to know each other a little better."

Lily swallowed hard, and felt her face heat with mortification. "Look, Jason, I know I'm not your type. I'm sorry I started trying to climb you like a tree. You came over here to hang out as friends, and I jumped to the wrong conclusion..." She loosened her ankles, which were locked against his back and tried to slide back from the edge of the counter in an effort to put some distance between their bodies.

Jason grasped her thighs to hold her in place. "That's not what I meant at all, Moonbeam. I want you." He pressed his erection against her core as proof of his statement. "I want the hell out of you, darlin'. I meant I want more than just sex with you."

The tension flowed out of her body at the obvious sincerity of his words. She smiled ruefully down at her pajamas. "I thought maybe the ensemble wasn't doing it for you."

He threw back his head and laughed—a deep, sexy sound she felt down to her toes. "I may never look at flannel the same way again. Or flamingos. I'm considering getting one of those pink, plastic ones to stick in the ground over at my place, and then I can think of you every time I look at it. The outfit is fine. I especially like the woman in it. The thing is, our first time in Vegas wasn't very romantic, and now here we are, about to do it on a counter in your laundry room…I bet this room has never seen so much action before."

She waved her hands in dismissal. "Please. My sister is Gloria Davis Diemer Vasquez Peterson Endicott. There's not a flat surface in this house that hasn't seen some action."

"Vasquez?"

"Argentinian polo player—so cliché. He's the only ex Gloria had to pay alimony to, she collects it from the rest of them."

He shook his head. "Gloria is a piece of work. Sorry. I shouldn't talk that way about your sister."

"Half-sister. And don't worry about it. We've never been close, or understood each other. I'm as big a puzzle to Gloria as she is to me." She flapped her hands. "And discussing her is a major mood killer. Can we please get back to what we were doing? I like the idea of getting to know each other better too, but we're both so worked up now, I don't know how well it would work."

He grinned, revealing sexy dimples. "So we take the edge off…"

She nodded. "And then we could finish our cold pizza and warm beer, and maybe stream a movie."

"You might just be my dream woman, Lily Davis.

Now, much as I love them, it's time to lose the pajamas."

He pulled her pj bottoms off with one smooth move, and Lily yanked his Henley out of his pants, where it was tucked in over his belt buckle only. His muscles bunched as he helped her lift his shirt over his head, and she actually shivered at the sight of his bare chest.

While she was distracted, Jason unbuttoned her pajama top, and pushed it off her shoulders. He wrapped his arms around her, and pulled her forward until her bare breasts were pressed against his hard chest. The light sprinkling of golden brown hair on his chest abraded her breasts in the most delicious way.

Jason pulled a condom out of his pocket and tossed it next to her on the counter. "Are you sure about this, baby?"

She lifted her hips to wriggle out of her sensible white cotton panties—man, she was so not dressed for the way this night had turned out. "Does that answer your question?"

A slow smile slid across his face as he undid his belt buckle. "It most certainly does, Moonbeam."

He lowered his head and pressed his lips to hers. Lily wriggled to try and get even closer to him, as if it were possible. Any closer and he would be inside her. Jason thrust his hips, and with one, decisive stroke he was.

Her head lolled back on her shoulders, and her eyes drifted shut as he moved, slowly. Tenderly.

"Uh uh uh, Moonbeam. Eyes open." He instructed in a quiet, but firm voice.

She obeyed without thought, and was rewarded

with the sight of his warm gaze, full of affection. For her.

Her body responded in a liquid way, and he groaned softly. She clenched her legs more tightly around his narrow waist, which pulled her more forward on the counter.

"Moonbeam, you feel so good," he murmured, never breaking their eye contact.

Her body began to ripple around him in response, and he threw back his head and called out, "Moonbeam. God. Moonbeam."

Their bodies both tensed, and then relaxed in release, but they stayed connected. Physically and emotionally.

*Huh.* This night had certainly not turned out the way Lily had expected it to.

## Chapter 11

Jason woke up before the sun, as per usual. He blinked and looked around the room. He was disoriented and a little bit like he was in a bedchamber at Versailles. Then he felt the soft, warm body snuggled up next to him and remembered. After releasing a little tension in the laundry room, Lily and he enjoyed a fun night, binge-watching a zombie television show he'd been meaning to watch, talking, laughing, and cuddling on the couch. When they'd finally made it to Lily's bedroom—with its straw-colored silk wallpaper, light blue drapes and bedding, and ornate frou-frou furniture, they'd laughed about how the décor did not in any way, shape, or form reflect Lily's free-spirited personality. Then they tossed the satin and lace decorative pillows aside and tumbled into bed together.

He settled back against the feather pillows and relaxed. It was like sleeping on a cloud—the style might not be his taste, but the luxurious comfort the bedding provided was pretty darned nice. Lily stirred in her sleep and pressed her round bottom against his thigh. Yeah. He could totally get used to this shit.

He traced Lily's side, where it curved in at her waist, before swelling up to her hip. There was something so feminine and beautiful about the shape of her body. It was so different from the women he usually dated—any curves the last girl he'd slept with had were courtesy of a plastic surgeon. Lily's body was soft and real, and he liked it; was maybe on his way to more than liking it, if he was going to be honest with himself, but only with himself, not with anyone else yet. It was too soon to make any kind of declaration about his feelings to Lily, wasn't it? He had no effing clue. This kind of relationship was uncharted waters for him.

Hell, Jason didn't think he'd ever woken up next to a woman before Lily. He absently traced the line from Lily's lush hip up to the round swell of her breast. Nope. He usually got gone as soon as possible after the sex. He didn't want the woman to have any false hope it would lead to a relationship. He slid his hand back down, over her ribs, past the dip of her waist again, back over her hip, and down to her thigh. Her skin was as soft as these ten-gazillion thread-count sheets, all stretched over her firm muscles. Speaking of firm—his body responded in a way that made him think waking up next to Lily was a great freaking way to start the day.

Lily moaned as his erection swelled against the cushion of her ass, and he wasn't sure if she was awake or asleep. His hand kept up its slow, lazy tour of her body, as he realized the only other time he'd woken up next to a woman it had been Lily in Las Vegas.

Lily squirmed and made a little noise low in her throat, which made him realize his woman was playing possum. The corners of his mouth quirked up as he pressed them close to the shell of her ear and whispered, "I know you're awake, faker."

She chuckled, and her breast jiggled under his touch. There was nothing like a natural woman, in his opinion. The fake stuff doesn't move like the real deal.

"What time is it?" Her voice was raspy from sleep.

"'Bout four."

"A.M.?"

He laughed and gave her breast a gentle squeeze. "Yep."

"We didn't get to sleep until after one. What are you doing awake and peppy at this hour?"

She nestled in even closer, and she couldn't possibly miss the part of his anatomy that was very 'up' at this hour of the morning, thank you very much.

"It's growing up on a farm. I always wake up early. Even on mornings when I don't have to get moving before the sun does, I still do, but usually I can drop back off and sleep in a little."

She snorted, and damned if even snorting was cute on her.

"Sleep in? 'Til when? All of six a.m.?"

"Hey, it's two extra hours for me. Don't knock it!"

Her only response was a moan that sounded more tired than aroused. That was not acceptable. Jason traced the line of her body again, but this time when he got to her hip, he took a right turn to her sex, where he found her so ready for him this time they both moaned, and it had absolutely nothing to do with being tired.

Lily rolled over, pushing him onto his back as she went. She straddled him, and reached for one of the condoms he'd tossed on the nightstand. He shuddered as she rolled one down his length, and then slid him home.

Home.

He felt at home with this woman. Even in this fancy-ass bedroom that was nothing like either of their personalities, he felt more at home than he'd ever felt in his life.

As she started to move, he put his hands on her hips and grinned. "This is way more fun than my usual morning ride."

\*\*\*\*

Jason tended the sizzling bacon in the frying pan. There wasn't much in Lily's fridge and cupboards, but they'd cobbled together enough to make a decent breakfast.

He heard the front door open, slam shut again, and Lily's footsteps as she padded into the kitchen.

She waved the newspaper over her head. "You were right! The paper was here this early on a Sunday. Who knew?"

"It isn't early any more, darlin'." He laid the Southern accent on a little thick, because Lily had said last night how much she loved the way he talked.

She rolled her eyes, tossed the newspaper on the counter, where it landed with a thump, then climbed up onto one of the stools at the kitchen island. He raised his eyebrows and couldn't hold back a grin as Lily methodically sorted the thick Sunday paper. Dividing advertisements from the actual newspaper and pulling out the comics to read first. "Guess this means you won't be helping with the cooking?"

Her sexy, pink lips tilted up at the corners, as she perused the first comic strip. "You said you would make breakfast. Aren't you a man of your word?"

He frowned. "Of course I am."

She peeked up at him and laughed. "You are so easy. I was teasing you! I may have only lived in Rivers Bend for five months, but even I know how honorable the Braden brothers are."

He rubbed his hand on the back of his neck. "You heard a lot about me, huh?"

She hurriedly went back to reading the funnies, and answered with studied casualness. "Uh huh."

He felt his cheeks grow hot. "Not all of it is true, you know."

"You mean you haven't slept with every woman from Cindy down at the mini-market to the old Widow Warren?"

He tossed a dishtowel at her, which she caught one-handed and promptly lofted right back at him.

"I have not slept with Mrs. Warren! Jesus. Do they really say I did? She's almost eighty! And Cindy's a kid! She's the same age as my niece Caitlin."

Lily snapped the comics and turned the page. She obviously was fighting a huge grin and losing. "Like I said. You are sooo easy."

He grinned and shook his head. "Just for that—you are on toast-making duty, woman."

****

The family room was the only truly comfortable room in the entire house. Lily settled in next to Jason on the sectional sofa. He sat in the corner, and Lily curled her legs up next to her and nestled into the crook of his arm, which he rested on the back of the sofa.

A country song played softly through the speakers. It had taken Jason a while to figure out Gloria's intricate sound system, but Lily was impressed he had done it. She said she could never get it to work without Hadley's help. Since he'd been the one to get it to play, he got to pick out the music.

"I didn't think I liked country music, but this is good. Who is it?"

Jason ran his hand lightly up and down her arm. He felt her shiver at his touch, and he felt ten feet tall. "I thought we'd start you out old school. This is George Strait."

She reached for the coffee table to grab the magazine section of the Sunday paper and a pencil. "I think after my wake-up call this morning, I might have a new favorite part of Sunday morning, but usually this is it."

He pressed a feather light kiss to the top of her head, and smiled against her silky hair. "Oh yeah? I like to know what my competition is—what are you up to?"

She folded the magazine to reveal one of the archenemies of his dyslexia. He took a deep breath, and rolled his head to crack his neck, which was suddenly full of tension.

"The crossword puzzle! I love doing it on Sunday morning. It's the most challenging one of the week. My roommate back in Baltimore, Roni, used to do it in ink. I'm not that sure of myself—I stick to a pencil."

Maybe he could sit and listen to George sing, while she did her crossword puzzle, and she'd never find out his secret. He liked the way he'd felt when he got the music to play. She'd been so impressed, and he'd felt like a genius. She was so smart. He didn't want her to know with neither pencil nor pen, he could no more do a crossword puzzle than he could walk on water.

"And today, we get to snuggle up and do the crossword together, so it's even better than it usually is!"

His heart sank straight down to the soles of his feet. He broke out in a cold sweat, his ears buzzed like a swarm of bees had taken up residence in them, and his heart pounded so hard in his chest there was no way Lily couldn't feel it.

His old panic set in—the same fear of discovery he'd experienced as a little boy, when all the other kids were taking to reading like ducks to water, and he'd struggled in a vain attempt to keep up with them. He swiped the clammy sweat from his brow, cleared his throat, and spoke in a voice he feared sounded as panicked as he felt. "Um, I forgot, sweetheart, there's something I need to do this morning. Somewhere else."

She peered over her shoulder at him through narrowed eyes. "Really?"

He nodded like a bobblehead doll. "Yep. At the farm. Uh…responsibilities there, y'know. All that stuff."

He jumped to his feet. "Don't get up. My boots are in the kitchen; I'll grab them and go out the back. Thanks for everything…"

"What the hell, Jason?" Her exclamation mercifully interrupted his lame excuses. "What's going on here?"

"Nothing. I just really have to go. Now. Bye, Moonbeam."

He was not proud of himself, but he was one step away from a full-blown anxiety attack, so he bolted from the room like a fox with a pack of hounds at his heels.

\*\*\*\*

"Man, that is pathetic."

His brother, Jeff, didn't mince words, as he leaned on the railing of their mom's back porch and watched Jason throw the ball for his hyperactive Australian shepherd, Dingo.

"Thanks, bro. I hadn't figured that out on my own, so good of you to make it clear for me."

"If you know, then how could you be such a colossal dumbass?"

Jason threw the ball with a little extra muscle, and Dingo bounded after it. "You don't understand how I feel about Lily…"

"You loooove her," Jeff interrupted in a singsong voice followed by smoochie noises.

Dingo was back already and dropped the ball at his feet. His doggie tongue lolled out of his mouth, but his avid gaze was locked on Jason's face, as if willing his master to keep throwing the ball, so Jason knew his pup still had energy to burn. He threw the ball even farther this time. "How old are you—twelve?"

Jeff's answering laugh was deep and hearty. "C'mon! After the load of shit you gave me when I was falling for Maggie, did you really think you'd get off scot-free when you met the woman who knocks you on your ass?"

"Point taken." Jason nodded his head, as he watched Dingo run toward him with the yellow tennis ball in his mouth. Were any of his four paws actually touching the ground? "I do like Lily. A lot."

"You loooove her," Jeff interrupted again.

"If you're going to do this shit, man, then you gotta come up with better trash talk. I mean, seriously dude, you played in the NFL for years, and the best you can do is 'you loooove her.'" He ended with an exaggerated falsetto.

"Sorry. Go on." Jeff waved his hand for Jason to continue.

"I respect Lily. I respect the hell out of her. And

right now, she seems to think I hung the moon. Sure, she gives me some shit, but it's funny, and I like it when she teases me, but it's because she seems to have a high opinion of me." He picked up the spitty ball Dingo had dropped at his feet. "Dog, you've got this ball slobbered up good." He threw it again, and wiped his hand on his good jeans—the ones he'd changed into for family dinner at his mom's house.

Jeff looked after Dingo. "Does that dog ever get tired out?"

"Nope."

"So, you're afraid Lily won't still have feelings for you when she finds out you're dyslexic?"

"Of course she won't feel the same way."

"Why not? You're the same guy she's gotten to know. And for some reason, which I don't completely understand, she thinks a lot of you. Nothing will change, except she'll know you're dyslexic."

Jason ran his non-dog spit covered hand over his face. "But it will change everything! Don't you see?"

"Like bolting out of her house as if your hair was on fire this morning hasn't already changed everything?"

Jason threw up his hands, and ignored the panting dog and ball at his feet. "You're really going to make me say it? Fine! Lily's smart—like Sunday paper crossword puzzle smart…"

Jeff narrowed his eyes and frowned. "I don't like where you're going with this, Jase. Nobody talks bad about my little brother, and I think you're about to say he's not smart. I happen to know you're crazy-smart, you just go about learning a little different than some folks."

Jason snorted in disbelief and threw the ball again without responding.

"It's true. And what's more, Lily will agree with me. She's a special education teacher, for God's sake."

When Jason took a deep breath to interrupt and respond, Jeff held up his hands. "And before you say it—Lily is nothing like your old teacher, Mrs. Wentworth. Lily knows her stuff. She cares about the kids she works with, and she'll realize how very intelligent you are."

Jason swung his head to look at his older brother, the man he'd looked up to his whole damn life, whose good opinion meant the world to him. "You really think so?"

"I do." Jeff shook his head and grimaced. "But, man, do you have some sweet-talking to do to get out of the hole you dug for yourself this morning. If I were you, I'd get my sorry ass over to her place right after dinner, and eat some serious crow for dessert."

\*\*\*\*

Lily pulled her jacket closed over the Baltimore Ravens jersey she wore underneath it. She tried to look at anything but the two blondes on the other side of the produce display, who were looking at her as if she was a disgusting bug on the berry display. Okay, so what, she didn't have make-up on, and she was wearing a football jersey and jeans? But she'd had a rough morning, and even on the best of Sundays, she couldn't imagine getting dolled up in full hair and make-up to go to the grocery store. She inspected a package of grapes for ripeness, and tried to tune out the women's voices, which were raised enough she knew they meant for her to hear them.

"Honestly! Whatever is Jason thinking?"

"I know! Bless her heart, she's a plain little thing."

Lily felt her cheeks heat up—from anger or embarrassment, she didn't know, but it was probably a combination of the two.

"They can't be too serious, or else she'd be at the Braden Farm for Sunday dinner. I always loved going there with Jason when we were dating."

"Me too!" The second blonde chirped her agreement, and then lowered her voice, although clearly not enough that it wouldn't still be heard. "Maybe he's ashamed for his family to see what he's stooped to. You know what my sister would say…"

"She must be mighty good in bed!" They quoted in unison, and Lily winced at the piercing sound of their shrill laughter.

"That's it! You know what they say when a good-looking man is with a homely woman, she probably lets him do stuff in bed girls like us wouldn't."

At their ugly words, Lily's head shot up from the grape display, and she glared at the two mean girls trailing after her through the produce department. Did they intend to follow her through the whole store spouting their filth? Honestly, she was here with a child, for Pete's sake! Lily wanted to cover Hadley's ears and rush her to the dairy aisle.

Hadley pried the bag of grapes from her clenched hands. "I do like the red ones best, thanks for remembering, Aunt Lily." She tossed the crumpled bag into the cart, and continued to talk in a clear, loud voice. "Sam's one of my best friends, so I've been to the Braden's house a lot for Sunday dinner, and Jason never has a girl there. As a matter of fact, Sam told me her Grandma Joyce told her if Jason ever brought one of the tramps he runs around with to her Sunday table, she'd be tempted to toss them out on their ear."

Lily grinned at her niece—man, did she ever love this kid to pieces! "That sounds like Joyce."

"I never!" one of the blondes exclaimed.

"I find that hard to believe," Lily said sotto voce.

Hadley giggled and pushed the cart toward the dairy department, right past the two women, who stood rooted in place with red faces, and jaws dropped.

"I love living with you, Aunt Lily. I hope we can always stay together. I'm sorry again I was such a brat to you."

Lily ruffled Hadley's brown hair, so much like her own. "Stop apologizing! We're good now, and I'm not going anywhere, so don't worry your pretty head about it anymore."

Hadley snorted. "I'm not pretty. Not like my mom is."

Lily tossed two four-packs of Greek yogurt into the cart and shook her head, "Your mom isn't pretty like your mom."

Hadley wrinkled her nose. "What do you mean?"

"When our dad, your grandfather Davis, died, I found a box of old photos. Pictures of your mom when she was a girl, and she looked a lot like you. A lot like I did too."

Hadley pushed the cart up the aisle and stopped at the milk case. "Really?"

"Uh huh." Lily put a bottle of low fat milk into the cart. "Her hair was the same color as ours…"

"She does color it to make it that raven's wing black to draw attention to her eyes," Hadley said.

"And that's another thing—her eyes were hazel, like ours, and she wore glasses like I do…"

"Purple contact lenses," Hadley explained.

"Her lips weren't nearly as full as they are now…"

"Injections."

"And she may have been a late bloomer, but she wasn't as big here," Lily held her hands in front of her own average-sized breasts.

"Implants," Hadley nodded and pushed the cart to the deli counter.

Lily pulled a number from the machine. "I thought so. The way I see it, your mom owes her beauty more to modern medical advances than to nature."

"Just like those two witches in the produce department."

"Right. Since they bought their attributes, there's no reason to compare ourselves to them and feel bad." Lily felt her own spirits lift as she gave her niece the pep talk. "We are who we are, Hadley Diemer, and we're darned fine people, inside and out!"

Her niece beamed at her. "You're right!"

"Twenty-five?" the deli person called out in a bored tone.

"That's me." Lily waved her paper number in the air. She ordered the oven-roasted chicken breast for their lunches this week, and thought over what she'd told Hadley, while she waited for the woman behind the deli counter to slice it for her.

She believed what she said, but she couldn't deny she'd let those two mean girls get under her skin today. Normally, they wouldn't have fazed her, but the way Jason ran out of her house like the hounds of hell were after him this morning, had left her feeling a little more insecure than normal.

She'd thought they were having a lovely, lazy Sunday morning together, and Jason seemed to be enjoying himself too. Until he wasn't. For the life of her, Lily couldn't figure out what had gone wrong.

"Miss, I asked you if you'd like anything else?"

She started at the sound of the deli man's voice. "Sorry, I was somewhere else. A half-pound of Swiss cheese, sliced thin, please.'

She shook off her funk. No sense in trying to figure out Jason Braden. They were a really mismatched pair, and it probably wouldn't have worked out between them in the long run.

She smiled at Hadley, who was sneaking a box of brownie mix into the cart. She could imagine such a treat would be verboten in Gloria's house, but she'd be happy to make brownies with her niece this afternoon. All the better to keep her mind busy, and stop obsessing on Jason Braden. She so didn't want to be that girl.

"Better go back and grab some eggs, so we can make those brownies today. We're all out."

Hadley cocked her head. "Really? I thought we had half a dozen at home."

Lily blushed as she remembered Jason's healthy appetite this morning, and the activities preceding breakfast that built up said appetite. "I was hungry this morning."

"You ate six eggs? Seriously, Aunt Lily, that can't be good for your cholesterol. A person your age needs to think about these things."

"A person my age? Jeez, Had, how old do you think I am?"

Hadley shrugged and rolled her eyes before she

doubled back to the dairy aisle to get a carton of eggs.

Lily grimaced as she waited for their deli order and watched her niece walk away. Jason probably was even worse for her than the big bacon and egg breakfast they'd shared this morning, but hoo boy, did she ever want another taste of him.

Chapter 12

Brownie therapy was definitely a good thing. Hadley and Lily sat at the kitchen island with a pan of chocolatey goodness between them.

"Adding the peanut butter chips was a stroke of genius, Hadley."

"I know! Yum, right?"

"Definitely. Yum squared, even."

The doorbell sounded loudly throughout the house. "I don't think I've ever heard the doorbell before; everyone usually comes to the back door." Lily frowned as the melody played again. "Is that 'My Heart Will Go On?'"

Hadley rolled her eyes and nodded. "Mom said it was her theme song."

"Yeah…we gotta figure out how to change that."

"Word," Hadley said solemnly, and popped another piece of brownie in her mouth.

Lily hopped off the stool and glanced up at the kitchen clock. "Seven o'clock on Sunday night! I wonder who it could be?"

With a mouthful of brownie, Hadley replied, "Must be someone we know, because they had the gate code."

"Good point," Lily called over her shoulder. "But please don't talk with your mouth full, sweetie."

She peeked out of one of the glass panels on either side of the door to see who was there, and her heart jumped so hard, she felt like someone had used a defibrillator on her.

Jason stood on the front steps, illuminated by the motion-activated exterior lights, with a droopy bouquet of mixed flowers clutched in his hands.

She stepped away from the window, swiped her mouth to try to remove any random chocolate there, and ran her tongue over her teeth. She took a deep breath, and threw open the front door. "Jason! I couldn't imagine who was here. I never dreamed it was you."

"Sorry I didn't call first, but once again, I was afraid you wouldn't want to see me, so I figured the element of surprise would be on my side. This is a pattern I sincerely intend to break. May I come in?"

"Sure." She stepped back and waved her arm for him to enter.

He stepped into the formal, marble entryway with a sigh of what appeared to be relief. The cellophane around the flowers crinkled as he fidgeted with it, and Lily was stunned to realize super-smooth Jason Braden was as nervous as she was.

He thrust the bouquet at her. "These are for you."

She hesitated a beat before she took them. "Thank you."

"Look, about this morning…"

She darted a glance over her shoulder, down the hall to the kitchen, and then whipped her head back to face him with her index finger over her lips, and whispered, "Shh…Hadley is in the kitchen, and she really doesn't need to know why you were here this morning."

She looked back again, and issued a silent prayer Hadley's sharp, young ears hadn't heard any of this exchange. She knew Gloria had a revolving door to her bedroom, but it wasn't an example she wanted to present to her niece. Plus what happened with Jason wasn't her normal behavior, in spite of the fact it had now happened twice with him. The man got to her in a way no one else did, and whenever they were alone together she seemed to lose both her good judgment and her panties.

In a too-loud voice that made him grin and roll his eyes at her, she said, "Hadley and I made brownies, would you like to come back to the kitchen and have one with us?" She lowered her voice, and spoke for only his ears, "We can talk about this morning later, and believe me, we will be talking about this morning."

He raised his voice to answer, "I love brownies, so that's an offer I can't resist."

Now it was her turn to roll her eyes, as far as she could tell, Jason didn't resist many offers of the female variety.

\*\*\*\*

As Lily walked to the kitchen, Jason paused, leaned his head to the side, and took a quick look at her sweet ass in those black yoga pants. Lord almighty, she was nothing like the girls he usually went out with, who would've run for their makeup case and flat iron if he ever caught them looking so casual. But man, she was fine. The fact she didn't seem to think so, made her all the finer to him. There was no posing or posturing—she was just Lily. All the time. And he liked her that way.

He straightened up before she caught him ogling her ass, and scooted to catch up with her. Even he knew she'd think checking out her butt was a caveman thing to do, and he was here to eat crow. No sense in getting things off on the wrong foot.

Her Ravens jersey made him smile. It wasn't one of those tight, baby-doll sized ones, it was the real deal, and it hung big and baggy on her medium frame.

They cleared the doorway to the kitchen as he said, "Baltimore Ravens, huh? We've got to see about getting you a Portland Pintos jersey before my brother Jeff sees you in this one, don't you think, Hadley?"

"Hi, Jason! Sure, Sam gave me a Pintos jersey for my birthday this year. I love it!" She looked knowingly between her aunt, the cheap grocery store flowers, and him. She raised one eyebrow and smirked, sometimes the kid was twelve going on thirty.

Oblivious to their exchange, Lily opened a door to yet another hallway. This house was huge; Jason couldn't imagine living here. She called over her shoulder, "Maybe I will, but I'm a Ravens girl. We lived near the stadium in Baltimore…"

"We?" Jason cut her off with a sharp question.

She stopped in her tracks and twirled around to glare at him. "My friend Roni and I shared an apartment. Is that acceptable to you, Mr. Braden?" She spoke with exaggerated politeness, and made Hadley snort in a way he knew her mother would disapprove. "I'm going to put these flowers in water. Hadley, would you please get Jason a brownie?"

Being a good Virginia girl, Hadley was already off her stool and cutting a gooey, dark chocolate square for him. By unwritten law, no guest in a Virginia home went without being offered food and drink, even one as unwelcome as he suspected he was by Lily tonight.

"Would you like a glass of milk to go with this, Jason?"

"Yes, please." Jason shrugged off his fleece-lined denim jacket and slung it over the back of a stool. He sat down on the stool where Hadley had placed his brownie. "These look so good; I could smell them as soon as I stepped into the house—"

"I'm sorry to interrupt, but we only have a couple of minutes before Aunt Lily gets back from the flower-arranging room—"

Jason gulped down his first mouthful of brownie to interrupt Hadley, "Flower arranging room?"

Hadley slid a glass of milk across the granite island, and then stood with her hands on her hips. "What part of only a couple of minutes didn't you understand?"

He slugged back some milk to get the brownie down, and his mind boggled over the fact they had a fricking flower arranging room! No wonder the house was so big, if they had a separate room for every conceivable activity. But Hadley frowned and tapped her foot, so he knew they had to get back to the topic at hand, whatever it might be. "Sorry to interrupt. Go on, Hadley."

Her frown turned into a full-blown scowl. "I don't know what kind of game you're playing with my Aunt Lily—"

"No game!" He held up his hands.

"But," she interrupted right back, in a firm tone of voice that matched her stance. She looked like an old-time school marm standing in front of a misbehaving class. "I love Aunt Lily. In my whole, big, messed up, crazy, blended family, she's the only one who's got my back. Always. And I've got hers now. Everyone in town knows you're a player—sorry, because I'm friends with your niece and I like you, but I don't want you to hurt Aunt Lily."

Seriously, this kid had a pair of brass ones. She was giving him the 'hurt her and I'll hurt you' speech he'd given to so many of his sisters' beaux. Well, Heather's boyfriends. Deidre had been with her husband, Hank, for as long as Jason could remember. He looked Hadley square in the eyes with the same level of seriousness she displayed. "I don't want to hurt Lily. I like her. A lot." More than he was comfortable with, to be honest, but he wasn't going to admit it to the fierce little warrior in front of him.

She seemed to consider his words, then nodded once. "See that you don't hurt her, because if you do, I'll hurt you."

He took a sip of milk to hide his smile. Apparently, he wasn't quick enough, as her brows drew together over a pair of hazel eyes that looked so much like her beloved Aunt's, and her mouth drew down even farther. "Okay. I can't hurt you, but I've got money, and I can hire people who can."

His smile faded, and he choked a little on his milk. The kid could be a scary little thing, but loyal, and he admired loyalty. "Point taken, Hadley. I will try my damned...uh...darndest, not to hurt Lily."

She relaxed her shoulders and smiled indulgently. "I'm not a baby, Jason. I've heard cuss words before."

"Not from me, you haven't." He did have a colorful vocabulary, but tried his best not to swear in front of kids.

Lily came back into the kitchen. She carried his flowers in a cut-crystal vase. It looked like the Waterford his mom had brought back from her trip to the Irish Derby last summer. Somehow, Lily had managed to make his cheap bouquet look like a million bucks.

Hadley put her glass and plate in the dishwasher. "I've got to finish doing my homework, so I'm going to head up to my room."

Lily placed the vase in the center of the island. "Okay, sweetie, let me know if you need any help."

"It's algebra, Aunt Lily. No offense, but it's not your best subject."

Lily grimaced. "No. I'm not very good with math."

"I am," Jason piped up with pride. "I've always been good at math."

Lily smiled at him. "Then maybe Jason could help you if you need it."

"Thanks. I think I'm good, but I'll let you know if I get stuck." Hadley walked for the door to the front hall, but then stopped in her tracks to peek over her shoulder, and say with a sly smile, "In the meantime...I'll be far away in my room. In a whole other wing of the house. Probably listening to music on my headphones. It will be like you two are all alone down here."

Lily blushed as red as the rose in her bouquet. "Go. Now. Before I kill you!"

Hadley giggled at her aunt's threat, and ran out of the room, leaving them blessedly alone. Now he could get on with his groveling for forgiveness.

Lily ran her finger over one of the daisies in the vase. "The flowers are lovely. Thank you."

"You're welcome. I wanted to get you something nicer, but the grocery store was the only place open on Sunday night. Gotta love the Bend, right? Sidewalks roll up on Sunday. Anyway, I picked that arrangement, because there were a couple of lilies in it…y'know…like your name."

Jesus Christ in heaven above, could he be any more lame? Sweat beaded on his brow, and it wasn't from being in the warm, brownie-scented kitchen. Nope. He was scared spitless he would mess up this apology. This was all new ground for him. He'd never let himself get close enough to a girl to care if she accepted his apology when he acted like an ass.

"I have to admit when you ran out of here this morning I didn't expect to see you again. I've heard the stories—Jason Braden gets some, and then gets gone. I thought what was happening today was you getting gone."

He winced. He'd never been ashamed of his lifestyle before, but it hurt to know Lily had heard gossip about him, and thought what they'd shared was the same old thing to him, because it wasn't. He cleared his throat, which suddenly felt thick. "Sorry about that. It wasn't my finest moment, but it most definitely wasn't me getting some and getting gone."

She frowned and raised her eyebrows, and he was reminded of how her niece looked glaring at him across this same kitchen island a few minutes before. "Really? Because I've got to be honest here, Jason, that's sure as hell what it felt like to me."

"I'm sorry." He held her steady gaze, and continued earnestly, "I don't want you to feel that way, because it couldn't be further from the truth."

She snorted in disbelief. "Oh yeah? Then what was it? I thought we were having a nice morning together…" Her cheeks flamed and she lowered her gaze to the flowers she fiddled with as she continued,

"After a freaking amazing night together—"

"We were," he rushed to say. "And, man, was it ever off-the-charts amazing—"

"So what was it then?" Her eyes flashed, as her head snapped up to look him dead in the eye, her voice laced with sarcasm. "You felt too much, and it scared you? Please. Spare me your line of b.s. At least show me enough respect to not give me the same lame-ass lies you give all the other women."

Now see—that made him see red. The fact she didn't think what they'd shared was something special to him. Something rare. Something to be cherished. She didn't think he believed she was someone to be cherished.

Okay, yeah, he had run out, and it had been a stupid, chickenshit thing to do, but he had his reasons. However, Lily didn't know why, and there's no way she would unless he manned up and told.

"I'm dyslexic."

Smooth, Braden. Lead up to it, explain, ease her into learning your deepest, darkest secret. Or you could just blurt it out like a total loser.

"I figured. So what? Being dyslexic doesn't turn you into an ass, and that's what you were this morning, make no mistake about it..."

His jaw dropped and his heart stopped. He held up a hand to slow her roll. "You figured?" Here he was, opening up to her in a way he'd never had with a soul outside of his immediate family, and she figured?

She shrugged. "Well, yeah. It is my field. I recognized the signs in Vegas, when we were signing the registry at the wedding chapel, but I'd never heard anything about it, and Rivers Bend is the gossipiest town in the U.S., so I wasn't positive, but I was pretty sure..." Her voice trailed off, she shut her eyes, and took a deep breath, which she exhaled with an audible whoosh. "The crossword puzzle. I didn't think. I'm so sorry! I wanted you to do a frigging crossword puzzle. That's what had you high-tailing it out of here."

Heat flooded his cheeks, as the old shame washed over him. Talking about his dyslexia was even harder than he expected to be, and he'd been expecting it to be one of the hardest things he'd ever done. But this smart, feisty, phenomenal woman deserved his honesty. She had earned his honesty. He swallowed hard against the lump in his throat. "Yeah. It was the crossword puzzle. I've developed lots of ways to work around my dyslexia in my day-to-day life. I listen to a lot of audiobooks, so I'm not a dummy—"

She held up her hands. "I never said you were! I never thought you were!"

No. She hadn't. And Lily had guessed his secret in Las Vegas, before they'd slept together. Wow. Lily had known the truth, or at least strongly suspected it, and she still had wanted him. He leaned back in his seat and took a moment for the truth to sink in, and a warm glow suffused him as it did. Lily had guessed his secret shame. And she still wanted him!

When he could finally speak, his voice was rough. "Thank you. Thank you for seeing something more to me than my dyslexia. I can't even begin to tell you how much that means to me, Lily. But you're right; it's no excuse for my behavior. You see, I've found work arounds for most stuff, but crossword puzzles do me in."

"Of course they do! They'd be near impossible for

151

you, and I should've thought of it before I asked you to do one with me. I always do the crossword puzzle on Sunday morning, and I wanted to share that experience with you." Her lips tilted up. "And in my defense, I was still so relaxed and muzzy-headed from a night of your good lovin' I wasn't thinking straight, or else I would never have suggested it. So, again, I'm very sorry."

Jason ran his hand over his jaw. He couldn't believe what he was hearing. Lily was apologizing to him. She knew his secret, and it didn't seem to matter to her one little bit. His world rocked on its' axis. He never dreamed a woman like Lily would want a man like him. "Please stop apologizing to me. I came here tonight to apologize to you, well really, to grovel at your feet. I am so sorry, I behaved badly to you, and if I could roll back time to get a do-over for this morning, I would do things differently."

"Me too." She smiled at him. "And for the record, I think you're the polar opposite of a dummy. I've seen how my students have found ways to work around their learning differences, and I think it takes a remarkably sharp mind, and real intelligence to do it. So, please, no more 'dummy' talk from you, okay?"

"Okay." He felt humbled by her words, and his supposedly 'sharp mind' couldn't come up with a more coherent response.

"Do you want another brownie? I could use another brownie." Lily picked up the knife to cut another square.

"Sure, thanks. They're mighty tasty." He squinted at her, like she was an exotic creature he'd never seen before. And, truth be told, she was. He pointed back and forth between them. "So…we're good here?"

"Yeah." She nodded and reached for his plate to put another brownie on it. "I mean, in the future I'd appreciate it if you stayed and talked to me if I do something that hurts you."

"Understood."

"Then, yes, we're good here." She plopped a giant brownie on his plate and slid it across the island to him, but he pushed off the stool and skimmed around the corner of the island to stand next to her.

Lily turned to face him, and he took her face, softly, reverently, in his hands, and was enough of a caveman to like how big his hands seemed, compared to her elfin face, and how little she was compared to him. Especially since she had nothing on her feet, but another pair of those fuzzy socks. Purple this time, to match her football jersey.

"Then is it all right if I kiss you now?"

She craned her neck to smile up at him. "Yes, please."

He chuckled, and stroked his thumbs along her jawline. "Such pretty manners. We'll make a southern girl out of you yet, Moonbeam."

He lowered his head and captured her soft lips in a tender kiss.

Lily pushed up on her tiptoes to twine her arms around his neck, and the kiss took on some real heat when her body pressed against his—all soft to hard. Habanero level heat, as a matter of fact.

He pulled back long enough to murmur, "What did I do to deserve you, Moonbeam?"

He felt her smile against his lips, before she whispered, "Right back at ya, Einstein."

This time the nickname didn't sting, because this

amazing woman didn't think he was dumb. She saw through to the heart of him, straight through his dyslexia to the man he was, and she liked him.

She wriggled her curvy, little body closer to his, and he couldn't hold back a grin. Oh yeah. She liked him. And she wanted him almost as much as he wanted her.

"Impressionable child approaching!" Hadley called from the hallway.

They broke apart with obvious reluctance, and Lily mouthed, "Sorry."

He shrugged. He liked everything about this woman, including her too-old-for-her-years niece. Sure, he wanted to keep kissing Lily, to kiss every square inch of the soft, creamy skin that covered her body, but it would have to wait for a more opportune time. But it was okay, because against all odds, Lily had forgiven him, and they'd have plenty of time together, if he didn't pull another dumbass move.

## Chapter 13

"Let me get this straight," his friend Ty Harris asked with amazement, as they wandered through the new little gift shop that had recently opened on Main Street. "Lily not only forgave you for acting like a total dumbass, she actually apologized to you?"

Jason nodded. Light glinted off a delicate crystal flower in a rainbow. Maybe Lily would like it. He stretched out his hand to touch it, but jerked it back to his side, as he thought about how fragile it was. Everything on the shelf of glass knick-knacks looked like they would shatter if he breathed too hard on them. Talk about a bull in a china shop! He sent up a silent prayer he would get out of this place without breaking anything too valuable.

Ty shook his head. "You are charmed, Jason Braden. Truly, unfucking believably, charmed."

Jason rubbed the back of his neck and grinned sheepishly. "I'm damned lucky; don't think I don't know it. It's why we're here. I need to pick out a special present for her. I want to show Lily how much she means to me."

Ty punched Jason in the arm. "And being your only gay friend, you naturally thought I could help? Hells bells, Jase, I don't know anything about this kind of stuff. You would've been better off bringing my sister. Or Mick."

"Mebbe. But I didn't think of Mick, and your sister Bethanne would've been texting Lily while we were still shopping."

Ty bobbed his head once, and his messy, reddish-brown hair flopped over his eyes. He swept it back and huffed, "I really need to get to the barber."

A cheerful voice called out from the back, as a man bustled out of the stockroom, "Sorry to keep y'all waiting! May I help you find something?"

The man was on the short side of average, and had a round, cheerful face. For the first time Jason understood the old expression about a face being wreathed in smiles. The man fairly radiated good cheer. Kind of a normal looking guy, but he had some sort of charm, or charisma or something, which made you want to smile back.

Jason tried to move closer to the shopkeeper, to throw himself on his mercy for help in finding a gift, as Ty had proved to be worthless, but his friend blocked him. Ty stood frozen in place, right in his way, rooted like a tree. Ty stared at the guy from the store like he was a cobra and the shopkeeper was a damned snake charmer.

Jason cleared his throat pointedly and thrust his hand past Ty. "I'm Jason Braden, Welcome to Rivers Bend."

The man clapped his hands together with glee. "Oh! I know your sisters! Since Heather and Mick are going to move into his place, I'm going to be living in Heather's old apartment over Deidre's café while I look for a house. Delightful ladies!"

"Thank you. They're not bad as sisters go." Jason smiled, but it was wasted on the man, who had just noticed Ty, and stared at his friend with the same intensity Ty was sending his way.

Finally he tore his gaze from Ty's and shook Jason's hand. "I'm Grant Weston, nice to meet you."

"I get it now—Wishes Granted—your store name is a play on your name," Jason said.

"It is." Grant beamed at Jason. "Your sister Deidre's café next door inspired me. The Nosh Pit is such a fun play on words."

Since Ty had apparently been struck mute in the last two minutes, Jason introduced him. "This is my friend, Ty Harris."

"Friend?" Grant infused the one word question with multiple levels of meaning, and it broke Ty out of his trance.

"Just friends," Ty hastened to clarify. "Jason is here to pick out a gift for his girlfriend."

"How sweet of him." Grant smiled at Ty. "So, you're…"

"Available," Jason interjected, only to receive a glare from Ty for his matchmaking efforts.

"Good to know," Grant said. "Very good to know."

Jason grinned unrepentantly at Ty, whose expression relaxed as he turned back to once again gaze in silence at Grant.

Jason looked back and forth between the two men and shrugged. You'd think Grant was Channing Tatum, the way Ty was eating him up with his eyes. But who was he to mock—he felt exactly the same way when he looked at Moonbeam.

"What type of things does your lady like, Jason?" Grant asked.

Jason screwed up his mouth as he craned his neck

to look around the shop. "Well...books, and the Baltimore Ravens and Orioles..."

"Reading and sports...a Renaissance woman." Grant smiled at him, though in a kind way that took the edge off his gentle teasing.

Jason's gaze stopped at a framed picture hanging on the wall. "And owls! She likes owls."

Grant took the picture off the wall and carried it over to Jason. "Fine choice!"

Jason took the picture from Grant and smiled at the little owl in red eyeglasses.

"The owl is silk-screened onto a page from an old dictionary. Very unusual, but fun, and it sounds like it would be perfect for your lady."

"It is! The owl looks just like the one..." Jason's voice trailed off, as the realized Lily might not like him announcing she had a tattoo in front of Ty and a complete stranger.

"Her tattoo!" Ty completed his unfinished sentence. "It looks a lot like the owl on Lily's tattoo!"

What the actual hell?

"You've seen Lily's tattoo?" He ground out through gritted teeth.

"Cool your jets, jealous boy." Ty grinned. "Lily and I swim together at the high school pool a few times a week. It's great exercise. I've seen her tattoo then, when she's in her bathing suit. Oh my God, are you totally gone over this girl or what? It's on the back of her shoulder for Pete's sake, not over her lady bits. And even if it was, you know I'm not a man who's interested in lady bits—not Lily's, or anyone else's."

"Also very good to know," Grant murmured.

"Sorry, man, I don't know what's wrong with me.

I've never been jealous before, and certainly never so crazy jealous I'd be upset over a friend seeing her tattoo. I'm twisted up in knots over Lily, like I've never been over a woman in my life."

"You care for her. It's new territory for you. I get it; no need to apologize," Ty replied.

Jason thrust the owl picture at Grant. "I'll take it. Would you please gift wrap it for me?"

"Certainly." Grant smiled and carried the frame behind the counter, where colorful wrapping paper for every occasion stood on giant rollers. "I'll do it up real pretty for you. And there are cards on the back wall, if you want to pick one out to go with it."

Jason hesitated, but Ty walked to the rack of greeting cards. "C'mon, bro, I'll help you out with these."

Jason exhaled with a whoosh, and smiled in gratitude at his old friend. "Thanks, man, I'd hate to pick one out because it had a pretty picture of lilies on it, only to find out when she opened it that it was a fricking sympathy card or something,"

Ty laughed. "That would truly suck eggs. So you told her about—" He glanced around the store and lowered his voice. "—your dyslexia, and she was totally cool with it?"

"Yeah." Jason studied the cards as he answered. "She was pretty steamed about the way her predecessor at the school disregarded my obvious symptoms, but she said she could help me learn some stuff that would help me."

Ty took the card Jason handed him and shook his head. "Birthday…anniversary…thinking of you/love. Here—look at this section."

They both shuffled to the right, toward the mushy love section of the greeting cards, and Ty asked, "Are you going to do it?"

Jason grimaced and shrugged. "I thought it would be weird for our, y'know, relationship…"

Ty laughed. "Jason Braden in a relationship with something other than a horse or his mirror; I never thought I'd live to see the day."

Jason shoved Ty with his shoulder. "Whatever, dude, we decided it might make for a strange dynamic in a new relationship, so her friend Roni from Baltimore is going to work with me via Facetime."

He handed Ty a card with a black and white photograph of a little boy presenting a little girl with a bright red rose, the only color item in the picture.

"You bring color to my world," Ty read from the inside of the card.

"This one is great," Jason said and took the card from Ty's hands.

They walked to the front counter, where Grant was busy constructing an elaborate bow to go on the shiny, silver paper.

He held it up for Jason to get a better look at it. "Purple and orange, for the Ravens and the Orioles. Perfect, no?"

"It is! Thank you for all your help."

"Please." Grant waved his free hand dismissively. "It's what I do. I'll finish this package up, and I'll be with you in a few moments."

Jason turned his back to rest his butt against the counter, and Ty stayed where he was, apparently so he could continue to stare at Grant.

"Our first session is tomorrow night. I'm looking

forward to it, but I'm also a little worried. I've kept my dyslexia a secret for so long, and now Roni will know, and she's Lily's best friend—I want her to like me. To think I'm good enough for her friend. It's just hard to do...oh, never mind. You wouldn't understand—you're so smart. You're a lawyer; everyone respects your intelligence."

Ty rolled his eyes. "No. You're right. A gay man in small town Virginia could never understand what it's like to have a secret he worries will change the way people think of him. A secret that makes him ashamed, even though he knows logically there is nothing wrong with who he is. It's just the way he's made. It might be different than the way a lot of folks are made, but that shouldn't make it shameful, or change the way people think of him. You never know though, even if nine out of ten people are cool with him, the tenth one can be a bitch to handle. You're right, Jase, I know nothing about how you might be feeling."

"Okay. Point made and received. Ratchet back the sarcasm a few notches, Lawyer-man."

Ty grinned at him. "It's just another way of coming out, and having done so in high school to my football teammates, I think I can help you with this one, Jase."

Grant fanned himself with the bow. "A lawyer and a football player? Oh my!"

Ty blushed to the roots of his hair, while Jason laughed. Looked like he wasn't the only one who was going to be embarking on a new relationship.

****

Jason sat on a stool at the breakfast bar that separated his living room from the kitchen. He swiped his sweaty palms on the legs of his jeans and exhaled with a whoosh before clicking the video call icon on his laptop. The smiling face of Lily's friend from Baltimore filled his screen.

He forced a smile to his face, even though his heart thudded in his chest like a racehorse. "Hiya, Roni."

"Hi, Jason." Roni waved at the camera. "Did you get the materials I sent you?"

Roni was in full-on teacher mode, and seemed ready to skip the small talk and get right into the lesson. It was probably for the best—no reason to put off the inevitable, even though he'd rather be dancing nekkid at the Super Bowl Half Time Show than having this lesson with Roni.

He nodded, and willed his voice to be steady, and not betray his anxiety. "I did. Thank you. I have it all right here." He gestured to the counter next to the laptop.

He looked at the magnetic letter tiles and whiteboard on the granite countertop, as if they were a venomous snake preparing to strike. Roni frowned. Uh oh...he must've let his emotions show on his face.

"No worries, Jason. I know it must seem overwhelming now, but we'll take it in small, manageable steps."

He flashed a broad grin, and sent up a prayer it would reach his eyes, and not look as phony as it was. "Worried? I'm not worried. Everything's cool."

Roni smiled in an encouraging way. "It really is." Her eyes twinkled and her smile could only be described as devilish as she continued, "It may be your first time, Jason, but I've got lots of experience."

He burst out laughing, and felt her joke ease his nerves a little bit. "It's been a long time since a woman said that to me."

Roni laughed with him. "I bet it has, Mr. Charm. Let's get started."

\*\*\*\*

Around an hour later, Jason's tension had returned. He clenched his fists against his thighs so tightly he was afraid he might draw blood. At the very least, he'd have little half-moon marks on his palms from his fingernails. His frustration threatened to bubble over, but years of hiding his dyslexia had made him a pro at putting on a relaxed face in situations where was feeling anything but relaxed. He itched to throw the board with its magnetic tiles from his lesson kit across the room; instead, he sounded out the combination of letters in a hesitant manner that made him feel two inches tall.

"Cr…ack…er."

In spite of his best efforts to hide his shame, he felt heat flood his cheeks.

"Excellent!" Roni said. "You're doing great, Jason. I think that's enough for today. Do you have any questions?"

He felt his shoulders drop as he relaxed at her words. Through most of the lesson, he'd felt like they'd been somewhere in the vicinity of his ears, he'd been so tense. "Nope."

"Okay, then." Roni jotted a note on the pad in front of her, and shoved a lock of her pink hair behind an ear. Yep. She was Lily's bestie all right—pink hair and all. She was her own person, like his Lily was.

She looked at the camera and smiled her encouragement. "I feel really good about the work we did today. How are you feeling?"

"Great," Jason grinned and bobbed his head. He felt like he must look like one of those toy dogs in a car window, and stopped bobbing. It didn't seem as though he was fooling Roni anyway.

She bit her bottom lip, and hesitated before she said, "It's okay to feel frustrated. Or embarrassed—angry, even. Those are all normal emotions to have as we start out, it must seem like there's a long, difficult road ahead, but you really did an amazing job today. I feel like we're off to a great start."

Jason rolled his eyed. "Riight…an amazing job sounding out words any six-year old could read with no problem. Pardon me for not busting with pride right now."

"I know the words seem basic and obviously you have a far more advanced vocabulary, but it's the process you're learning. Once you get it down, you'll be able to use this system to break down the most complicated words into workable parts. And I have no doubt in my mind you'll get there. You are one of the most quick-witted men I've ever met."

Jason snorted out a brief laugh, one without any actual humor behind it. "Please, spare me the fake compliments, Roni. I know what I am, and smart is not it."

Roni leaned forward and narrowed her eyes. "Now you're making me mad, Jason. You are clearly a highly intelligent man. You've worked out some of these techniques on your own over the years, and it's amazing to me. I'm sorry you didn't get any support in school when you were a kid, but I'm here for you now. This was only our first lesson, so give yourself a break."

Jason heaved a sigh. "Thanks, Roni. I appreciate you taking time to work with me. I'm sorry if I was a jerk. I just wanted to—"

As he hesitated, Roni interjected, "Figure it all out in one hour-long lesson?"

He shrugged. "Mebbe."

"That's not a realistic expectation. If you were teaching me to ride a horse, after one hour would I be able to jump like Hadley can after years of riding?"

He shook his head. "Of course not."

She turned her hands palms out and nodded. "Right, and that's where you are now. You're learning the basics, and setting the foundation for more. I can tell you...as the more experienced one in this scenario...you did a kickass job today, Jase. Really good, solid work. And if you give our lesson a fair chance, and continue to put in the work, you will get there. A lot sooner than I'd ever be able to run a steeplechase on one of your horses."

He thought about Lily, and how he wanted to be the best possible version of himself for her. Resolve steeled his spine. "I'm all in, Teach."

Roni beamed at him from the screen. "I'm glad to hear it. So...same time, day after tomorrow?"

Jason picked up his whiteboard and waved it in the air. "I'll be here with my letters."

Roni chuckled. "Good. See you then. And give Lily a hug for me."

He winked at the screen. "That might be the easiest homework assignment I ever had."

\*\*\*\*

Sunday brunch at the Bradens was wonderful. As different as a Sunday meal with her parents as turkey from Tofurky, but still warm, loving, and fun.

Lily cradled the stoneware mug of hot, mulled cider in both hands to ward off the nip in the air, as she stood lined up at the railing of the back porch with Heather, Bethanne, and Magda. They watched while the guys burned off some of the calories from the massive feast they'd just indulged in, with a vigorous game of touch football.

"Nice view," she said.

"They play shirts versus skins in the warm weather." Bethanne sighed.

"They're mostly my brothers, so…meh! But I have to say, my husband is looking mighty fine," Heather said.

"And mine," Bethanne added.

"And mine," Magda chimed in.

All turned their head s to look expectantly at Lily.

"What?" She asked with wide eyes. "Jason isn't mine like the other guys are yours. This thing between us is very new."

"Are you kidding?" Heather snorted. "You are the first woman Jason has ever brought to the family Sunday gathering. You're like the Braden Whisperer, y'know, like the horse whisperer, taming the untamable…"

"Stallion," Bethanne interjected.

"Yuck! No. He's my brother, remember? I was going to say Lily is taming the untamable Braden."

"I don't know if anyone could tame Jason, or if I'd even want to. I like him the way he is. He gave me the most thoughtful present from that new little gift shop on Main Street."

"My brother told me about the new store. He's

totally smitten with the new shopkeeper," Bethanne said with a happy smile.

"What did Jason get you?" Magda asked.

"A piece of art, and it turns out my stepfather was actually the artist. It's an owl in red eyeglasses, silk-screened onto a page from an old dictionary. Jason had no idea it was my dad's work. He picked it out because it reminded him of my tattoo." Lily took a sip of her cider and loved the explosion of cinnamon, apple, and clove in her mouth. It was like the holidays in a mug. "Which actually indicates a good eye for art on Jason's part, because my dad designed my tat."

A stunned silence greeted her statement. Jason's shout, calling his brother Jeff a "dirty, rotten cheater," broke the silence.

Since the other women still stared at her with jaws dropped, Lily cleared her throat and forged ahead to fill the silence. "I called my folks to tell them, and they couldn't believe the coincidence either. They seemed very interested in Jason. And they'll get to meet him sooner rather than later, since they decided to spend Christmas here in Rivers Bend with Hadley and me."

"That's nice of them. I guess they really want to check out your new guy, huh?" Heather asked.

Lily grinned. "Not entirely. They're passing through Virginia on their way to a music festival in Florida on New Year's."

"You have the most unusual parents," Bethanne said. "I mean, not only are they driving the length of the East Coast to go to a music festival, but they're going to spend Christmas with the grandchild of one of your mom's ex's other wives."

"Mom doesn't hold a grudge about the end of her

marriage. She always said once she let her inner flower child free, she knew her marriage to my birth father was the biggest mistake of her life." Lily shrugged. "Not that she'd ever put it that way. She thinks there are no mistakes—merely situations that help advance us on the roads of our lives to our ultimate destiny."

"Very evolved." Magda nodded.

"And they love Hadley. I think my mom hopes she can steer Hadley off the path of 'crass commercialism' Gloria is on, so they always have her up to Westport for a visit during summer vacations. They live on Compo Beach, which is always fun for Had and gives my mom a chance to show her another way of life. A patchouli-scented way of life." Lily winked. "They're like honorary grandparents to Hadley."

Heather bobbed her head. "Wow. You're good. You totally deflected the Jason questions, but it won't work with me. Back to the topic of the gift that my idiot brother—"

"Hey!" Lily cut her off with a fierce scowl. "Jason is not an idiot!"

Heather's eyes bugged out of her head. "Whoa. A woman defending Jason to me? Not berating him? Or hounding me about why he won't return her calls? Give me a moment to wrap my head around this development. It's serious End of Days stuff." She paused, sipped her cider, exhaled deeply, and waved her hand in front of her face. "Okay. Mind reset. My evidently, newly-thoughtful brother bought you a silk-screen of an owl? A real piece of art—not like the velvet Elvis painting I bought in Vegas?"

"In all fairness, I have to admit my dad did go through a velvet-art phase. It was supposed to be ironic, but I think he secretly had a thing for big-eyed children painted on black velvet," Lily said with a fond smile.

"And," Heather continued as if Lily hadn't spoken. "Jason picked out said piece of art, because it reminded him of your tattoo?"

Magda's eyes were alight with interest and humor. "I can't believe you have a tattoo; I've always been too afraid of the pain to get one. That's so badass, Lily!"

Bethanne snorted a sip of cider. "Only to a woman who went to your snooty prep-school and is now a small-town librarian."

Magda scowled, and looked as indignant as her adorable Kewpie-doll appearance would allow. "Hey! You're a small-town librarian too!"

"Focus, ladies!" Heather slashed her hand across her throat. "Bicker over your respective coolness factor on your own time. Now is the time to interrogate Lily about what's going on between her and my little brother."

Lily laughed, in spite of Heather's fierce expression and harsh words. She'd only known Heather for six months, but she knew her friend's bark was worse than her bite, and Heather was thrilled with Lily's budding relationship with Jason.

"There's not much to get out of me. Like I said before, it's all very new. Like a week old, new."

"Yet still, it is farther into the relationship pool than Jason has ever dipped his toes before," Heather said.

Bethanne laughed. "And he's going to have meet Lily's folks at Christmas. Has he ever had to meet anyone's parents before?"

"Nope." Heather popped the 'p' at the end of the

word. "Jason has always been the master of roaring into the driveway in his big ole truck, honking the horn, while the girl squealed and ran out the door to him."

Lily giggled. "Sounds like a country music video. Like the girl's father would be cleaning his gun on the porch, or something."

Bethanne smiled, and bumped Lily's shoulder with her own. "Be that as it may, it's always worked for Jason, so meeting your parents is going to be a first for him."

"My parents aren't your usual parents. They're very mellow, and pre-disposed to like him, because he picked out a piece of Dad's artwork. And you guys did catch the part about them passing through here on their way to a freaking love-in music festival? They are totally not intimidating parents."

Her friends laughed, and Bethanne wheezed and wiped her eyes as she attempted to get her mirth under control.

"What's so funny up there?" Jeff yelled from the backyard.

Lily turned to look at the guys, who had stopped their game to stare at the women, as they cracked up on the porch. Her gaze was drawn to Jason like a compass to magnetic north. He had the football tucked under one arm, with both his hyper dog and Magda's one-eyed Shih-Tzu at his feet, and the look in his eyes as he stared back at her, was so hot she was afraid the soles of her shoes were going to melt.

"Oh my," Magda murmured.

Bethanne fanned her face. "I know. I've seen Jason flirt with women. I've seen him deflect them with his charm when they try to get too close, but I've never seen him look at one the way he's looking at Lily. It's inspiring." She raised her voice to call out to her husband, "Cisco, are you ready to head home?"

The women all laughed while the men exchanged confused looks.

Jason continued to be oblivious to anyone but Lily. He strode toward her, the dogs at his heels, and flicked the football to Jeff without looking. Jeff caught the ball one-handed.

He reached Lily, put his arm around her, and tucked her into his side. He rubbed his jaw against her hair. "Have I mentioned how fine you're looking today, Moonbeam? Going home sounds like a damned good idea to me. Want to see my place? It's closer than yours."

Lily felt her cheeks heat up. "But, Hadley…" She flapped her hand in the direction of the house.

Jeff grinned. "Don't worry about Hadley. We'll take her home with us. She'll be glad to hang out with Sam for a bit longer. Y'all can swing by our place to get her when you're done getting the tour of Jason's…"

Magda smacked him on the back. Hard. "Do *not* finish that sentence."

Jeff widened his eyes, and managed to look like the very image of wounded innocence. "Maggie! I'm shocked at where your mind went. I was going to say Jason's apartment. What are you thinking?"

Magda's answer was lost to Lily, as Jason grasped her hand and tugged her down the steps of the porch. She barely had time to put her mug on the railing and say, "Thanks, Jeff. I'll be by the Retreat to get her in a little while."

"Take your time!" Jeff chortled, but it stopped in a

choked cough, as Magda whacked him on the back again.

****

Lily walked straight to the wall of glass overlooking a field and the hills beyond. Her jaw dropped, and her head whipped around to look at Jason, who watched her reaction with interest, from the front door to his apartment.

"Wow. I mean…wow. What an amazing view!"

Jason heaved a sigh of what appeared to be relief, and walked toward her. When he reached her, he stood behind her, wrapped his arms around her, and rested his chin on her head. She felt his jaw move against her scalp when he spoke.

"I'm glad you like it."

She chuckled. "When you said you lived over a barn, I was expecting something much more primitive."

The rumble of his answering laugh vibrated against her back. "Before I moved in, it was pretty rugged, but we fixed it up the way I wanted it."

Lily's spine stiffened a bit. "We? Who was the other part of 'we'?"

She peeked at him over her shoulder, only to be greeted by a grin. She squirmed out of his arms and turned to face him with a glare. "What's so funny?"

He put his hands on her shoulders, and gently kneaded the tension she held there. "It wasn't a girlfriend, if that's what you're thinking. I worked with an architect. The same guy who renovated the Retreat at Rivers Bend for Jeff and Cisco."

"And my misunderstanding is amusing to you, why?"

"Not amusing, it's a relief. I almost popped Ty in

the jaw the other day when he told me he'd seen your tattoo, so I'm glad I'm not the only one here who is exhibiting ridiculous jealousy. These feelings are new to me, and I'm glad to not be alone in them."

She grinned and rolled her eyes. "You're not. At the mere mention of the word 'we' I had visions of you planning this amazing view with another woman. And picturing you both curled up on that sectional sofa, looking out at it together."

He slid his hands down her arms and grasped her hands in his. He walked backward, and gently tugged her along with him. He sank down onto the soft, brown leather sofa, and pulled her onto his lap. "Why don't we admire the view together?"

She curled up against his warmth and hard body like a contented kitten. He pressed a kiss to the top of her head, where it rested on his shoulder.

"This is nice," she murmured.

"It is."

"I feel bad I ran off without thanking your mom for dinner, though."

"We can stop by her place after, and you can thank her then."

"After what?"

"After this."

Jason shifted her, so she was lying on the sofa, and propped himself up on top of her. His eyes twinkled, as he lowered his head to capture her lips in a kiss, which she returned enthusiastically. He was right. She could thank Joyce later.

Chapter 14

Lily heaved a sigh, as she reached in her desk drawer for her insulated lunch bag. She was looking forward to the holiday break from school. They really needed more than one special education teacher at the school, and her workload was demanding. It looked like it was going to be another day of eating alone at her desk, while she forged on with the never-ending paperwork that was a big part of her job.

She pulled out her sandwich, and had just taken a bite, when her phone vibrated against her desk. She could tell by the ringtone it was Gloria. Noon here, it would be around ten o'clock in the godforsaken country, where her half-sister lived with her elderly, diplomat husband.

She chewed hastily, and tapped the screen to answer. "'Lo, Gloria."

"Are you eating?" Disgust dripped from Gloria's voice.

She gulped down her bite of sandwich and answered. "Sorry. It's lunchtime here. I didn't want you to go to voicemail. Is everything all right?"

It was unusual for Gloria to call her. She'd call Hadley once in a while, but rarely called Lily.

"As a matter of fact, no, everything is not all right."

Gloria sounded annoyed, but not scared, so Lily's visions of civil unrest in the turbulent part of the world where her half-sister was living quickly dissipated. "What's wrong?"

"I spoke to Hadley yesterday. She told me something that disturbed me."

Lily frowned. As far as she knew, everything was great with Hadley. Her niece was looking forward to vacation as much as she was and spending Christmas with Lily's folks. "Really?"

"Yes." Gloria's voice was clipped and tight. "She told me your parents are going to be spending Christmas in my home. I am not pleased."

Lily clenched her fist, and her heart pounded in her chest. Gloria could irritate her like no one else in the world. In those two, brief sentences, she'd managed to both insult her parents, and make her feel unwelcome in the home where she was living. Through gritted teeth, she ground out, "I'm sorry. I didn't think you'd mind. After all, you send Hadley to stay with them for a couple of weeks every summer."

"That's a very different thing than having them stay in my house. You've certainly made yourself at home…inviting people to stay there, without asking me for permission first."

Lily shut her eyes and took a deep breath, before she answered. "A couple of points. One—I do not like the way you said 'people,' as though my parents are strangers I found on the side of the road—"

"That man is not your father. Our father is your father."

"Biologically. He's not the man who raised me, though." At Gloria's silence, Lily continued, "And two—I am living in your house, at your request. I would prefer somewhere smaller and cozier, but you

175

insisted I live there. I didn't think I needed to ask your permission to have my parents stay there for a couple of nights over the holiday. I was clearly wrong."

"Yes, you were."

Gloria's snapped response stung, but Lily reminded herself she was here for Hadley, not for Gloria, and bit back the sharp retort she longed to make. Instead she said, "I'll make arrangements for them to stay elsewhere."

"Good."

It was a lucky thing they weren't on a video call, as the smug reply caused Lily to actually shake her fist at the phone. "Anything else?" she asked tersely.

"As a matter of fact, yes, there is something else. It has come to my attention you're involved with Jason Braden. I do not want him sleeping with you, in my home, while my impressionable, young daughter is under the same roof. The man has a reputation as a playboy, and I'm not comfortable with your relationship with him."

That was rich, coming from the woman who'd slept her way through several counties, before marrying husband number five. Lily couldn't hold back the sarcastic answer if she tried. "You do appreciate the irony of you, of all people, implying I'm being promiscuous? I mean, seriously, Gloria, you've seen more of the male residents of Rivers Bend naked than the town doctor."

"How dare you!"

"And I'm also insulted you feel the need to tell me not to have a male visitor stay overnight, when Hadley is home. I would never do that in a million years!"

"Not just any male visitor, but one who is clearly

only with you for some sort of deviant sexual reason. Jason Braden does not do relationships, and if he did, it wouldn't be with a plain Jane like you."

"Sorry to prove you wrong—oh, wait, no I'm not—Jason *is* in a relationship, and it *is* with me."

"Given his history with women, he won't be around long, so there's no sense in me getting worked up about him being in Hadley's life. I need to get going, we're entertaining tonight, but I slipped away to call you. I didn't want another day to go by, before I told you about my concerns."

Lily jiggled her leg, as she considered how to answer. This woman was her half-sister, and her beloved niece's mother, so she needed to try to maintain some sort of civil relationship with her. "Fine. Concerns expressed, and received. As I said, I'll make other arrangements for my parents over Christmas—"

Gloria interrupted her, "And you will not do whatever it is you're doing with Jason Braden in front of my daughter."

"Good bye, Gloria."

"Ta-ta, Lily."

She disconnected the phone and tossed it on her desk, then picked up her sandwich. Her stomach churned after that unsettling phone call, and she screwed up her mouth before tossing her sandwich back down too. Lily's appetite was gone. She leaned back in her chair, and heaved a sigh. Seriously, it was hard to believe Gloria and she shared any DNA.

The phone call to her parents was going to be awful. How could she tell them, after all their kindness to Hadley over the years, Gloria didn't want them in her home? Maybe Jeff and Magda would let them stay at the Retreat over Christmas. She needed to call them to ask, but couldn't do it right now. Her heart still raced. Her cheeks felt heated, and that one bite of sandwich she'd managed to eat before Gloria's call, tossed around in her stomach like a tiny sailboat in a hurricane. Later. She'd ask them later. It would also give her time to think of a way to explain this all to Hadley, which wouldn't be easy, given she didn't really understand it herself.

****

Lily felt a definite lightening of her spirit, as she bopped to the cheery Christmas song playing in the store. Normally, she enjoyed a trip to the mall as much as going for dental surgery, but today was different. It was fun being with Magda, shopping for Hadley and Sam, and the decorations and music were going a long way to dispelling the lingering bad mood from her talk with Gloria.

She held up a flowing blouse that she loved, and Magda wrinkled her nose and shook her head so hard her blonde curls bounced.

"Not for Hadley. For you—yes, it would look great, but it's not Hadley's style."

"I guess it is a little hippie chick for Had." Lily hung the top back on the rack with reluctance.

Magda searched a pile of sweaters for her soon-to-be stepdaughter's size. "I can't believe Gloria refused to let your parents stay in her house. What a bitch!"

Lily shrugged. "She can be. Luckily, my folks are happy to stay in their camper. They're going to be driving it to the music festival anyway, so they didn't mind at all. It's really sweet of Jeff to let them park it on Retreat grounds; please, thank him again for me."

Her friend hoisted a blue cashmere sweater in triumph. "I found one in Sam's size! And, of course, I'll thank Jeff again. Although I think you thanked him plenty, before we left the house today."

"I don't know," Lily shrugged. "It's so nice of him, I feel like I should do more."

"You brought the man homemade Christmas cookies. He would do almost anything for a cookie." Magda waggled her brows. "Which has paid off for me on more than one occasion."

Lily held up her right hand. "I do not even want to know."

"Plus, you're dating his brother now. The Bradens are a loyal bunch, and you're one of them now. There's not much any of them wouldn't do for you."

Gloria's harsh words regarding her relationship with Jason caused Lily's cheeks to flame. Magda frowned at her. "Why did that make you frown and blush? Are you and Jason having problems?"

The two women moved toward a display of denim, and Lily focused all her attention on looking for Hadley's size to avoid eye contact with Magda. Gloria's snide insinuations shouldn't have the power to embarrass her, but they did.

"Everything is fine with Jason. It's something my sister said."

"Gloria? Don't let her get under your skin. She's a master at making other women feel like dirt. What did she say?"

"She said a man like Jason could only possibly be with me for some sort of deviant sexual reason. That he would never be in a relationship with someone as plain as me."

"Plain?" Magda yelled. "She wishes! You have such a cool, funky look. She's jealous."

Lily rolled her eyes. "Of me? Please."

"Yes, of you. You have all kinds of things Glo doesn't."

"Name one."

"I can name several off the top of my head. Give me a little time, and I could write a book on the subject. First of all, you're smart, attractive, confident, funny. You've made lots of friends in Rivers Bend. Real friends, not like Gloria's phony society friendships. Hadley loves you, and shares things with you Gloria never will, because she's so shallow. You have two parents who love you to the moon and back, and are more grandparents to her daughter than her blood relations ever have been. Plus, you're dating a Braden man, which Gloria was never able to do."

As Lily took a breath to respond, Magda put her finger against Lily's lips. "Shush. I don't want to hear it. You are all of those things, and they are why Jason is with you, not for whatever perverse reason Gloria thinks he is. She doesn't want to admit it, because it means you have so much more going for you than she does, and Jason sees it and appreciates it."

Tears burned at Lily's eyes, and Magda hugged her. It was a little awkward, what with Maggie holding a sweater, and her clutching the pair of jeans, but it made her feel better. "Some women in the grocery store said the something similar. I guess I let it get to me, because Gloria echoed their words."

Magda patted her back and laughed. "Trust me. Jason could get those women in the store to do whatever he wanted. They were doing the same thing as

Glo, trying to justify why he doesn't want them by dragging you down. Maybe it makes them feel better, but it's not true, so you have to ignore it as best you can. Now, let's buy these things, and then go get some hot cocoa. Something about all the Christmas cheer in this place has me craving a mug."

Chapter 15

Lily shivered against the chill in the air during her student pick-up duty at school, and pulled her lightweight down jacket tighter around her. She was a New Englander, she shouldn't be this cold in Virginia in December, for goodness sake! Her blood must be getting thin. A familiar pickup truck pulled up in the carpool lane with a cheery toot of the horn. Suddenly, she felt a little warmer.

Jason hopped out of the truck, and loped over to her. Looking hotter than the sun in his fleece-lined denim jacket and jeans that were worn in all the right places. And who knew cowboy boots would do it for her like nothing else?

"What are you doing out here on such a cold day? I'm bringing Hadley back to the farm with Sam. It's her riding lesson today."

He pecked her on the cheek, and she felt heat flood her face. She glanced around and said, "I'm on dismissal duty today."

A slow grin spread across his face. "What you're telling me is that little kiss is as far as it's going to go right now."

Lily rolled her eyes. "Yes. This is official business, mister."

"Here come the girls anyway."

Jason jerked his head to indicate their two nieces

strolling out of the school. She seriously didn't know how Hadley could see where she was walking, with her head down over her phone.

"Hiya, Uncle Jase! Hi, Ms. Davis." Sam waved at them both.

"Hey girls. Why so glum, Hadley?" Jason asked.

Hadley lifted her gaze off the small screen of her smartphone and frowned. "I got a really weird email. It's from the Admissions office of the boarding school in Switzerland Mom was so hot on me going to."

Lily frowned. "What does it say?"

"It's thanking me for my interest in their school, and there's a brochure for their riding program attached. Why do you think they're sending it to me? Do you think my mom is still trying to make me go there?" Her sentence ended in a worried whisper that tore at Lily's heart.

"She hasn't said anything to me, sweetie. I'll call her this afternoon and get to the bottom of it. Maybe their Admissions office is behind on their responses, and this was supposed to come to you sooner."

Hadley screwed up her mouth. "That doesn't seem likely."

Lily didn't think so either, but she didn't want Hadley distracted and worried through her whole riding lesson. "Go and enjoy your riding lesson, and don't worry about it anymore. It's probably all a misunderstanding."

"Hop in the truck, girls. I'm going to say goodbye to Lily."

"Ooooo…" The two girls called out in unison, mischievous smiles on both their faces, but they climbed up into the monster truck and shut the door behind them.

"What do you really think is going on with that boarding school?" Jason asked with a frown.

Lily shrugged. "I have no idea. But, I've had the distinct impression Gloria isn't completely happy Hadley and I are getting along so well. She might want Had to go to that ritzy school in Switzerland to get her away from me." She looked up at Jason and felt the sting of tears behind her eyes. She blinked rapidly, it wouldn't do for Hadley to see her upset. "It's on another whole continent."

Jason put his hands on her shoulders and squeezed. "Don't you worry, either. We'll figure it out."

"Figure what out?"

Lily jumped at the sound of Ty Harris's voice behind her. She put her hand to her throat. "Jeez, Ty! You scared me—I didn't see you coming."

"Sorry." Their friend was still dressed in his lawyer clothes, a charcoal suit, and wool overcoat, but carried a gym bag in his hand. "It's free-swim in the pool today. Did you forget we were going to swim laps together this afternoon?"

Jason gave her another peck on the cheek and smiled at his old friend. "I've got to get the girls back to the farm. See if you can cheer Lily up, okay?" He climbed into the truck and carefully pulled out into traffic.

"Why do you need cheering up, Lily?"

She heaved a sigh. "My sister."

"Ah. Gloria, the she-demon of Rivers Bend. What has she done this time?"

"I think she might still be trying to get Hadley to go to that boarding school in Switzerland."

"And Hadley and you don't want this to happen?"

"No. Hadley wants to stay here, and I do too. This is her home. Plus, we've worked past our problems, and we're really happy living together."

"If you don't mind me putting on my lawyer hat for a moment, I can tell you in Virginia, the law will take the child's point of view into account in custody disputes. So, if Hadley doesn't want to go, her feelings would be considered. You are currently Hadley's legal guardian, are you not?"

Lily nodded. "I am. I had to become her guardian, in order to live here with her after Gloria moved. I need to be able to sign forms for school, medical issues…that kind of thing."

"Right. So, if Gloria decides to force this issue, you would have legal roads you could follow to stop her."

Lily rolled her neck, and some of her tension released with an audible crack. "Right. Like a special education teacher in a public school has the resources to fight a woman with Gloria's money in court. Her lawyers would eat me alive."

Ty grinned. "But you have a secret legal weapon." He jerked his thumb at his chest. "Me. I'd take your case, gratis."

"I couldn't ask you to work for nothing!"

"Fine. Give me a dollar."

The people in this town were the best! Lily pulled Ty in for a quick hug. "Thank you, Ty. Hopefully, it won't come to a court battle. I think I'm going to have to skip our swim this afternoon, though. I want to get my call to Gloria over with before I have to pick Hadley up from her riding lesson."

\*\*\*\*

The warm, humid air and chemical smell of chlorine slapped her in the face like a wet towel. Usually, especially on a chilly day like today, Lily enjoyed the feel of the air in the swimming pool area of the school's field house. Today, it made her a little queasy, but it probably had more to do with her call to her half-sister. Looking around the room, she spotted Ty, toweling off poolside and hurried over to him. When she got close, she reached into her pocket and pulled out a dollar bill, which she waved in the air and smiled ruefully.

"Is your offer for dollar legal representation still on the table?"

Ty stopped in the middle of drying off, and his shoulders slumped. "Does this mean you reached Gloria, and she still wants to send Hadley away?"

"Yes and no. I reached Gloria, and she did contact the school in Switzerland, but it doesn't seem like she's going to push the issue immediately."

"That's good, isn't it?"

"For the moment. I was afraid she was going to send Hadley away after the holidays, but Gloria said she's not. Maybe because she can't arrange it that quickly, but in any case, she said it's for the future. Which will not thrill Hadley, but takes the immediate pressure off the situation."

"Why is she so hot to send Hadley away, when the kid doesn't want to go?" Ty asked with a frown.

Lily took a deep, fortifying breath before she answered. "She said she wants Hadley to be away from public school in Rivers Bend by high school, as she's approaching dating age."

"What?"

"Gloria doesn't want—and this is a direct quote here—she doesn't want Hadley to start dating inappropriate young men. Like I am."

"Like you are? Jason? Gloria doesn't approve of Jason Braden? That's rich, considering how she pursued his brother relentlessly for years."

Lily laughed, but there was no humor in it. "She said my hippy parents have filled my head with ridiculous notions about society, and she's worried I'm passing them on to her daughter. And, as a result Hadley will start dating, and again this is a quote, some yokel who didn't even go to college, like I'm doing."

Ty twisted the towel so tightly, Lily was afraid her normally mellow friend was going to tear it apart. "What a bitch! Sorry. I know she's your sister—"

"Half-sister," Lily said.

"I can't believe how judgmental Gloria is."

"Believe it. And let's face it, Gloria wishes she was half the person Jason is! All the money in the world can't buy integrity or kindness."

"What do you want to do? If she's not taking Hadley away right now, there's not much we can do yet on a legal front."

"I understand, but it's coming, and when the time comes, if Hadley still doesn't want to go, I think I want to fight Gloria to keep her here with me."

"Fine. I'll stay on call, but maybe it won't come to that."

"Maybe Gloria will grow a heart before Had gets to high school, and she won't be so set on her leaving. Or maybe, by then, Hadley will want to move to Switzerland, but if neither of those things happen, will you help me?"

"You got it, Lily. I'll be happy to represent you if it comes to a legal battle."

"Thanks, Ty. I appreciate it more than I could say. Now, I've got to get over to Braden Farm to pick up Hadley and fill her in on the latest developments."

"She'll be relieved. It's a couple of years before high school, and to a twelve-year-old that will feel like a lifetime."

Lily smiled. "True. I don't want to have to tell Jason what she said about him, but I don't want to keep secrets from him either. That's no way to start a relationship."

Ty waggled his eyebrows. "So, you kids are in a relationship now…I never thought I'd see the day Jason Braden would settle down with one woman. You're one hell of a person to make it happen, Lily Davis."

"You don't want to know why my sister thinks he's with me."

"No, you're right, I don't want to know. I think I've had enough of a glimpse into the workings of Gloria's twisted mind for one day already."

\*\*\*\*

Hadley gulped down her last mouthful of pasta and slid off the stool at the marble kitchen island. She put her plate in the sink, and hugged her aunt tight. "Thank you so much for talking my mom out of Switzerland, Aunt Lily! You're the best!"

Lily hugged her niece back and replied with a warning tone. "It might not be permanently off the table, Had, but we're okay for now."

"It will all work out," Hadley said with confidence. "I need to get to my homework, is it all right if I don't help with the dishes tonight?"

Jason smiled and answered for Lily, "No worries, kiddo, I'm on dish duty tonight. It's the least I can do, since y'all fed me."

Lily turned her head to smile at him with gratitude shining from her eyes, and he felt like he was ten feet tall.

"Thanks, Jason!" Hadley called out as she ran out of the kitchen.

Jason stacked the dishes remaining on the island, and carried them over to the sink. "You've been awful quiet tonight. Was the call with Gloria really bad?"

Lily shrugged. "A little. She's really a piece of work."

"What did she say this time?"

"She's still hell-bent on Hadley being in the Swiss boarding school by the time she's high school age. She's worried about her dating the wrong element."

Jason rinsed his dish and placed it in the open dishwasher, and laughed aloud while he did. "The wrong element? In Rivers Bend? Who does she think Hadley is going to meet here that is so bad for her? We're a pretty nice little town."

Lily's face flamed as red as the marinara sauce on their pasta. She cleared her throat, and busied herself pouring the leftover spaghetti into a container. Was it his imagination, or was she actually avoiding eye contact with him?

"Um…well…here's the thing. Gloria doesn't want her dating someone like I am."

Jason froze in place, with a dish under the steaming water pouring out of the faucet. "You mean…me?"

Lily inclined her head, and still didn't look at him. "Yes. She said specifically she didn't approve of my choice of man, and didn't want Hadley making the same mistake." She made air quotes around the last word.

"Oh." The hot water burned his hands and Jason snatched the dish out from under it and slammed it in the dishwasher with a clatter.

"But what does she know? Like Gloria has the best taste in men? C'mon! That polo player was only after her money. She wouldn't know a quality man if he hit her in the face." She frowned and continued, "Well, a quality man wouldn't actually hit her in the face, but you know what I mean—metaphorically."

"Got it." Jason took the pot from Lily and squirted some dish soap in, before turning the hot water back on, and adding it to the shiny, stainless steel pasta pot. "Gloria doesn't think I'm a quality guy."

Lily rolled her eyes. "I repeat—what does she know? You're a great guy."

"But Gloria doesn't think I'm good enough for you?" Jason scrubbed the pot energetically, and chuckled without humor. "She's not wrong."

Lily put the salad dressing in the refrigerator door, and slammed it so hard the bottles rattled. "Yes, she is. If anything, it's the other way around. I'm not good enough for you. I mean, have you seen the women you dated before me? *Vavavavoom!*"

Jason dropped the sponge in the pot, and turned his head to stare at her. "You're gorgeous, Moonbeam."

Lily leaned against the fridge and rolled her eyes behind her tortoise shell glasses. "Yeah, right."

"You are your own person, with your own distinctive style. Those other women are all cookie cutter imitations of each other. You're you. And in case you haven't noticed…I like you. A lot." He dried his hands on a dishtowel, and walked over to stand in front of Lily, where she still leaned against the fridge. He put his hands on her shoulders and squeezed. He bent his knees and scooched down, so they were at eye level with each other. "Not one of the other women I've dated has ever made me feel the way I do when I see you."

"What do you mean?" Lily bit her bottom lip, which drew his attention to her rosy lips, and he wanted to kiss her more than he wanted to take his next breath, but he had to make her see herself the way he saw her.

"When I pulled up to the school today and saw you on the sidewalk, my heart about pounded through my chest."

She peeked up at him, because with their height difference, even him scrunching down wasn't enough to make them the same height. "Really? Mine did too, when I saw you."

He smiled. "That's good news, because here's the big difference between you and anyone else I've gone out with—how you feel and what you think matters to me. I know it makes me sound like a total jerk, and I'm starting to think maybe I was before I met you, Moonbeam. I didn't much care about those things with anyone I went out with before you. See—you make me a better man."

"You already were a good man."

He shrugged. "In some ways, but where women were concerned, not so much. I never had to make any effort, but you challenge me to be a better man and damned if I don't want to live up to the challenge."

He straightened up, and walked back to the sink

and resumed cleaning the pot. "Like meeting your parents when they get into town. It's going to be a first for me."

Lily pushed off the fridge and stood next to him. She picked the cheery, red dishtowel off the counter and held it out. He finished rinsing the pot and handed it to her. She dried it and said, "You've never met a girl's parents before? How is that possible?"

"I kept things breezy. I never pretended a relationship was something it wasn't. I never brought a girl home to my mom, and I never met any of their folks either. I'm a little nervous about it, to tell you the truth."

"My parents aren't your typical parents." Lily crouched in front of a cabinet, to put away the now shining pot.

"Which might not work in my favor, given their views on animals and what I do for a living."

"They'll see how gentle you are with the animals, and how much the animals all love you, and they'll be fine." Lily rose up, and took the pasta drainer from him to dry.

It was nice doing these little domesticated chores with Lily. It felt good. Right. And damned if it didn't shake him to his core.

## Chapter 16

A custom-painted psychedelic van, towing a small camper pulled up in front of the Retreat, horn tooting cheerfully the whole time it approached.

Lily peeked up at Jason from the corner of her twinkling eyes. "I told you they weren't your normal parents. Nothing to worry about."

If that was the case, then why was his heart pounding like a horse in the final furlong at Preakness. He surreptitiously wiped his damp palms on his jeans, and watched as a beaming woman, hung out the passenger side window, waving and grinning from ear to ear.

"Lily! My beloved daughter!"

In spite of her jokes about the Fletchers not being normal parents, Lily glowed like she was lit up from the inside, as she waved back enthusiastically. "Hi, Mom! Hi, Tommy!"

Lily's parents' rig ground to a halt in front of the porch where they waited, and the loud clunk its engine made, caused Jason to wonder if it would make it all the way to the music festival in Florida, where they were headed after their visit here in Rivers Bend.

Lily's mom was out of the van as soon as it stopped, and ran toward the porch, but Lily hurried down the stairs and met her halfway, where they hugged each other tightly, and Mrs. Fletcher rocked her daughter back and forth. A tall, lanky man with a full head of flowing, dark hair, graying at the temples, skimmed around the front of the van. There was a lopsided grin on his face as he watched his wife and stepdaughter greet one another.

Hadley rushed toward them. "Jane! Tommy! I'm so happy you're here!"

Jane continued to hug Lily with one arm, but spread her other arm wide, to make room to include Hadley in their embrace. The girl was enveloped in their hug, and Jason noticed for the first time Lily's mom had what appeared to be holly leaves and berries woven in a wreath, perched on top of her unruly mop of shoulder length, gray-streaked brown curls.

"Happy Solstice, everyone!" Jane called out to one and all.

Thomas Fletcher reached the ladies and held out his arms. "Happy Solstice!"

Lily and Hadley pulled away from Jane's loving hold, and both hugged Mr. Fletcher.

"Let me introduce you to everyone," Lily said.

She pulled back and waved Jason forward.

Showtime. Jason swiped his hands on his pants one more time, as he walked down the steps toward Lily and her family. Man, how do other guys do this every time they go on a date? It was torture. Or maybe, it wasn't always this nerve wracking. Maybe, it was extra, special terrifying today, because he cared so much about Lily and really wanted her folks to like him. He extended his hand as he got closer.

"Mom, Tommy, this is Jason Braden. Jason, these are my parents, Jane and Thomas Fletcher."

Jason shook hands with Lily's stepfather, who may

look like a mellow, aging hippy, but had a grip that would have twisted a weaker man to his knees. He'd heard about fathers doing this to their daughters' beaux before. Jason knew he could squeeze harder and didn't want to appear to be a wuss, so he returned the firm grip, but not as hard as he was capable of doing. Based on the knowing smile and head bob Mr. Fletcher bestowed upon him, Jason thought it had been the right move.

"Nice to meet you, Mr. Fletcher, sir."

With one last squeeze, Lily's stepfather released his hand, and threw back his head and laughed. "Tommy, son. Call me Tommy. Mr. Fletcher was my father."

"Tommy," Jason replied with a smile.

"And I'm Jane." Lily's mom beamed at him, and threw her arms open wide, the flowing sleeves of her gauzy tunic top fluttered in the breeze.

Clearly, a handshake wasn't going to cut it with Mrs. Fletcher; a hug was in order here.

Jason could see a little of Lily in her mother's intelligent, kind eyes and radiant smile, and felt his nerves begin to ratchet down a notch. He went in for what he intended to be a brief embrace, but Jane pulled him tight and patted his back.

"Wonderful to meet you, Jason."

Much taller than Jane, he could see Lily over the top of her head, and she watched with an amused grin. He winked at her over her mother's head, before he said, "You too, Jane. I see a lot of Lily in you."

Jane pulled back, but kept her hands on his shoulders and squeezed them once before releasing him. "Oh, you're a charmer!"

"That he is." He heard the chuckle in his own mother's voice behind him, and remembered they weren't alone here. In all his nerves, he'd forgotten the whole Braden clan had assembled to welcome Lily's folks to the Bend.

Jason made the introductions, and Jeff and Magda steered everyone toward the kitchen, where their housekeeper, Mrs. Wilson, had laid out a huge spread for lunch. Cooking vegetarian fare had been a challenge for the older lady, who was used to cooking for their family of enthusiastic carnivores, but she'd done herself proud with this feast.

Their two families were chatting away together as if they'd known each other for years, and cheery Christmas music played on the Retreat's sound system. Lily slid into the seat next to him, with her plate full of Mrs. Wilson's cooking, the aroma of the spicy, Mexican-inspired tomato and bean casserole wafted up to his nose.

"See—it wasn't so bad," Lily whispered.

He felt her warm leg press against his under the table, and the pressure he'd been feeling in his chest eased at the contact. "Says you. It was one of the hardest things I've ever done," he whispered back out of the corner of his mouth.

"They love you," Lily replied, before taking a bite of the casserole. Her eyes fluttered and closed, and he remembered her making a very similar face, in a very different situation last evening. "Mrs. Wilson, this is delicious."

"Thank you dear." The housekeeper's raw-boned face turned ruddy at the compliment.

"It truly is," Jane replied. "It was so kind of you to

prepare a vegetarian Solstice feast for us."

"And to let us park the camper on your property, Jeff," Tommy added.

Hadley scowled. "I can't believe my mother won't let you stay with us."

He felt Lily's leg jolt against his, before she said, "What do you mean, Had?"

The child rolled her eyes. "I know you told me they wanted to camp, but I'm not an imbecile, Aunt Lily. I knew my mother had to have something to do with why they're not sleeping in our house. It's not like we don't have the room; besides, I overheard Jeff and Maggie talking about it here one day."

Maggie's blue eyes opened wide, and she mouthed at Lily, "Sorry."

Lily grimaced and waved her hand dismissively at her friend. "No worries, Maggie. I should've told Hadley the truth; she's almost a teenager now."

"That's right," her niece piped up, before shoveling in a forkful of Spanish rice.

"It's fine," Jane said. "We honestly do prefer the camper to rattling around in that big, old house. It's cozy. And we have a lovely view of the river here."

"And we'll still get to spend plenty of time with our girls," Tommy added, and swung his head to fix Jason with a stare. "And to get to know Jason a little better."

Oh good. Evidently, the protective father thing was not over as soon as Jason had hoped it would be.

He hastily swallowed a mouthful of the casserole, which suddenly tasted like sawdust and said, "Looking forward to it, Tommy."

\*\*\*\*

"You know, it really is cozy in here," Lily said, as she cradled a warm mug of tea in her hands and looked around the interior of the trailer, where she sat in the booth seating across the tiny kitchen table from her mother.

"It is. Tommy's and my needs are simple, so there's plenty of room for us on our travels."

"Even if you can't stay with Hadley and me, you could've come over to hang out today."

"I wish I was more evolved, Lily, but the truth is, I'm not far enough along on my journey I would be able to set foot in that woman's house. Hadley is always welcome in our home, but like the old saying goes—I don't want any part of a club that doesn't want me as a member." Her mother fluttered the fingers of one hand dismissively, held her tea in the other hand, and blew on it. They were in close enough quarters Lily was able to feel the steam from it as it curled around her face.

"I don't think it has anything to do with you, Mom. What I think is going on is Hadley and I are getting along and happy, and Gloria can't stand it. She always has to be the center of everything, and is being eaten up by jealousy her daughter can be happy with me." Lily took a sip and rolled her eyes. "Not to mention her fear I might have some influence over Hadley, and she might not turn into a little Gloria-clone after all. When I talked to her about her forcing Hadley to attend that boarding school in Switzerland, Gloria mentioned specifically, her fear Hadley might follow my example and start dating someone inappropriate for her social position."

Jane held the mug to her lips, but before she took a

sip, she waggled her eyebrows, grinned, and said, "Enough negativity and talk about Gloria. Speaking of dating, let's discuss your new young man. He's a beautiful soul…and, my oh my, hubba hubba."

Lily felt heat wash over her cheeks, and it had nothing to do with the hot drink and close quarters in the trailer. "Mom! Please. Hubba hubba?"

"I stand by my hubba hubba." Her mother raised one shoulder in a graceful, elegant gesture, which allowed a peek into the debutante upbringing she'd abandoned to marry Tommy and follow her heart. "Jason is very handsome, and he has a beautiful soul. His aura is lovely, and complements yours; I'm very happy you found each other."

"We've only been seeing each other a month." Lily protested. "It's not like we're soul-mates or anything."

"Ah, but you are. I see it in the way your auras dance together around you."

"You don't think we're a little mismatched?"

"Please, Lily, I hope you're not taking Gloria's talk about his lack of formal education to heart. I'd like to think I raised you to be less shallow than to think that way."

"No, it's not that—I think Jason is highly intelligent. And really gifted with the horses; I know you don't approve of the Braden's farm—"

"I might be changing my opinion on the farm, since our visit there yesterday. The animals are clearly loved, and the family's connection to them is beautiful to see. Jason, in particular, has such a strong link to the horses and his dogs."

"Wow. I never thought I'd hear you talk this way about domesticated animals."

"I'm not going to order a steak any time soon, but I can see there is another side, which I want to learn more about in the future. But, you've distracted me from our original conversation…what do you mean by mismatched?"

"Gloria and some of the other women in town here he dated in the past have suggested he is out of my league in the looks department, and it makes them wonder what he sees in me."

Jane put her mug down with enough force it thumped and the tiny table shook. "Ridiculous! You are beautiful, Lily, inside and out. Jason is lucky to have you in his life. And if the way he looks at you is any indication, he knows it. These women are just jealous."

"I know. In my heart, I know it. But, we are very different people."

"Not at your cores. In your values and in your spirits, Jason and you are soul-mates."

"Again, Mom, it's only been a month. Cool your jets with the soul-mate talk."

Her mother dismissed her objection with a languid wave of one hand. "You'll see. Your mother is right, as always. Jason Braden and you are fated to be together in this life."

Chapter 17

The little church looked magical decorated for Christmas, with pine boughs, red bows, and candles twinkling everywhere. The organist played Christmas carols as the population of Rivers Bend filled the pews for the early Christmas Eve service. Lily arrived with her parents and Hadley, and noticed there were open seats near the front. She gestured to them, and her stepfather nodded and strolled toward them, holding her mom's hand like they were still newlyweds after all these years. Lily really hoped she found love like that in her life—maybe Jason was the one. Her heart beat a little faster at the thought. Lost in her daydream, she realized her family had gotten ahead of her down the aisle, and she scurried to catch up with them. It was easy to spot them, and not because the church was tiny. Her folks definitely stood out among the population of this small Virginia town. Her stepdad's idea of suitable Christmas attire was a red velvet frock coat, which he wore over a paint-splattered pair of black jeans. Her mom was in a flowing, gauzy green dress, and she wore the wreath of holly and berries in her hair again tonight. She loved how they were their own people, wherever they might be. She truly admired Tommy and her mom, and was so grateful they were the people who raised her.

She felt a tap on her hand, and turned her head to

look down at Heather Braden, who was seated at the end of the pew opposite her family.

Heather smiled up at her. "Merry Christmas!"

"Merry Christmas." Lily leaned down and the friends hugged. She smiled over Heather's shoulder at her friend's new husband, Mick Evans. "Merry Christmas, Mick."

Model handsome, Mick was something to see, and he never looked happier than he had since his whirlwind Vegas wedding in November. "Merry Christmas, Lily. Glad your family is joining us tonight."

"Me too. It's so nice of your family to include us in everything, since Gloria has made her house off limits to my parents."

"Happy to do it. Your folks are a kick!" Heather laughed.

Lily glanced over her shoulder at them standing out like exotic orchids in a field of wildflowers, and smiled. "That they are. See you after the service."

She felt a tingle of awareness and knew Jason was looking at her. She didn't really understand how she knew; Lily had never shared this sort of connection with anyone else before. She looked down the pew, and saw the man in question, seated between his mom and his sister, Deidre. She smiled at him, and raised her hand in greeting.

Jason grinned, winked, and mouthed, "Merry Christmas."

She shoved her glasses up on her nose and mouthed the words back to him. The organist struck the opening chords of the processional, and Lily hastened to her seat across the aisle. As she slid into the pew next to her niece, Lily tried to squash the very not church-appropriate thoughts, which filled her mind at the sight of Jason dressed up for church in a suit. Her mother was right about one thing...hubba hubba indeed.

****

Lily warmed her hands on her stoneware mug of mulled apple cider, and took in her surroundings. It was like she'd landed in a Christmas movie on television. The Retreat at Rivers Bend was an old plantation-style home, and Jeff, Magda, and Sam lived on one side of it. The other half was reserved for Retreat guests. Tonight, they were gathered in their personal living room. The pine scent of the massive Christmas tree, positioned at the front window, mixed with the smoky aroma of the crackling fire in the fireplace. Christmas music played over the sound system, and cheerful conversation and laughing surrounded her.

Lost in her own thoughts, Lily started when she heard someone clear their throat directly behind her. She looked over her shoulder and saw Jason's smiling face, as he held a sprig of mistletoe over her head.

"Look at that—you're under the mistletoe. You know what that means, Lily."

"Does it count if you're actually carrying the mistletoe around with you?" She asked with a laugh.

"According to Jason Braden's Official Mistletoe Policy...yes. Yes, it does."

"If it's official, I guess there's no question." Lily stood on her tiptoes and pressed a quick kiss to Jason's cheek.

He shook his head. "Not to be a stickler or anything, but again, according to JBOMP—" He pronounced it as a word, jay-bomp.

"Jason Braden's Official Mistletoe Policy?" Lily interrupted.

"Right. According to JBOMP, a peck on the cheek doesn't count. Lips on lips are required at a minimum. Tongue may be waived, as we're at a family gathering, but lip contact is a strict requirement."

Jason put his hands on her shoulders and leaned in, slow and sexy, holding eye contact the whole time. When their lips were a millimeter apart, her heart raced, and her breath caught. Finally, Jason kissed her. Her head spun, and her cheeks heated, and she heard someone hoot in the background, and became aware they were not alone. They were actually in a room filled with their loved ones.

They pulled apart with reluctance, and Lily glanced around the room, to discover all eyes were on them.

"Okay, folks, show's over," Jason called out to the crowd.

"Aw, it was just getting interesting," Ty Harris walked over and said. By his side was the owner of the new gift shop in town, Grant Weston, whom Ty had been seeing of late.

Jason playfully punched Ty's bicep, and the three men all laughed. Lily smiled, but couldn't help but feel a smidge embarrassed. One, little Christmas kiss from Jason, and she totally forgot they were on public display. No man had ever affected her so much before.

"Merry Christmas," she said.

Ty kissed her cheek, and Grant smiled at her.

"Merry Christmas," the two men said in unison, and then looked at each and laughed.

"Thank you so much for letting me crash your family's Christmas Eve celebration. I wanted to keep the gift shop open today for last minute shoppers, so there wasn't time for me to travel to see my family. This is so much nicer than sitting alone in my apartment—thanks!" Grant said to Jason.

Ty added, "Me too. My folks decided not to travel to the Bend this year, since Dad just had knee surgery, and the trip would be too much for him. I had to be in court today, but I'm heading down tomorrow to spend a few days with them. I'll be back for New Year's Eve though."

"No worries, y'all. The Braden family motto should be: The More, the Merrier. We're happy to have you with us tonight," Jason said.

Lily's parents joined the group, and her mother said, "We're very fortunate it's your motto, because we're having a lovely time tonight! And Jeff and Magda invited us for Christmas morning too. Lily, they'd like Hadley and you to join us bright and early for present opening and brunch. Will that work for you?"

"Sure will!" Lily said with a smile. "Hadley will be thrilled she gets to open her presents with Sam."

"Let's go tell her," Tommy said with a boyish grin.

Her mother clapped her hands together with pleasure and her parents drifted off to find Hadley and give her the good news. Ty and Grant were lost in conversation—and each other's eyes—so, she and Jason were once again on their own.

"Mom and I are coming over here tomorrow morning too," Jason said. His cheeks grew ruddy, and his beer appeared to be the most interesting thing in the world, based on the intense way he stared at the bottle. "I have a little present for you...nothing big...maybe I could give it to you then?"

Lily squeezed his arm. "I have a little something for you too. That sounds perfect. I'll bring it over tomorrow."

Jason looked up from his bottle, and smiled at her. Lily found it completely freaking adorable the Playboy of Rivers Bend seemed nervous about giving her a Christmas present. Seriously. What did he think she was going to say? Keep your present? No way in hell! She couldn't wait to see what he'd gotten for her.

****

Christmas morning found much of the same crowd gathered in Jeff's living room. Once again, a fire was lit in the fireplace, and Christmas music played in the background. A mountain of presents surrounded the huge tree in the window.

Jason took a swig of coffee, and looked at Lily, who sat between Magda and her mom on the sofa. All three women were also enjoying some fortifying coffee, and laughing at something Jane had said. Lily was dressed casually, as his mother had instructed last night. Christmas morning was a laidback affair, when he was a kid, they'd stay in their pajamas…too excited about their presents to take the time to get dressed. Lily looked great in her jeans and fuzzy, red sweater. Jason wondered if it felt as soft as it looked. Maybe later today, he'd be able to get Lily alone and find out.

"You're not going to unwrap her in front of my daughter, so get that look out of your eyes, Jase." His brother Jeff stood beside him and said in a low voice only Jason could hear.

"What look?"

"The one that says, she's your present, and you're

fixing to unwrap her in front of God and everybody."

Jason rolled his eyes. "She looks pretty in that sweater; get off my back. Speaking of presents, isn't it time to hand them out?"

Jeff nodded. "It is. Want to help me play Santa?"

"Sure."

Jeff whistled to get everyone's attention, and when all conversation ceased, and only Bing Crosby could be heard singing in the background, Jeff said, "It's present time, y'all!"

A cheer went up around the room.

He waved his hands to quiet everyone, so he could be heard. "For those of you new to the whole Braden Christmas experience, Jason and I will pass out presents to everyone, so we all have one, which we will open. Then repeat until finished."

Jason eyed the huge stacks of gifts under the tree. "And judging by the mountain of boxes over there, I'm hoping we'll be done in time for the New Year. Y'all must've been good this year."

Hadley and Sam had the most presents by far, as was right, since they were the only kids in the group. Hadley's mother had shipped a lot of presents to her, and Lily had lugged them all over this morning, in addition to the ones she had gotten for her niece. Jason loved how much Lily cared for her niece, who wasn't always the easiest child in the world. Underneath it all, she was a good kid, and he was glad she had her Aunt Lily in her life.

Hell. He was glad he had her Aunt Lily in his life, who was he kidding? He didn't want to think about when Gloria came home, or decided to send Hadley away to boarding school. What would Lily do? Would she stay here in Rivers Bend, or move back to Baltimore with her friend, Roni? Jason didn't want to consider the possibility Lily might move away from him. It had only been a month since they started seeing each other, but already, he couldn't imagine his life without her in it. He shook his head once. These were all new feelings for him.

"Earth to Uncle Jason! It's your turn to open a present," his niece Sam called out with exasperation.

He smiled. "Sorry, y'all. I guess I need more coffee, I drifted off there for a minute."

Jason picked up his present, a medium-sized box wrapped in paper with owls in Santa hats on it. He smiled over at Lily, as he shook the package. "Hmm...owl wrapping paper...whoever could this be from?"

Lily laughed, and her cheeks flushed with pleasure. "You got me. It's from me. I hope you like it."

"I'm sure I will."

As eager as a kid on Christmas morning, he opened his present from Lily. He couldn't wait to see what she'd gotten for him. The box had the sticker on top, which indicated it had come from Ty's new beau's gift shop, Wishes Granted. He lifted the top, and saw holiday tissue paper. Pulling it aside, he pulled out a beautiful carved wooden horse, which was polished to a high shine. He whistled between his teeth.

"This is amazing, Lily."

"You like it?"

"I love it."

"It's hand-carved. I thought of you when I saw it in Grant's shop."

"Thank you, sweetie. It's perfect."

Sam interrupted, "Okay. Magda, it's your turn."

The present opening continued on, but Jason wasn't watching. He ran his hand over the smooth, wooden horse, and smiled at Lily across the room, in what he feared was a goofy way. He'd never been this gone over a woman in his life. She blushed and smiled back, before turning to watch Magda open her present. Magda held up a pretty, little bracelet with a charm dangling from it, which was a present from Sam.

"Now it's your turn, Aunt Lily," Hadley said.

Jason recognized the package in her hands, and knew it was his present. He felt a little nervous, and hoped Lily liked her present half as much as he liked his.

Lily read the tag. "This one is from Jason."

"Oooo..." Hadley and Sam called out in teasing voices.

Lily smiled and ignored them as she carefully opened the present without tearing the paper.

"She's always opened her presents that way," her mother said with a fond smile. "So careful and precise. I don't know where she got it from...certainly not me! I tear into them like a greedy child."

Lily glanced up from the box and looked at him. "Great minds think alike. It seems like we both shopped at Grant's store."

"I think everyone did this year." His mom laughed. "It's very convenient having a place to get nice gifts here in town."

"Oh, Jason, I love it!" Lily pulled the framed photograph of them at Heather and Mick's Las Vegas wedding. The frame was silver, and decorated with crystals. Grant had said it was fitting to bedazzle a picture from a Vegas wedding.

Lily held it up to show everyone and a collective 'aww' sounded throughout the room.

"From our wedding!" Heather called out from her perch on her new husband's lap, where she'd sat to save room. At least that was her excuse. Jason suspected she just liked sitting on Mick's lap.

"Grandma, it's your turn." Sam had no time for sentiment…she was bound and determined to keep the present opening moving along at a good pace.

He snuck a glance at Lily, who held the frame to her chest and mouthed, "Thank you."

He felt his cheeks heat up and smiled at her. These feelings might be new, but damned if he didn't like them. A lot. Maybe too much? It would hurt like hell if Lily didn't feel the same way, or decided to leave town when her responsibility to her niece here was done.

Jason stood up, and walked over to the tree. Time to hand out another round of presents. Today was Christmas, and he was here with Lily and their families. He would enjoy today, and let the future work out however it was going to.

Chapter 18

Lily shivered in the chill of the early morning air, as she stood on the driveway of the Retreat next to her parent's psychedelic traveling rig.

"Time to get on the road," her stepfather said. He shook Jeff's hand. "Thank you so much for your hospitality. It's much appreciated."

Her mom pulled her into a tight embrace, and Lily hugged her back. It was warm and comforting, and she felt tears sting her eyes at her parents' departure. It had been nice having them here, and she would miss them when they were gone.

"Farewell, my beautiful daughter. It was lovely spending this time with you, Hadley, and all your new friends." Jane pulled back, but kept her hands on Lily's arms. She squeezed and added, "Especially Jason. I really like him. I'm so happy for you."

"Jason was so sorry he couldn't be here to see you off, but early mornings are a busy time on the farm."

"We understand, we said our goodbyes last night after Christmas dinner," Jane said.

Tommy hugged her and said, "I have to admit I reserved judgment on him at first, but he won me over. I like him very much, and think he might…just might…be good enough for my second favorite woman on this planet."

"Only this planet?" Jane put her hands on her hips

211

and a mock scowl on her face.

Tommy threw back his head and laughed. He gestured with a sweep of his arm at the colorful depiction of the galaxy painted on the side of their van. "Fine, woman. In the entire universe! Is that enough for you?"

"Yes," her mother smiled in satisfaction.

"I'm going to miss you," Hadley said with a sniff.

Tommy and Jane pulled the girl into a group hug.

"We'll miss you too," Jane said.

"But we'll see you at our house this summer," Tommy said.

"If mom lets me go."

"Oh, she'll let you go." Lily was adamant—she had no intention of letting Gloria interfere in Hadley's summer visit to her parents' house on the beach in Westport.

Tommy and Jane pulled out of the driveway the same way they pulled into it, honking the horn and waving out the windows. Hadley and Lily waved until the van was out of sight, and they couldn't hear the cheerful beeping any more.

****

The week after Christmas went by in a blur of lounging and celebrations with friends. Lily enjoyed it very much, and a week later she was standing in another driveway, seeing off another family with a wave. This time it was her own driveway, and Hadley looked out the back window of the town car her father had sent to pick her up for the weekend. Jason stood at her side, waving at Hadley as they drove down the long driveway to the gate.

When the car was out of sight, Lily sighed and

turned to go into the house. "I hope she has fun. She wanted to stay here and spend New Year's with Sam and Madison."

Jason draped his arm around her shoulders as they walked up the steps to the front door. "She'll enjoy it. She doesn't get to see her dad too often, so once she gets there I'm sure it will be nice for her."

"I hope so." Lily opened the front door, and led the way into the marble entryway, with its grand, curving staircase and massive crystal chandelier.

"You know how much I like Hadley, but to be honest, I'm actually looking forward to having a little alone time with you." He pulled Lily to his side and pressed a kiss to the top of her head.

"Me too," Lily said, but felt her heart sink. Jason had been the consummate playboy before they met. He played the field, and liked it that way. Now, he not only had a girlfriend, but she came complete with a tween girl, for whom she had complete responsibility. What if he got tired of the extra responsibility of a child? Felt tied down and confined?

Lily had never been one to worry too much about tomorrow; however, she couldn't help but think Jason might get bored with Hadley and her, and decide to return to his old, carefree lifestyle.

"We've got this whole, giant mansion to ourselves," Jason said. "What do you want to do? If you don't have any ideas, I have a couple of suggestions…but no pressure."

She looked up at him, and saw a twinkle in his eyes, and his lips twitched at the corners, as if he was holding back a laugh.

"I wonder what you have in mind?" She tapped her

index finger to her chin.

Jason clasped her in his strong arms, and she felt the solid floor vanish beneath her feet as he picked her up as easily as if she weighed no more than a feather. "I have to admit to a certain liking for the laundry room."

Lily blushed as she remembered their previous adventure in the laundry room. "I've looked at it in a different light since that night."

\*\*\*\*

"Wow! It looks so festive in here," Lily looked around the Retreat dining room, where Jeff and Magda were having a big New Year's Eve bash. It seemed like the entire population of Rivers Bend was here and dressed in their holiday best.

Lily wore a forest green velvet sheath dress, with a gauzy overlay that draped over the top. She picked it out, because she thought the gauze would flow nicely when she danced. Jason stood at her side and held her hand in his. Never one to get really dressed up, Jason was in a pair of khaki slacks, a button-down shirt, and a sports coat. Even if he was more casually dressed than some of the men at the party, he still managed to be the most handsome man in the room...at least in Lily's opinion. Although, Rivers Bend did seem to have a disproportionate number of wildly attractive men living in it.

A small band, Lily recognized them as teachers she knew from the school system, who played together in a band during their off hours. Lily smiled to herself as she saw their band name on the banner behind them. *Teachers for Sale.* Clever.

There was a buffet set up on one side of the room, and a bar at the end of the room opposite the band. All around them, people danced, ate, talked, laughed, and generally had a great time.

"They certainly did it up right," Jason said.

Lily wrinkled her nose and looked up at him. "You seem surprised; did they do something differently than they have in the past?"

Jason shook his head. "This is a first. I think it's Maggie's influence on Jeff. Do you want a drink?"

"A glass of champagne would be nice."

"You got it. I'll be right back." Jason released her hand and made his way through the crowd to the bar.

Popular in the small town, Jason kept getting stopped to talk to people. At this rate, it would be after midnight by the time he got back to her. Lily frowned as she watched a group of young women, in much more revealing outfits than hers, swarm around Jason. Each one seemed determined to get closer to him than the rest. Jason smiled, but Lily knew him well enough now to know it wasn't his genuine smile; it was the one he reserved for situations when he wanted to be a good, southern gentleman, but wasn't happy with what was happening.

A noisemaker sounded right next to her ear, and Lily jumped.

"Happy New Year! A little early, but what the heck!" Jason's oldest sister, Deidre, yelled to be heard over the band and the buzz of conversation in the ballroom.

Magda and Bethanne joined them, added their New Year wishes, and the women all hugged.

"You look amazeballs!" Bethanne said.

Lily spun so the gauzy part of her dress floated around her. "Thank you very much. You guys all do too!"

"When are we going to get you two Connecticut Yankees to say 'y'all', instead of 'you guys'?"

"Old habits are hard to break," Magda said.

"I have to admit 'y'all' is a useful word," Lily said.

"Where's my brother?" Deidre asked.

Lily craned her neck to look for Jason, and saw he had finally made it to the bar, although a couple of the persistent women were still glued to his side. "He's getting our drinks." She smiled at Magda and said, "He tells me this party is new thing, and thinks it's due to your influence on his brother."

Deidre nodded. "Maggie has brought a lot of improvements to Jeff's life in the past year. A lot of happiness."

Magda's eyes grew dreamy. "A lot changed in a year, and it was definitely for the better."

"You're a good influence on Jason too, Lily," Bethanne said.

"Oh, I don't know about that!" Lily protested.

"You are." Deidre nodded. "He seems more calm and settled now."

Lily's lips turned down, and she pushed her glasses up on the bridge of her nose. "That doesn't sound good. What if he doesn't want to be calm and settled? He used to have a lot of fun."

"He still does have fun," Magda said. "Just a different kind of fun."

Yeah, right. The boring kind of fun. Lily's fears from earlier in the week, that Jason would miss his former lifestyle and leave her at the curb, reared their ugly head.

The man in question joined their group, a beer

bottle in one hand, and flute of champagne in the other. He smiled and handed the glass to Lily, and held up his beer in a toast. "Happy New Year, y'all!"

Lily clinked her glass to his and thought he looked happy now, and she should live in the moment and be happy too. No sense borrowing trouble.

\*\*\*\*

The song ended, and Jason mopped the sweat off his brow, before applauding the band. One of the things he really liked about Lily was she liked to dance as much as he did, and once they started tonight they hadn't gotten off the dance floor. Lily's face was a little dewy—a lady never sweated according to his mother—as she applauded the band and added a little whoop. He'd ditched his sports coat several dances ago, and wondered if Lily was hot in her pretty, green dress.

His brother Jeff stepped up beside him, Magda by his side, and smacked him on the back. "Almost midnight."

He pulled his phone out of his pants pocket and checked the time. "So it is. Great party, Jeff."

"Thanks. Glad you came."

The lead singer in the band, Jason thought he was the woodshop teacher at the high school, stepped up to the microphone and said, "Get ready, y'all, grab someone to kiss…it's almost midnight. Ten…nine…"

Jason grinned at Lily and pulled her tight against him, as the countdown continued. Everyone yelled, "Happy New Year!" at the same time, and the band played the traditional "Auld Lang Syne."

"Happy New Year, Lily."

"Happy New Year, Jase."

He leaned down and kissed her, maybe a little

more passionately than his mama would approve of in public, but, hell, it was New Year's Eve. And Lily didn't seem to mind, she returned his kiss in kind, and twined her arms around his neck as she tried to pull him even closer against her. This was another thing he really liked about Lily—her passionate nature.

When he could hear the conversations around them begin to resume, he pulled away from her with reluctance. Jason's dad used to say the way you rang in the New Year, was the way you were going to spend the year. If that was true, he couldn't think of a better way to spend a year, than with Lily in his arms, and all their loved ones partying around them.

The band started playing a slow song, and they rocked to it together.

"You look serious. What are you thinking about?" Lily asked.

He rested his forehead on hers. "I'm thinking how happy I am right now. Tonight has been just about perfect."

"Only just about perfect? What's missing?"

Lily broke their eye contact, and if he wasn't mistaken, she seemed anxious about his answer. Weird.

He whispered his answer so close to her little, shell-like ear his lips brushed against it. "Having you all to myself, alone. Preferably naked."

He felt her cheek heat up against his, and knew he'd made her blush. He smiled.

"It's after midnight. Ready to head home?" Lily asked.

Jason grabbed her hand and pulled her off the dance floor, to the chair where he'd placed his jacket. "Am I ever! Let's go."

Chapter 19

The one cozy room in Gloria's mansion is where Lily had decided to put up the Christmas tree this year. Hadley said her mother normally had a giant tree in the vast marble entryway, but Lily didn't want to do it that way. She wanted the tree in the den, with its comfortable seating, warm fireplace, and built-in bookshelves. Somewhere they could sit and enjoy the lights.

Today they were taking the tree down, with Jason's noble assistance, and her niece was being decidedly grumpy.

"Putting up the tree was a lot more fun than taking it down," Hadley said with a huff.

"Always is," Jason said.

"Yep. That's why I put it off until this weekend. I hate taking the tree down," Lily said.

"We used to have servants who did it. It would be down and whisked away by January second, and I never knew anything about how or when." Hadley frowned as she took an ornament off the tree, and put it in a box.

"Must've been nice," Jason said with a head bob.

"It was," Hadley replied with a much put-upon sigh.

"At least y'all have an elevator to the attic. At my mom's house we have to lug the boxes up the stairs to stow them," Jason said.

A voice called from the front entryway, and Lily froze in place at the sound. Unfortunately, it was not a very dignified place to be frozen, bent over and stretching to reach a hard-to-get-to ornament.

"Helloooo…where is everyone?"

"Mom?" Hadley's voice sounded as confused as Lily felt.

"Gloria?" And Jason's sounded as appalled as she felt.

Lily stood up and answered, "We're in the den."

The deep sigh could be heard from the entryway. "The library. A den is so plebian."

Lily had her back to Hadley, so she rolled her eyes at Jason, who ducked his head and suddenly seemed completely absorbed in arranging the ornament storage container.

Gloria swept into the room along a wave of expensive perfume, and then stopped short, her perfectly manicured hands on her slim hips. "Whatever are you doing?"

"Taking down the Christmas tree"—Hadley answered, before adding—"Hello, mother. What are you doing here?"

Gloria turned to her daughter and held her arms open as a clear invitation to greet her. "Hadley, dear, it's so good to see you."

Hadley walked to her mother, and Gloria turned one contoured cheek to her daughter and allowed her to kiss it.

"You too, mother. We weren't expecting you."

"Hello, Gloria. Forgive our surprise, but we thought you were on another continent. Is everything all right?"

Gloria waved one hand in a graceful, yet dismissive, gesture. She sank down on a soft, leather chair. "It was a long trip, but everything is fine. It is time for Walter's annual physical exam, and he wanted to have it in Washington, with his own physician. I tagged along to do some shopping."

Hadley's eyes grew wide, and Lily thought she glimpsed a glimmer of tears before her niece blinked and her expression froze into the too-sophisticated ennui, she'd affected when Lily had first arrived in Rivers Bend. Over their time together, Hadley had begun to behave much more like other girls her age, and less like a character from Sex and the City.

Gloria appeared to have realized her error, and hurriedly added, "And of course to see you, Hadley darling."

"Of course." Hadley's answer was stiff, and she pointedly didn't look at her mother. The girl looked up at Jason and asked, "Shall we bring these boxes up to the attic; they're full."

"Good idea," he replied and hoisted the bigger box with no visible effort.

Hadley picked up the smaller container and walked out without another word.

Jason nodded at Lily and Gloria. "We'll be back in a jiffy."

"My goodness, Lily, you're all dewy. You're a complete mess. We used to have people to do this sort of thing. I don't understand why you have to try to do everything on your own. You were always such a stubborn girl."

Lily swiped her bangs off her forehead, and realized she was perspiring a little. She pushed her glasses up on her nose and blew out air in an attempt to cool off her face. Gloria always was so elegant and put together, but Lily fought the urge to explain her torn jeans and long-sleeved T-shirt. It was practical for the job she was doing.

"It's nice to see you too, Gloria. Will you be staying here? I can get your room ready for you."

"No need. We're staying at the Hay Adams in Washington. Much more convenient for what we have to do. I wanted to run up and see how things were going here, and I have to say, I am not pleased."

"Because we're taking down our own Christmas tree? Please. Millions of people do it every year."

"Not because of that...well, not entirely because of the tree. I'm not at all pleased to see Jason Braden here. I thought I'd made my position on your redneck beau perfectly clear."

Lily's hands formed into fists at her side, and she had to unclench her jaw to reply, "I am going to choose to ignore your redneck crack. With regard to Jason's presence here, I thought it was fine with you, as long as he wasn't sleeping over when Hadley was home. As we weren't doing that anyway, it was no problem. He came over earlier this afternoon to help us with the tree."

"I'm going to be frank with you, Lily, since subtlety does not seem to work with you. I do not appreciate the influences you're bringing into my child's life." Her lavender eyes narrowed.

A pretty color, and highly unusual, but Lily knew they were colored contact lenses. She frowned and took a breath to reply, but before she could say anything, Gloria spoke again.

"And I want to remind you, Hadley is my child.

Not yours."

"That sounds a little like a threat."

"Not a threat. That would be highly uncivilized." Gloria raised one small shoulder, and opened her eyes wide. "Consider it a reminder. Possibly, a warning. Hadley is my child, and if I deem you a poor influence on her, I will take steps to remove her from the situation."

"Maybe it's the time I spent living in Baltimore, which I'll admit can be a bit of a tough town, but that sounds an awful lot like a threat to me."

"Take it as you will."

Lily heard the hum of the elevator descending back down to the entryway, and lowered her voice, so Hadley wouldn't hear her when she got off the elevator. "I have something for you to take as you will as well, Gloria. I am currently Hadley's legal guardian, and if you want to send her to school in Switzerland, which she does not want to do, I will take steps to stop you."

Gloria tsked her tongue. "That does sound like a threat, Lily, so déclassé."

Jason and Hadley's footsteps echoed on the marble, so Lily took a step closer to Gloria, who sank back in her seat, as though afraid Lily would strike her. She might want to pop her one, but Lily would never act on it. Instead, she would hit Gloria where she lived.

"Just so you know, I have retained legal counsel, and I will take whatever steps necessary so Hadley's wishes are taken into consideration with regard to your plans for her future. I've been informed the Commonwealth of Virginia takes the child's wishes very seriously."

Gloria gasped. "You—" but couldn't answer before

Jason and Hadley walked back into the room. Instead of whatever scathing retort she'd been going to let loose on Lily, her half-sister composed her expression, and smiled benignly at Hadley. "Darling child, why don't you run upstairs and change into something presentable. I'm going to take you to lunch at the club."

\*\*\*\*

Jason had heard the expression 'you could cut the tension with a knife,' but he'd never really experienced it before. Hadley had gone upstairs to change, and left him alone with Gloria and Lily. The women glared at each other from their seats across the room from each other, and the air between them was so thick with tension, Jason was amazed he couldn't see it covering the room like a thick fog. He walked over and sat next to Lily on the sofa. He picked up her hand, and rubbed soothing circles on the top of her hand, which she clenched and was cold as ice. As he stroked her, he felt her flesh warm up, the tension begin to ease, and her tight fist gradually loosened.

He could feel Gloria's eyes burning into them, and looked over at her, and was amazed to see anger burning in her improbably lilac colored eyes, as she stared at their joined hands. What the hell had happened in here, and why did it piss Glo off so much to see them holding hands? She knew Lily and he had been seeing each other, so it shouldn't be a shock to her.

"You see this…this arrangement of yours, is precisely why I want my daughter removed from your influence," Gloria said through clenched teeth.

Lily's hand tightened again in his, and he felt her take a breath to respond, and jumped in before she did. He knew Gloria wasn't much of a sister, but she was

Lily's only one, and he didn't want the two women to say words that couldn't be unsaid.

"Now, now, Gloria." He used the same voice he did with a skittish horse on the farm, in an attempt to soothe the angry woman. "You don't mean it. You know Lily is a wonderful person."

He smiled down at Lily, who had peeked up at him with gratitude shining in her eyes.

"What I do know, is she's too good a person to throw herself away on a man like you, and I won't have my daughter do the same thing, when she begins to date."

Okay. Now Jason was pissed off too.

Luckily, Hadley came back in the room just then.

"I'm ready to go."

Gloria's expression changed in a flash, and she turned on the charm offensive Jason had seen her use on men before, but never on another female. Seemed Glo was going to try to woo Hadley back to her side.

"And don't you look beautiful, my darling child. Shall we go?" Gloria rose in a graceful movement, and walked over to her daughter. She cupped Hadley's face in her hand and beamed at the child.

"Um…yeah…that was the plan." Confusion reigned in Hadley's eyes, and while she was probably shooting for sarcastic with her expression, her voice wobbled a little, and Jason thought Gloria's rapid mood change made Hadley nervous. *Join the club, kiddo.* It was scaring him too.

The child jerked her head out of Gloria's hands, and hurried over to her aunt, where she leaned down to kiss her cheek. "Bye, Aunt Lily. I'll be home soon. Sorry to bail on helping with the tree."

"No worries, Had. Jason and I have got it. There's not much left to do anyway. You go and enjoy your mom's unexpected visit."

Lily's voice wobbled too, and Jason knew she was thrown for a loop by Gloria's surprise invasion. Because, that's what this felt like...not a friendly visit. This was an attack. He'd learned enough about Lily to know she didn't like to argue, but to protect Hadley, she would go to the mat against Glo. He watched Hadley leave with her mother, who didn't spare another word for either Lily or him, and felt uneasiness gnaw at his gut. This situation was not going to end well.

He waited until he heard the front door close, and then asked, "What the hell happened here while I was in the attic? Are you okay?"

"I'm fine." Lily squeezed his hand, and then pulled hers away from his and stood up and walked back to the tree, where she removed an ornament. Unfortunately for her attempt to act cool and collected, it had a bell on it, and the ringing noise made it obvious her hand was shaking.

Jason missed the warmth of her by his side, and stood. He walked to her and wrapped his arms around her waist, and pulled her back up against his front. Resting his chin on her soft hair, he said, "Try again, Moonbeam. I know you're not fine; you don't have to lie to me. I'm here for you."

"How dare she say those things about you...about us?" Lily's voice shook with anger.

"She wasn't completely wrong. You are way too good for me."

"Please. I am not."

"You're smarter than me."

"Book smart, maybe, but you're smarter than I am about a lot of things. You're very savvy about people, and you're so good with animals. You know so much about the science behind breeding—"

Jason interrupted her, "Speaking of breeding...your family is in a completely different social orbit than mine. I'm not saying better, mind you, but different. Old stock. Gloria looks down on us Bradens on account of it."

Lily snorted. "She's wrong. Your family is wonderful. Close and loving and loyal...all things she is not."

"She wants better for Hadley." It wasn't a question. Jason knew he had a reputation around town as a playboy, and it had never bothered him before. It had always amused him, truth be told, but things with Lily were different. He was different.

"She never seemed that interested in what was best for Hadley before. She married a string of different men, and raised Hadley to be too mature, too soon. I can't help but think jealousy is at the root of all this sudden interest. I think it bugs Gloria Hadley and I are getting closer, and Hadley is happier now."

"There has been a change for the better in Hadley, since you moved here. She seems to be a happier kid. To have come into her own."

"And I don't think Gloria likes it, but that's too darned bad. I love my niece, and as long as Hadley doesn't want to go away, I'm going to fight for her right to stay in Rivers Bend." Lily squirmed out of his embrace, and pulled her phone out of the back pocket of her jeans. "I better call Ty, and let him know what's happening."

Jason felt a chill, and it wasn't from the loss of her body heat next to him this time. What was happening between Lily, Gloria, and Hadley could tear their little family apart. He hoped he wasn't any sort of contributing factor, and sent up a little prayer things would be resolved before it got to the point of no return for all of them.

Chapter 20

The den looked empty without the tree...and
without Jason and Hadley. Hadley hadn't returned from
her lunch at the country club with her mother, and
Jason took off as soon as the last box was stowed away
in the attic. Lily felt a pang of sadness at the turn the
day had taken—it started out so pleasantly, but it all
changed when Gloria swept in, with her threats and
ugly talk about Jason.

Lily decided she needed a little BFF time, and
pulled out her phone to Facetime Roni. A smile tugged
at her lips, when her friend's cheerful face filled the
little screen. "Hey, Roni."

"Hey, yourself. You look sad. What's happening?"

Her shoulders slumped and Lily heaved a sigh.
"You know me so well. Gloria is back in town."

"Ugh. No offense, Lily, but I can't stand your
sister."

"I'm not feeling too crazy about her at the moment
either."

"Is she back permanently?"

"No, it's just an unpleasant cameo appearance.
She's threatening to send Hadley away again."

Roni rolled her eyes. "Why is she so hell-bent on
this Swiss boarding school, when Hadley so clearly
doesn't want to go there?"

"She's afraid, now that Had is almost a teenager,

she is going to start dating the wrong kind of boys. Like I am. With Jason."

"What?" Roni's jaw dropped and her pretty blue eyes bugged out of her head.

"And better yet, she said it in front of Jason."

"Did he rip her a new one?"

"No. He's too much of a Southern gentleman, but I could tell it hurt his feelings. After she left, he told me she's right about me being too good for him. Which is so not true."

"Gloria is poison. Where is she now?"

"She took Hadley out to lunch at the country club—probably to show her all the fine young men she could meet there. Luckily, her husband and she are staying down in D.C., so I won't have to put on a happy face all weekend here. I'm not sure I could keep up appearances for Hadley's sake for a prolonged period of time. I need a little while to decompress."

"Where's Jason now?"

"He left. I'm afraid he took her nasty cracks to heart, and I don't know what to do."

"I've gotten to know him a little better during our sessions, and he's a great guy. Show him what he means to you, and how you feel about him."

Lily heard the front door open. "I think Hadley is home now, Roni, I better run. Sorry I dumped all my problems on you, I didn't even get to ask you what you're up to."

Roni smiled. "No worries. We can talk later. I love you, Lil."

"Love you too, Ron." With a tap of her phone, Lily disconnected the call.

Hadley came into the room, and collapsed on a

chair and heaved a much put-upon sigh. Dramatic in the way only tween girls can be. "Hi, Aunt Lily."

"Hi, Had. How was lunch?"

"It was nice to see Mom, but she's really pushing that Swiss school on me. It was all she wanted to discuss."

"How did it make you feel?"

"It made me feel like I want her to back off! I mean, seriously, what is her deal with this school? Do they have her on commission or something?"

Lily huffed out a quick laugh, in spite of her dark mood. Hadley did have a good sense of humor. "I don't think so, but I'm not sure; it would explain things."

Hadley giggled, but her expression quickly darkened. "It would've been nice if we could've seen each other and talked about...I don't know...life and stuff. What we've been doing. What we got for Christmas. Like normal people. Sometimes I feel like she's not really interested in me for me, as a person. Do you know what I mean?"

Lily had to proceed with caution here. She shared the same suspicions Hadley did regarding Gloria's feelings for her daughter, but didn't want to say or do anything to further drive a wedge between them. Since Hadley didn't want to leave Rivers Bend, she was willing to fight for her niece, but if possible she wanted to do it, without destroying the tenuous relationships between the three of them. "I wish your mom would take your opinions on this school into account—"

"Thank you!" Hadley interrupted with a dramatic wave of her arms and epic eye roll.

"But"—Lily held up her index finger—"I believe she is doing what she thinks is best."

"Do you think it's best for me?" Hadley narrowed her eyes and frowned.

Lily squirmed in her seat. "Well...um...no. No, I don't, because you don't want to do it. I just want you to understand, Gloria isn't doing what she's doing to torment you. She really thinks she's doing the right thing."

"It doesn't make it any less annoying."

"No." Lily couldn't disagree with that statement.

"And what's her deal with Jason? He's such a great guy, why is she so snippy about him?"

"She was talking about Jason at lunch?" Lily's pulse pounded. Honestly, she didn't want to have to drive down to Washington tonight and tell her sister off, but she would.

Hadley screwed up her mouth and pointedly avoided eye contact. "I probably shouldn't have said anything to you."

Lily took a deep breath, and willed her voice to sound calmer than she felt. "It's okay, Had, I always want you to be honest with me. Even when it's something you think I won't like. Maybe, especially when it's something you think I won't like."

"She talked a lot about him being"—Hadley made air quotes—"not our kind. What does that even mean? Like he's a different species or something, because his family didn't come over on the Mayflower? And like the world's going to end if I date a boy from Rivers Bend too?"

Lily knew her father and Gloria's mother had always emphasized the importance of their lineage, but that sort of thing never mattered to her own mom and stepfather. They judged people based on their actions, not their ancestors, and raised Lily to do the same. Again, this conversation had taken a sharp left turn onto a minefield, and Lily didn't know how to respond. She wanted to encourage Hadley to be the kind of person she'd been raised by Tommy and Jane to be, but she didn't know if it was right to contradict Hadley's own mother.

After a long pause, she said slowly, "I think the way people behave, is more important than who their parents are."

Hadley bobbed her head in agreement. "Exactly! I mean look at that whack-a-doo Ms. Magda was engaged to before she moved to Rivers Bend. Is he the kind of guy Mom wants you to date? Because he might be from an old family, but he was seriously looney-tunes."

The child looked around for the first time since her entrance into the room. "Y'all finished taking down the Christmas decorations. The room looks empty without them."

"I was thinking the same thing before you got home."

Hadley stood up and said, "I'm going to go upstairs and change out of these clothes. I have some homework to do."

"Okay, Had. Maybe later we can order a pizza or something."

"You're not going out with Jason tonight?"

Lily shook her head. "Nope."

Hadley put her hands on her hips and scowled. "It better not be because of what Mom said about him."

"No."

At least Lily hoped it wasn't, but she feared it was.

Jason had really seemed to take Gloria's snide words to heart, and when he'd left he said he'd talk to her later— no mention of seeing each other. Lily liked Jason more than any other guy she'd ever dated, and if Gloria's snobbery came between them...cancel that thought...she refused to let it happen. Hopefully, Jason would come around all on his own and realize Gloria's old-fashioned ideas were bull. She bit her lip and thought over Roni's words. She needed to find some way to let Jason know how amazing she thought he was, but in a way that wouldn't scare off the recently reformed playboy. Their relationship was still pretty new—they hadn't even mentioned the 'L' word yet, but there had to be a way to make him see how good they were together.

She picked up the remote and turned on the television. In the meantime, there wasn't any problem so big it wouldn't be helped by a little binge-watching of reality TV shows.

****

"Hello!" Magda poked her head around Lily's office door, a red, knit hat partially covering her blonde curls. She held up her hands to reveal two to-go cups from the Nosh Pit. "I'm here to pick up Sam after auditions. I think it's so great the girls are trying out for the spring musical. I hope they all make it. I thought I'd get here a little early to visit with you, and I come bearing cappuccino. Fixed the way you like it, according to Deidre."

Lily pushed the report she'd been working on away from her and leaned back in her chair. "Bless you. Seriously. You must've been sent from the caffeine gods.

Magda laughed and handed her one of the cups. She put the other down on the little round table, where Lily worked with her students, and unwound her scarf from around her neck, pulled off her coat and hat, and tossed them on the table too, before sitting in one of the chairs. "Bad day?"

"Bad week, at least so far." Lily pulled off the lid of the cup. In her opinion, sipping the hot coffee through the cool foam on top was the best part of a cappuccino, and didn't understand people who drank them through the little hole in the lid.

"We missed you at Sunday brunch at the Bradens."

"Wasn't invited." Lily shrugged and took a sip. She closed her eyes and savored the strong coffee and creamy foam.

"You weren't?" Magda's blue eyes opened wide in shock.

"Nope."

"Did Jason and you have a fight, or something?'

"No, but we haven't seen each other since Saturday. My sister stopped by—"

"I heard about her visit from Sam. What kind of person comes home from thousands of miles away without any notice, and then doesn't stay in her own home, with her own daughter? I don't get it."

"Me either. She hasn't seen Hadley for months, and just takes her out to lunch. And it seems like she mainly only did it to push her boarding school idea on Had."

Magda shook her head, and took a sip of her coffee. "She's a pill. But, I don't see how her visit has anything to do with Jason and you."

"Jason was at the house when she arrived. He was

helping Hadley and me take down the Christmas tree. When Hadley went upstairs to change, Gloria said—right in front of Jason, mind you—the reason boarding school was so important to her is because she doesn't want Hadley dating someone who is beneath her, like I am."

Magda choked on her coffee, and for a second, Lily feared she was going to do a spit take. "That's nuts!"

"Even more nuts, is the way Jason seems to agree with her."

"You two are perfect for each other. Yeah, you're different kinds of people, but you fit together like puzzle pieces."

Lily smiled at her friend, grateful for the support, but feeling a heaviness in her chest at the fact Jason didn't seem to feel the same way about their relationship. "He said some stuff about my ancestors coming over on the Mayflower." She waved her hand in the air, and rolled her eyes.

"Trust me, lineage means nothing with regards to a person's character." Magda snorted. "Remember my ex?"

"I know." Lily bobbed her head in agreement. "I said the same thing, but he said something about breeding horses."

"And then he left?"

"Not right away. He helped me finish taking down the Christmas decorations and stowed them in the attic, but then he beat feet outta there."

"Have you spoken since then?"

"Yes, on the phone. And texting. But, it has been a little awkward, and he's been busy on the farm, and I've been busy with work and chauffeuring Hadley to all her activities, so we haven't seen each other in person."

"Do you want me to talk to him about this horse-breeding-Mayflower thing? I could set him straight on it," Magda asked.

Lily shook her head. "No thanks. I'm not sure it's the whole problem. I feel like something else is bothering him."

"What could it be? He's been so happy since you've been seeing each other."

"I have been too."

"What's the problem, in that case? He's happy...you're happy"—Magda flapped her hands at Lily—"Be happy."

"It is really different dating someone when you have a kid in your life."

"I learned that too, when I started dating Jeff. I love Sam to bits, but it adds a level of...I don't know how to put it...complications?"

"I love Hadley too, and I'm treasuring this time I get to spend with her. But, yeah, complication is a good word. It's a lot of responsibility—"

Magda interrupted with a wave of her paper coffee cup. "Especially if you're making an effort to do it right. Not just sweeping into town for lunch at the country club."

"True. I guess if I didn't care as much as I did, it would be easier, but I do care. So, I'm putting Hadley's needs first, and I guess there's a part of me that feels like it's not completely fair to Jason. We can only go out if I don't have to be home with Had, and sleepovers are out, unless she has one too and will be out of the house. It takes away some of the spontaneity. I'm not complaining, but I'm wondering if Jason is getting a little tired of having a girlfriend who can't run down to D.C. to see a concert or go dancing on the spur of the moment."

Magda frowned. "Maybe he's feeling that way, but I don't think he is. He seems to enjoy spending time with Hadley and you both."

"He does!" Lily agreed one hundred percent. "Jason really likes Hadley. But, I think in his previous relationships there's been more...y'know...um...sexy fun time than there has been with me." She finished in a rush, and could feel her cheeks blazing from embarrassment.

"First of all," Magda held up a finger. "Jason has never actually had a 'previous relationship,' he's had hook-ups, so they've been all about the sex. With you, there's more. It's a deeper connection, so I'm sure he's willing to sacrifice some of, what did you call it? Sexy fun time, if it means he gets to spend time with you."

"Or maybe he's decided I'm not worth all the trouble."

"How long does Gloria's husband's ambassadorship last? This isn't forever; when she comes home, you can go back to being a normal aunt, not a legal guardian. And then...let the sexy fun times commence!"

Lily bit her bottom lip. "Or not. You see, if Gloria keeps pushing this Swiss boarding school, and Hadley doesn't want to leave Rivers Bend, I'm going to fight to retain guardianship, so Hadley doesn't have to go. I've consulted with Ty about my legal options."

Magda slowly put her cup on the table. Her jaw was somewhere in the vicinity of her knees. "I had no idea things had gotten to this point. Wow. Serious stuff."

"It is, but I love Hadley, and want her wishes to be taken into account."

"So, you're talking about the possibility of a minimum of six more years of being Hadley's legal guardian."

"Which is fine. I'm happy here in the Bend, and I love being with Hadley, but it's not what Jason signed on for with me. Maybe he's had enough, and he doesn't know how to tell me."

"Aw, Lily, I'm sure that's not the case." Magda leaned forward and covered Lily's hand with her own.

"I hope so. Against all my instincts, I really let myself fall for Jason."

\*\*\*\*

Madison's eyes grew wide and her jaw dropped as if she were going to gasp, so Hadley covered her friend's mouth with her hand and dragged her down the school hallway, away from her aunt's office. Sam scurried to keep up with them.

When they opened a door and ducked into a stairwell, Hadley released Madison and said, "I'm sorry, Mad. I didn't want Aunt Lily to know we heard her."

Sam patted her back. "Do you think Uncle Jason is really trying to dump her? It seems harsh, and not at all like him."

Hadley shrugged. Her stomach was in knots, and the lump in her throat made it hard to answer. She swallowed hard and said, "I love my Aunt Lily. She dropped everything and moved here when I needed her; I don't want to be the reason she loses Jason."

Madison grew pale, and her eyes were wide and brimming with tears. "What are you saying, Had?"

It suddenly became crystal clear to Hadley. It didn't make her happy, and it wasn't what she wanted, but she knew deep down it was the right thing to do. This trying-to-be-a-good-person thing really sucked eggs. "I need to give that Swiss boarding school a chance. I'm going to fill out the application when I get home today."

## Chapter 21

Jason waved at Heather as he pulled his rig up to the barn at the Retreat. She looked up from her phone and waved back, but wasn't smiling. Uh oh. Looked like he was in trouble with his big sis about something. He looked at the clock on the dashboard. Nope. He wasn't late. He stopped the truck and hopped out to greet her.

"Hey, Heather. Where's Jeff? He usually helps me load the horses to go back to the farm."

"After he led this group on their morning trail ride, he went on a sales call with Mick and Cisco. It would be a big deal for us, it's a huge company, and they would send lots of meetings our way, but they wanted to meet Jeff and Cisco before they agree to sign."

"I guess I'm on my own."

Heather squared her shoulders and tilted her chin. "I'm perfectly capable of loading horses onto a trailer. I may not ride any more, but I grew up on the farm too."

"Settle down, Rocky. No need to fight, I know you're capable. I just didn't want to interrupt your work."

"Okay." Heather nodded once, before adding in a softer tone of voice, "Do you want a soda, or a cup of coffee or something before we start?"

"Did Mrs. Wilson bake cookies today?"

"Her specialty—chocolate chip with dried

cherries."

Jason grinned and patted his stomach. "In that case, I'd love a cup of coffee and a couple of cookies."

Heather walked to the back steps into the Retreat, and waved for him to follow. Mrs. Wilson's fresh-baked cookies...didn't have to ask him twice! Jason trotted after his sister into Jeff's kitchen.

Heather pointed to a plate of cookies in the center of the kitchen table. "Have a seat. I'll get our coffee."

He slid into the booth side of the table, grabbed a cookie, and took a huge bite. He closed his eyes in bliss and groaned as the tart cherries and delicious chocolate chunks combined with the chewy cookie in a heavenly taste. "Best. Cookies. Ever."

Heather smiled over her shoulder, as she slid the coffee pot back into place and carried their two steaming mugs over to the table. She placed one in front of him, and kept one for herself. Jason reached for the sugar and creamer and fixed his coffee up the way he liked it—hot, creamy, and sweet. Kind of like Lily, now that he thought about it.

Either his goofy smile at thinking of Lily gave him away, or Heather read his mind, because she said, "I missed Lily at brunch on Sunday."

Her voice sounded casual, but Jason knew his sister pretty darned well, and could tell it was too casual. Heather had something on her mind, and he suspected he was going to get blasted. To brace himself, he took a swig of coffee.

"I guess you lasted longer with one girlfriend than I thought you would."

He swallowed the scalding liquid, and felt it burn all the way down. "So basically, you lured me in here with cookies to attack me. Very Wicked Witch of you, Heather. I feel like I'm in Hansel and Gretel."

"Attack is a little strong," Heather said with a frown.

"Okay. How about insult?"

"I didn't mean it to be insulting. Just truthful. You have been with Lily longer than any other woman, and I shouldn't be surprised it didn't go any further than it did. I guess it's a good first step into the relationship world for you."

"Why are you acting like we broke up? I didn't invite her to brunch. It's no big thing."

Heather leaned back in her chair across from him, and pursed her lips. "You've seen her this week then? Since Sunday?"

"Well...no..."

"If you're going to dump Lily, please have the decency to talk to her before you do. Don't just ghost on her."

"I'm not dumping Lily," he ground out through clenched teeth. "Why do you keep saying it?"

"What's going on, if you're not dumping her?"

He shrugged, and stuffed a cookie in his mouth. Heather didn't speak while he chewed; she stared at him expectantly, until he was able to speak. She had learned well from their mom.

He swallowed and said, "I saw her sister Gloria on Saturday, when she was in town. I was over at their place, helping take down the Christmas tree. She said I wasn't good enough for Lily."

"Who cares what Gloria says? I learned the hard way not to listen to the poison that comes out of that woman's mouth."

"But even a blind squirrel finds a nut now and then, and this time, Gloria is right. I'm not good enough for Lily. I'm not smart enough, educated enough, successful enough—"

"Stop right there!" Coffee sloshed on the table when Heather slammed down her mug. She swiped at it with a napkin. "That's a bunch of bull. You and Lily are great together."

"Yeah, but—"

"Yeah, but nothing." Heather wadded up the paper napkin and tossed it on the table while she glared at him. "It makes me furious you feel that way. Does Lily make you feel that way?"

His eyes bugged out of his head. "What? No! Lily makes me feel ten-feet tall."

Heather's shoulders relaxed a smidge, and while she didn't smile, at least she wasn't scowling anymore. "Good. That's how it should be."

She picked a cookie off the plate, and took a bite. They sat in silence for a minute, but he could practically hear the wheels turning in Heather's head. "Mick felt the same way when we were dating. Like he wasn't good enough for me. It caused a lot of stupid problems between us, and Gloria was involved in all of that too."

They heard a car engine, and the slam of car doors before the deep rumble of male conversation could be heard from the back driveway. Heavy footsteps clumped up the stairs. The back door opened, and Jeff, Cisco, and Mick entered the kitchen. All three were dressed to impress, in really sharp-looking suits and ties. See…that's what he meant. This was the kind of guy Lily deserved. A successful businessman, in a nice suit. Not some dyslexic horse wrangler, in shit-kickers and jeans, who never even went to college.

Mick moved to Heather like he was pulled to her by an invisible force, and leaned down to kiss the top of her head. He smiled and said like he was a 1950s sitcom character, "Hi, honey. I'm home."

Jeff looked between his brother and sister. "Things seem tense in here. Is everything okay?"

"Wow, that is unusually sensitive of you, Jeff. Maggie is having a good effect on you," Heather observed with a wry grin.

Jeff pulled out the chair at the end of the table, plopped down in it, and loosened his tie. "Damn straight, she is."

"Let me ask you something," Heather said to Jeff, but stared at Jason, with a raised eyebrow. "Do you think you're good enough for Maggie?"

"Hell no! I'm nowhere near good enough for her." Jeff replied with a snort of laughter.

Heather's head swung around to pierce Cisco with an intent gaze, and asked like a prosecutor questioning a witness in the courtroom. "And you, Cisco, do you think Bethanne is out of your league?"

"*Meu Deus*, what do you think? Of course Bethanne is out of my league; I just hope she never realizes it," the handsome Brazilian said with a twinkle in his dark eyes.

"See! They all feel the same way. It doesn't mean it's true."

Jeff looked at him through squinted eyes. "Problems with Lily?"

"Courtesy of Gloria," Heather said with the scowl firmly back in place.

"Oh, man...don't listen to Gloria," Mick said in a heartfelt manner. "Like...ever. Seriously."

"She had some valid points," Jason objected, but he felt his cheeks flame up in embarrassment.

"Please. If I know Gloria, she had some points designed to hurt Lily, and come between the two of you," Heather said.

Mick sat in the chair next to Heather and reached for a cookie. "What she said."

Cisco leaned his backside against the counter next to the coffee maker, as he took a sip out of the mug he'd poured for himself. Jason didn't understand how his friend could drink the bitter brew black, but that's how Cisco liked it—and the stronger, the better. "I'm with them. She always left me alone. Well, mostly. But, I saw Gloria play her games with these two." He pointed at Jeff and Mick. "And she's trouble."

"With a capital 'T'," Mick put in his two-cents worth.

"And Lily's got enough problems right now," Jeff added.

"You mean with Gloria trying to force Hadley to go to that boarding school in Europe?" Jason asked.

"Yeah. I had lunch with Ty yesterday, and he told me Lily has a fight on her hands to get Hadley's wishes honored by the court."

"Maybe she's trying to stir the pot between Jason and Lily to distract her sister from the fight over Hadley," Mick suggested.

"That sounds like something Gloria would do." Jeff nodded in agreement.

"Okay. We've established I'm an idiot for falling for Gloria's manipulation, but what if she's right?"

"She's not!" All four of them shouted in unison.

"And now we have also established none of you think Gloria is right," Jason continued with a grin. "And I agree she was trying to hurt or distract Lily…or both…but, you can't deny Lily could do better than me."

"True. She could," Jeff said like any brother would. "But, against all logic and reason, Lily wants you."

His sister, brother-in-law, and friend all laughed. Nice. Real nice.

He took a breath to reply, and Heather interrupted him before he could speak. "Don't. Just…don't. I haven't talked to Lily this week, but I'm sure she's hurt about how you've abandoned her when she could really use some support."

"I haven't—"

Heather held up her hand like she was stopping traffic. "Stop. This stuff with Gloria and Hadley is really stressful for her, and you haven't seen her since Saturday. This is time for her boyfriend to step up and be there for her." She narrowed her eyes and studied his face. "Or are you freaked out about the responsibility of being with Lily, if she's going to have custody of Hadley until she's in college? Is that why you're bailing?"

"I am *not* bailing. Jesus, how many times do I have to say it?"

"Then after you get the horses home and settled, go over to Lily's. See her, let her talk about what's going on with Gloria. Be a boyfriend. I don't mean to freak you out, but that's what you are now. A boyfriend. Deal with it," Heather said.

Jason slid out from behind the table and stood. He

shook his jeans down over his boots. "Stop the presses. I'm gonna take Heather's advice for the first time in my life."

"About damn time." His sister snorted.

"I'm going to load the horses, and then go over to Lily's. Wish me luck."

Jeff grabbed another cookie. "More cookies for us. I thought he'd never leave."

Jason fought the urge to take his well-dressed brother in a neck-lock and give him a noogie. He was trying to be more worthy of Lily, right? Oh, hell, she would have to take him as he was. He wrapped one arm around Jeff's neck and messed up his brother's hair with the other hand.

Chapter 22

Jason pushed the button, and his truck window rolled down smoothly. He squinted at the box, and pressed in the code. The large, wrought iron gates at the end of the driveway swung open with a creak. He put the window back up against the chilly January air and followed the winding road up to the huge mansion, but drove past the circular driveway at the front door. Instead, he pulled around the house and parked in the back by the kitchen door, where he was most likely to find Lily at six on a weekday evening.

He parked the truck and trotted up the back steps. He rapped on the door, but there was no response from inside the house. Hopefully, it didn't mean Lily was well and truly pissed off at him for pulling back from her this week, and she wasn't going to let him in the house. He craned his neck to peek in the kitchen window, and noticed the only lights on in the kitchen were the dim ones, built in under the cabinets to illuminate the counters. Huh. Looked like Lily and Hadley weren't home yet.

He pulled his phone out of the back pocket of his jeans, and pressed a button to call Lily.

"Hi, stranger."

He could hear the edge in Lily's voice. Okay. So, yeah, he was in trouble. Time to get back in her good graces.

"Hi, Lily. I've missed you this week, and I stopped by to see you. I'm on your back steps right now—where are you?"

"I'm still at work."

Her response was curt, and not exactly friendly. It didn't look like it was going to be as easy to charm Lily as it had always been with other women. Made sense. She was a lot more important to him than any other woman had been. He wasn't really sure what to do.

"Long day." He hoped his brief answer would buy some time to come up with a plan. He probably shouldn't have barreled right over here without a course of action plotted out—he had thought if he came over and smiled and acted like normal Lily would do the same, and everything would be fine. Not so much.

"Yep. Hadley made the play, just a bit part, but they have a cast meeting tonight. I always have reports to do, so I'm working until she's done, and then we can come home together."

Her voice was still as chilly as the air, but at least it was a lengthier response than her previous ones, and there might've been the slightest hint of a thaw in her tone.

"Oh, okay. Yeah, Jeff told me Sam had gotten a little role in the play too. That should be fun for them."

"Yep."

A brief silence ensued, and Lily was the first to break it. "If you've missed me, where have you been? And why are you at my house now? Is there something you wanted to say?"

Jason cleared his throat. "I wanted to apologize. I let Gloria get in my head on Saturday, and I was wrong. I guess—"

"You guess?" Lily's voice didn't sound cold any more, she sounded hot under the collar as she interrupted him.

"I'm always going to think you're too good for me, Lily, but it was pointed out to me this afternoon, most of the men I know feel the same way about their women. And it doesn't stop them from being together, so if you'll forgive me for being a giant jackass, I'd love it if it didn't have to stop us either. Because I like us. Together, I mean. Jesus, Lily, I'm bad at this feeling-sharing business, help me out here!"

Her laughter sounded through his phone, and Jason's heart skipped a beat. Maybe things were going to be all right after all, in spite of himself.

"I've missed you too this week. And I like us together..."

He heard a voice in the background, and Lily trailed off before he thought she was finished with her sentence. Damn. He really wanted to know what she had been planning to say.

"Okay. I'm on the phone with Jason, hang on a second," Lily's voice was muted, like she'd pulled the phone away from her mouth.

He heard a muffled response in the background, and then Lily spoke to him again, "Hey, Jase, sorry about that. Hadley is done with her meeting, so I'm going to finish up here and then we're going to head home. Can you wait and have dinner with us tonight?"

"Sure. I'd love to. Why don't I run to Mancini's and pick up subs for us, while you're finishing up at work."

"That would be great. Would you grab a salad for us to share too? It would ease my guilt about the meatball sub I'm going to order for dinner."

He laughed, and listened while she got Hadley's order. Once their dinner orders were placed, he said, "See you back here in a little bit."

"Sounds good," Lily said, and he could hear the smile in her voice. "And, thanks, Jason. For dinner, and for calling to explain. I appreciate both."

\*\*\*\*

Lily tried to eat her meatball sub with a modicum of restraint, but she was starving! She'd been trying to eat a salad at lunchtime, instead of a hot meal in the cafeteria, as their menu was designed to keep growing kids active all afternoon, but it only served to make her sleepy and chubby. The salad at noon seemed like it was eons ago and combined with this late dinnertime; she was ravenous. Hadley was distracted enough these last few days she didn't notice Lily's complete and total absorption in her meatball sub, but she glanced at Jason and saw one corner of his oh-so-sexy mouth tilted up in a dry half-smile.

She swallowed hastily and said, "Sorry. It's been a long time since lunch."

She didn't say she'd been eating like a vegetarian bird at lunch, in the hope she might drop a few pounds. That information was on a need-to-know basis, and Jason so didn't need to know.

"I need to get to my homework. This play stuff is really going to cut into everything else I have to do," Hadley hopped off her kitchen stool and picked up her plate.

"You haven't finished your sub," Jason said.

"I can bring it for lunch tomorrow," Hadley replied.

"I'll wrap it up for you, Had. You can head upstairs and start your homework." Lily smiled at her niece.

"Thanks, Aunt Lily!" Hadley put her plate back on the marble island, and rushed to the door. She stopped, and called over her shoulder, "By the way, I did an online application to that school in Switzerland. I need you to fill out some stuff and sign it."

The sub, which had been so delectable a few seconds ago, now sat in Lily's stomach like a heavy ball of lead. Hadley seemed determined to bolt out of the room after her pronouncement, until Lily's words stopped her in her tracks.

"Hold it, Had."

Her niece didn't turn around, so Lily couldn't see her face, but her voice sounded uncertain. "What's the prob?"

Jason looked between them like he was at a tennis match, and his jaw was roughly in the vicinity of his knees.

"What do you mean you filled out an application to the boarding school? I thought you wanted to stay here in Rivers Bend. What changed?"

Hadley shrugged. "Nothing. I just thought maybe I should go."

"Because…?" Lily prompted with a wave of her hand for Hadley to continue.

"Just because."

"That's not an answer, sweetie. Is something going on at school? What made you change your mind? I won't stand in your way, if it's what you want, but I don't understand what happened to make you change your mind."

Hadley turned, and she had a bright smile on her

lips, which didn't reach her eyes. When she spoke, her words didn't ring true either. "Nothing happened. I just changed my mind. Everything is fine, Aunt Lily. Thanks for understanding!"

Lily's head spun with the rapid about-face in Hadley's attitude, but before she could formulate the words to ask another question, Hadley whirled around and ran out of the room.

She turned her head to look at Jason, whose furrowed brow and frown told her he was as confused as she was.

"What the hell was that?" he asked.

She shrugged. "I have no idea."

"Maybe boy stuff?" Jason suggested.

"Could be. But I don't know of any boy she's especially interested in right now."

"She's almost a teenager, maybe she's getting more into boys."

"Or a girl at school might be bullying her."

Jason shook his head. "I don't see it. I know she's a great kid with a big heart, but on the surface, Hadley can seem like a tough cookie, and bullies are cowards, I don't think one would want to take her on."

"I haven't heard or seen anything at school to indicate bullying either. I'm grasping at straws here. The last time we talked about the boarding school, her position on the subject was she'd prefer to walk barefoot over hot coals than to go to school there. I don't understand what changed in the last couple of days."

"Her mom's visit?"

Lily shook her head. "I don't think so, we talked after Gloria left, and Hadley was still totally anti-boarding school. Whatever changed, it happened after Gloria was here."

"I'm just happy things between us are back to where we were. I meant it before—I missed you, Moonbeam."

Jason reached and stroked her hand with his, running his thumb over the pulse point at her wrist. Over and over. So gently. It always amazed her how gentle, such a rough-and-tumble guy could be.

And it completely turned her to jelly. She bit her bottom lip, and peeked up at Jason. What she saw was capable of incinerating her.

His gaze scorched Lily, as he looked at her as if she were his world. Her heart pounded, until she was sure he'd feel it in her pulse as he continued to stroke that sensitive spot on the inside of her wrist.

"I missed you too," Lily said.

"I know it's a school night and all, so a sleepover is out of the question, but do you think we could head into the family room and mess around a little?" Jason said with a smile and a wink.

His sexy dimples and playful wink made Lily melt a little bit more. Pretty soon there was just going to be a puddle on the tall kitchen stool where she'd been sitting. She knew she needed to clean up the kitchen, but she was tired of adulting today.

"Sounds like a plan," Lily said as she turned her hand, so it clasped Jason's, slid off the stool, and pulled him toward the family room. She threw a glance over her shoulder, where Jason followed with an eager grin.

They were too wrapped up in each other as they passed through the front hall to notice Hadley crouched on the grand, curving staircase, but if they had, they would've seen a sad smile on her lips, and satisfaction in her eyes.

## Chapter 23

"Wait there," Jason said as he hopped out of his truck and skirted around the hood. He opened her door for her with a flourish.

While she knew she was perfectly capable of opening it and getting out of the monster truck on her own, no one had ever done it for her before and his chivalrous gesture made her heart go pitter-pat. He reached up to lend her a hand as she climbed down.

"Thank you, Jason. That was a first for me."

"Me too." His grin was crooked, and damned if that didn't get her heart racing again.

"Really? I thought helping a woman out of a car was taught in Southern Gentleman 101."

He placed his hand low on her back as they walked across the parking lot to the restaurant he had chosen for their dinner date. It looked very elegant, and based on the high-end models of the cars in the parking lot, Lily really hoped this dinner wasn't going to deplete Jason's finances. She wasn't her sister, and didn't need a man to spend a fortune to impress her.

"I've helped my mom and my sisters, but that doesn't count."

She flashed a smile over her shoulder at him. "They'd be thrilled to hear they don't count."

"You know what I mean." He grinned at her as he opened the door into the restaurant and gestured for her to precede him. The hostess looked him up and down with such intensity; it was like she was starving and he was the last roll in the breadbasket. Lily slipped her hand into Jason's as he said, "Reservation for two. The name's Braden."

The pretty young woman tore her gaze from Jason's body with obvious reluctance and looked at her book on the podium. "Here it is," she picked up two menus and beamed at Jason. "Follow me."

As they followed the hostess in her white blouse and snug, black slacks, the woman definitely put a little extra sway in her hips. For Jason's benefit, no doubt. Lily had never gone out with someone as drop-dead gorgeous as Jason before, and other women's reactions to him always amazed her. They were obviously on a date here, what was up with the blatant flirting?

Jason pulled out her seat, and as she sat down, the hostess lingered next to Jason, but as his attention was focused strictly on Lily, the woman finally heaved a sigh and returned to her hostess stand.

They sat down, and ordered drinks from the waiter who appeared as soon as they did so.

Jason picked up his menu and studied it as Lily spread her white, linen napkin on her lap. She hadn't wanted to pry into his sessions with Roni, and hoped the menu wouldn't be too difficult for him to interpret. She looked at her own, and realized a lot of the words could present a challenge to his dyslexia.

While she pondered a way she might actually help him, without seeming like she was and embarrassing him, Jason continued to study the menu and read out loud in a casual voice without looking up at her, "The twin lobster tails or the chicken piccata both sound good. I can't decide which one I want."

There was a slight hesitation before a couple of the trickier words, but he read it perfectly. He peeked up at her from the menu and winked. "Based on the way your jaw is hanging on the table, I would say you're surprised at my progress?"

Lily realized he had set up this situation to show her how well his lessons had been going, and her heart felt so full of pride it felt as though it might burst. She held up her water glass in a toast, since their cocktails hadn't arrived yet. "Jason, that was wonderful! I'm so proud of you."

His cheeks grew ruddy, and he lowered his gaze. "Thanks, Lily."

"I didn't want to pry, so I didn't ask either Roni or you how your lessons were going, but it seems like everything is going great!"

He looked across the table at her and nodded eagerly. "It really is. At first, it was a little rough, but I kept working away at the methods Roni was teaching me, and one day—*BOOM!*—it was like the pieces of a puzzle fit together and I broke the secret code."

"A lot of students have told me that's how it feels for them too. I'm so thrilled for you, Jason."

The waiter approached with a tray and interrupted to place their cocktails on the table as he asked, "Are you ready to order?"

"Not quite yet," Jason said.

"I'll let y'all enjoy your drinks, and be back in a little while to tell you the chef's specials."

"Thank you," Jason said with a smile, and the waiter nodded and walked away.

Lily lifted her Manhattan and said, "To you and

Roni!"

He blushed again, but poured a little beer in the glass and lifted it in response. "To you for being so supportive and connecting me with a great teacher like Roni."

She felt her cheeks heat in response, and they both sipped and went back to reading the menus.

Jason closed his and put it down on the table. He leaned back in his chair, took another sip of beer, and asked, "How are things going with Hadley? Is she still hell-bent on going to that boarding school?"

Lily nodded. "Yep. I don't understand it."

"She is a tween girl. Maybe she'll change her mind back again."

"She doesn't have to change her mind for me. I mean if it's what Hadley really wants, I'll support her in it, but it seems kind of sudden to me," Lily said with a frown and a shrug.

"I wasn't around much this week, so I didn't spend much time with you two. Are you sure nothing happened? Did y'all argue about anything?"

Lily shook her head. "Nope. Everything was fine. Maybe it has something to do with the school play." She wrinkled her nose and thought as she carefully took a sip of her cocktail, which was full to the brim of the martini glass in which it was served. "Now that I think about it, the day of her audition was the when I noticed a change in her attitude. When we got home that night she was different."

"Different, how?" Jason asked with a frown.

"Distracted. Quiet. Not like herself."

"Did the audition scare her? It can be intimidating to be on stage in front of a crowd, especially at that self-conscious age."

"Not Hadley. She loves being the center of attention." Lily shook her head.

"So what happened between her audition, and her distracted behavior? Did anything out of the ordinary happen?"

Lily bit her lower lip as she put down her glass with a thunk. Some amber liquid sloshed over the rim, and onto her hand. She wiped it on her napkin. "Magda had stopped by my office with coffee for us. She was picking up Sam from her audition, and we visited for a while."

"Doesn't sound like anything that would upset Hadley," Jason said.

"Nooo..." Lily said and felt her cheeks flame as she remembered what Maggie and she had been discussing. "But if she overheard us, we were talking about..." Her voice trailed off, and she picked up her menu and became absorbed in putting in a show of studying it.

"What were you talking about with Maggie?" Jason asked.

"Well, um, you."

"Me?" Jason's eyebrows raised.

"Technically, about you and me, and how there was a little distance between us after Gloria's visit."

"Could Hadley have overheard you and Maggie?"

Lily shrugged. "I guess. My office door was open, and the girls did come there when they were done with their auditions."

"Did y'all discuss anything else that could've affected Hadley's decision about boarding school?"

"Maybe," Lily glanced at Jason. "I told Maggie

about my plans to fight Gloria if she insisted on sending Hadley away against her wishes, and how it would be a big responsibility for the next several years."

"True, but Hadley's a smart kid, she must've figured that one out on her own already," Jason said.

"I also might've mentioned...well...um...I was afraid that responsibility was what had scared you off after Gloria's visit."

"What? Why would it scare me?"

"I'm not exactly footloose and fancy-free right now. And if I get full custody of Hadley until she's done with high school, I won't be for a long time. I thought maybe it was all too much for you."

Jason stared at her, and he didn't look pleased. He actually looked hurt, and Lily felt like a terrible person.

"Do you really think I'm that shallow?"

"No. No! It's just..."

"Are you ready to hear the chef's specials?" the waiter interrupted before Lily could finish her sentence.

"Sure," Jason said to the waiter before he swung his head to stare pointedly at Lily and said directly to her, "We're going to enjoy our dinner now, but you and me, Moonbeam...we'll finish this discussion later."

\*\*\*\*

The rest of dinner had passed pleasantly enough, but Jason's mind kept going back over Lily's words. He wasn't angry, but he was curious...and maybe a little hurt. He glanced over to the passenger seat as he drove Lily home. She was silhouetted in the semi-darkness as she stared out the window, a tiny frown on her lips. The glow of the dashboard lights reflected off her glasses, and he thought he saw moisture in her eyes, as she blinked. Oh crap on a cracker. Was she crying? They spoke at the same time.

"Don't be sad, Moonbeam."

"I'm so sorry, Jason."

"There's nothing to be sorry about—you feel the way you feel. Although, I have to confess it does bother me a little you don't trust us. Trust me."

Her skirt rustled as she turned in her seat to face him. "But I do trust us. And you."

He looked forward to the road unwinding before him, in the orange glow of the streetlights, and tilted his head. "Not if you think I'm going to bail on account of you caring for your niece. I thought you knew I'm all in on this relationship."

"I guess I do." She shrugged.

He pulled up to a stop sign and looked both ways before proceeding. "There's a ringing endorsement."

"It's a lot of responsibility. My time isn't my own right now, and to be honest with you it's even a little bit of a bummer to me, so I imagine it's a huge bummer to you. I'm used to doing what I want, when I want to, and with Hadley I can't. And you were even more carefree than me before we started dating. Now it's all carpools, and very little...y'know...alone time together."

He felt his lips curl up in a smile, in spite of the seriousness of their conversation. "I've been trying to make our alone time extra exciting when we get it, to make up for the limited opportunities."

She swatted at his arm and laughed. "Mission accomplished. Trust me, I have zero complaints about our alone time. Best alone time I've ever had, as a matter of fact."

"Okay then."

"But I worry you're going to want more alone

time—"

"Moonbeam, I'm a guy…I think about alone time with you every minute of every day, but I understand you have other things going on in your life. Important things."

"And what if those things become too much for you to want to deal with?"

He hung a right turn onto River Road and drove toward her house. "Don't you think I worry my lifestyle won't be what you want in the long term either?"

She wrinkled her cute little nose, and pushed her glasses up on it. "What do you mean?"

"I work on a farm. The animals don't wait for anyone else's schedule, and let me tell you, sometimes their schedule sucks. They get up early. Like zero dark thirty early. And expect me to feed them right off. They get sick or have babies in the middle of the night, and need me to help them. And my job doesn't transport very easily. It's here. In Rivers Bend. Or another small town like it, and you're a city girl."

He glanced over and saw her roll her eyes. "I know you haven't been to Westport yet, but technically, I'm a suburban girl."

"I looked it up on my map app. You grew up less than an hour from New York City. At the risk of sounding like a rube, you come from a pretty sophisticated place, and I'm from the sticks. Hell, I sound like a rube, because I am a rube. So, trust me, I wonder what you see in me. And I worry about when the novelty of dating someone so different from you is going to wear off, and when it does that you'll be gone."

She shifted in her seat to face forward and the car

was silent except for the click of the turn signal he'd flicked on before turning into her driveway. He stopped and entered the gate code.

As it creaked open, Lily said, "Okay…so neither of us have plans right now to go anywhere in the near future, but I guess there are no guarantees as we go forward."

"I may be a rube, but you see a lot of life in a small town, and I can tell you—there are no guarantees about anything in this world, Moonbeam."

She sighed. "That's true."

He pulled around to the back of the house, and stopped the truck. He turned to face her, and took her little, elfin face in his big hands. "Whaddya say, are you willing to take a chance on us, and let whatever happens in the future happen?"

She leaned her cheek into his hand and rubbed against it, her eyes closed behind her funky eyeglasses. "Mm hm. Sounds like a plan."

"I happen to know your niece is sleeping over at my niece's house tonight. What do you say to a little of that alone time we both enjoy so much?"

"Race you upstairs!" she said with a cheeky grin, as she opened the door of the truck and bolted for the back door.

## Chapter 24

The rest of the weekend with Jason had been carefree and fun, but Lily was paying the price for it on Sunday night. Surrounded by dirty clothes, in the laundry room.

Hadley entered and said, "I finished the dishes."

"Great. Thanks, Had, I really appreciate the help."

Her niece frowned and put her hands on her hips as she looked around the room. "That's a lot of laundry!"

Lily blew her bangs off her forehead, as she sorted white clothes out of the mountain of laundry on the sorting table in front of her. There were some advantages to living in her sister's mansion, and this palatial laundry room was one of them, but it was still a lot of work. "I think people sneak in here while we're sleeping and leave their dirty clothes for me to wash. It's the only reasonable explanation."

Hadley laughed, and Lily felt her heart warm. Her niece hadn't laughed much in the past week. She poured the bleach into the dispenser in the washer, and glanced over her shoulder at Hadley. "Do you have a couple of minutes?"

"Sure." Hadley shrugged. "I have a little homework, but not too much tonight."

"That's good. I wanted to talk to you a little bit about this boarding school application."

She banged the lid of the washer shut, pressed

some beeping buttons and the washer started with a hum. She turned and leaned her backside against the washing machine. Hadley's eyes were wide, and she looked like she was poised for flight at the mention of the topic under consideration.

"Um…actually, I just remembered a math quiz I need to study for, so…"

"It can wait for a little while. You're great at math. I'm sure you'll ace the quiz."

Hadley's shoulders slumped and she leaned against the counter behind her. "What do you want to know?"

"I guess I need to know what I have to do for your application."

A bright smile spread across Hadley's face. "Really? Great! I thought you were going to try to talk me out of going there."

"No pressure from me, Had. If you want to go to boarding school in Switzerland, I'll support you. I'll always support you, sweetie. If anything in your life is certain it is my love and support for you."

"I know, Aunt Lily. I can always count on you."

The heartfelt words, and the slight quaver in Hadley's voice made Lily frown a little. What the hell was going on with her niece?

"I want to be sure you're doing what you want to do. It's a big change from how you felt a week ago, so I don't understand."

Hadley shrugged, screwed up her mouth, and turned her head to break eye contact with Lily. "I changed my mind. What does it matter why?"

Lily crossed her arms across her chest and sighed at the snippy tween tone of voice, and then realized it might be considered a negative, aggressive posture. She went back to sorting laundry to get the next load ready, and to keep her hands occupied. "It matters to me, because I want you to be happy. If you're happy here in Rivers Bend, that's fine. If you're happy at boarding school in Switzerland, that's fine. Heck, if you're happy living with crocodiles in Australia...well, until you're done with school, I might have a problem with that one, but you get the idea. I want you to be where you want to be. And, I guess I'm afraid you might be making this choice for reasons that aren't going to make you happy in the long run, so I want to understand why you changed your mind. When your mom left, you still were really opposed to the idea, and then all of a sudden, you're filling out an application. I don't get it."

Now Hadley crossed her arms and stared at a point on the wall to her side. She looked small, and young, and scared, and Lily hated it. Clearly, a direct line of questioning was not working here.

"I'm seriously not pressuring you, Had. Don't look so sad, I love you and I want to understand. Look—let's talk about something else. How was your weekend? Did you and Madison have fun at Sam's house?"

Hadley blinked a couple of times and then nodded. "We did, and we got to ride horses at Sam's grandmother's farm on Sunday. Which you would've known if you and Jason had been there. Where were you?"

"We went out for brunch, and for a drive. It was such a pretty day today. That's one advantage to living in Virginia, as opposed to New England. Sometimes, in the middle of winter, you get these warm, sunny, glorious days."

"So, you guys got along this weekend? Everything

is good with you two?"

"We did, and it is."

Hadley nodded once, and squared her shoulders. "Good. That's good. Look, Aunt Lily, I appreciate you looking out for me, but I know what I'm doing, and I want to go to that boarding school in Switzerland. It's all good."

"Yeah, but—"

Her niece continued as if Lily hadn't spoken, "I'm going to go up to my room and study for that quiz now, okay?"

She turned on her heels and ran—literally ran out of the room—before Lily could answer.

Lily rubbed her breastbone, where her chest had tightened, closed her eyes, and did deep breathing exercises to relax, the way her mom had taught her to do. Next time she talked to her mother she really needed to ask if she was ever this much of a pain in the ass to her parents, and if so, apologize to her. Because, man, this being the guardian of a tween girl was not for the faint of heart.

\*\*\*\*

"It is so good having you here for the weekend, Roni!"

Her friend's suitcase bumped against her side as she pulled her old roommate in for a second, tight hug.

"It's good to be here, but I can put my suitcase down now?" Roni laughed, and returned Lily's embrace with one arm, while awkwardly holding her overnight bag with the other.

"Fine," Lily laughed too as she released Roni, and called up the stairs, "Hadley, Roni's here!" She reached for Roni's bag, "I can carry that for you. C'mon, I'll show you to your room."

"Room? You mean there isn't a guesthouse, bigger than the house I grew up in for me? I'm disappointed."

Lily gestured with her free hand for Roni to follow her up the curved staircase. "There actually is a guest house, but I thought you'd rather stay in the main house."

"Get outta town! I was joking about the guest house."

"Never joke about my half-sister's love of excess."

Hadley stuck her head out of the doorway to her room. "Hi, Ms. Roni."

"Hiya, Had. Good to see you,"

Hadley stepped into the hall and Roni pulled her in for a hug, which the tween returned with fervor, before drawing away and hanging her head. "I'm in the middle of something. I'll talk to you later." She turned on her heel and rushed back into her room, shutting the door firmly behind her.

Roni swung her head to look at Lily and raised one eyebrow.

Lily mouthed her response, so Hadley wouldn't hear, "Later." Aloud, she said, "This way to your room."

She opened the door to the room next to hers, and led the way into the luxurious guest room. She dropped the bag on a fancy bench at the end of the bed. The tufted golden upholstery matched the bedding and draperies.

Roni's eyes were wide as she pivoted around to survey the room. "Wow. This is really something else. Very grand. Way grander than I'm used to."

"You and me both, sistah." Lily snorted.

Roni flopped on the bed, and patted the coverlet next to her. "Sit. Tell me what's happening here. The kiddo seems sad for someone who insists she's doing what she wants about this boarding school business."

Lily sat next to her and sighed. "I wish I knew what was going on, but I don't. I think maybe she overheard me talking to a friend about Jason, and our problems, but things between us are okay now, so if she was worried me being her guardian was the issue between Jason and me—"

"And it didn't occur to you Hadley might think things are okay now, because she's going away?" Roni interrupted her, with words that might have seemed harsh, if not for the gentle smile on her face.

Lily smacked her forehead with the heel of her hand. "Duh! No. I did not. Why didn't I realize she might think her leaving is what triggered Jason and I to make up?"

"I don't know...I mean, it's not like you're a professional educator, who works with kids all the time or anything."

Roni winked at her, and Lily swatted at her friend's arm.

"Okay, oh-wise-one, since you're so smart, tell me what I do to fix things?"

"I'm not really sure. You could talk it over with Hadley."

"She might not believe me."

"I guess you've got to try though, because, let me tell you—for two people who claim to be so happy with their choices, you both seem pretty darned miserable to me."

\*\*\*\*

"Did you and Roni have a nice visit this weekend?" Jason spoke to Lily, but watched Hadley as she took another pass around the indoor ring to practice her horse jumping.

"We did. How was your weekend?"

"Lonely without you, but I'll survive." He glanced away from Hadley to wink at Lily, and then turned his attention back to the ring. "She really is getting better all the time. She said that school in Switzerland has a good equestrian program; do you think it's why she wants to go there?"

"I don't think she does want to go there." Lily jutted out her chin.

"She seems pretty hell-bent on going. Not happy, mind you, but determined. Maybe we're wrong— maybe she really does want to move."

"Roni had a good thought, which I need to talk over with Hadley, but I haven't had a chance to yet."

"Oh, yeah? What does Roni think?"

"That Hadley knew you and I were having problems, and thinks me being her guardian was the cause. She decided to make the sacrifice to go to the school—which she doesn't want to do—to free me up, and solve our problems." She gestured between Jason and herself to indicate they were the 'our' in question. "And when you and I did make up, Hadley thinks it's because she's going to Switzerland, and I won't have to be her guardian anymore."

"Kind of convoluted, but I guess it makes sense."

Hadley took the last jump flawlessly, and trotted her horse over to Jason and Lily.

"Good job, Hadley. You get better every day."

"Thanks, Jason." Hadley smiled, but Jason could

tell it didn't reach her eyes.

"I think that's enough for today. Why don't you take Flash back to the barn. I'll be over in a couple of minutes."

"Okay."

The clump of hooves was the only sound as Jason and Lily watched her go.

"That is one sad kid," Jason said with a shake of his head.

"I'm going to talk to her tonight. Try to clear the air, but I'm afraid she won't believe me."

Jason thought Lily could be right. She would do anything for her niece, and Hadley knew it, so she might think Lily was sacrificing her happiness for Hadley's. "Why don't you let me take a whack at it? I can talk to her while we're grooming the horses. She might listen to someone who isn't a family member more than she would to you."

He hated the hopelessness he saw in Lily's eyes and the dejection in her slumped shoulders. "All right. Give it your best shot. I'll go up to the house and visit with your mom."

His two favorite ladies. Jason smiled at the thought. "She'd like that."

They exchanged a quick kiss, and even that brief contact stirred Jason's blood, and threatened to derail his mission. There was something about Lily that caused him to feel things he'd never felt before, and it scared the crap out of him.

Lily sighed and blinked owlishly up at him. Looked like their kiss had affected her too. Good. "See you at the house when you're done. Good luck."

\*\*\*\*

Jason didn't know what he'd been thinking...offering to talk to Hadley. What he didn't know about talking to kids on serious matters could fill a book. Hell, it could fill an entire encyclopedia set. But he knew his mother and he had shared some good talks in this barn. Both of them being occupied with caring for the horses, freed him up to talk openly to his mom about difficult subjects. And, since his dad had died when he was a little kid, his poor mom was forced to discuss topics with him normally reserved for a father and son.

Now, if only he could figure out how to start. Hadley took care of it for him, when she said with a deep sigh. "I sure am going to miss Flash, when I'm in Switzerland."

"I promise to take good care of him for you, until you get home." Jason continued to muck out a stall as he spoke. "They have horses there, right? You said there's a good equestrian program. Is that what changed your mind, or was it something else?"

She shrugged, and continued to brush down her beloved horse. "It wasn't just one thing, I guess."

"No? Because I think maybe it was one thing. Your love for your Aunt Lily," Jason kept his voice quiet and gentle, like he would with a skittish colt.

He risked a glance in Hadley's direction, and saw her hand freeze mid-brush for a few seconds, before she started up again. "I don't know what you mean."

"I think you do. Y'know, one of the things I like best about you, Hadley?"

"No."

"You're a straight-shooter. You always tell it like it is; even if something is uncomfortable, you don't let it stop you. So many people aren't that honest and straightforward. It's refreshing."

"Thank you. I think."

He chuckled. "You're welcome; I meant it as a compliment. But, right now, I don't believe you're being one hundred percent honest with me. I think you know what I mean. You think your Aunt Lily would be happier if she wasn't your guardian. Maybe you think she and I would be happier, am I right? And don't hold back—tell me the truth; I can handle it."

"Maybe that's part of it. You can't pretend things wouldn't be easier with me out of the picture." Hadley's voice sounded small and scared, but a little defiant at the same time.

"It might be a little easier, but it sure wouldn't be happier."

She peeked at him over her shoulder, and patted Flash on the neck. "What do you mean?"

"I appreciate your honesty, so I'm going to be just as honest back, okay?"

After a moment's hesitation, Hadley responded with the barest of nods.

"When you're not responsible for anyone besides yourself, life is easier. You do what you want, when you want to do it. Easy-peasey."

He heard Hadley snuffle at his words, and continued, "But...what kind of life is that? A darned lonely one. I know for a fact, your Aunt Lily is happy here, and being with you is a huge part of her happiness."

"Being with you is a huge part of it," Hadley corrected him.

"We both are a part of her happiness, how's that?"

he asked with a smile.

"Fair enough. But you can't deny, you and Aunt Lily were having problems, drifting apart, and when I said I wanted to go to that school in Switzerland, things between you got better."

"I know you probably won't believe me, but you leaving is not what made things better between us. It was a sort of trigger, because it got us talking—"

"See? I'm right," Hadley interrupted.

Jason shook his head once. "No. You're not. We talked about how we didn't want you to go, if it wasn't what you really wanted to do. And it forced us to discuss some stuff that was bothering both of us, some of it about you, some of it not. But, at no point did either of us think 'Hadley is going away—yay! Now we can be happy together'. We're both happy now. With each other, and with you."

"Really?" Hadley whispered, with a quaver in her voice.

"Really. If you want to go, kiddo, then fine. But, I don't think you really want to leave Rivers Bend, do you?"

Hadley stopped brushing Flash, and turned to Jason. Tears glistened in her eyes, and she shook her head. "No. I so don't want to go. But I thought it was the best thing for Aunt Lily, and she's given up so much for me, I wanted to do something for her."

"If you really want to do something for her, tell her what you just told me."

"You think?"

"I think it will make her happier than anything on earth, kiddo. C'mon, let's finish up in here, so you can go talk to her."

## Chapter 25

"That's the whole truth, Aunt Lily. You gave up so much for me; I wanted to be a good person like you. I thought if I went away, things between Jason and you could get back to the way they had been."

Hadley concluded her explanation with a pathetic snuffle, and Lily reached across the Braden's rustic kitchen table to squeeze her niece's hand. Jason stood next to the stove, a mug of hot coffee cupped in his hands. His expression was solemn, but when he caught Lily's eye, one corner of his lips tipped up and he gave her a slow wink of encouragement.

"Oh, Hadley, I'm so sorry you thought our problems were your fault. They weren't. You get that, right?" She tilted Hadley's chin up, to look her niece straight in the eyes, and gently wiped a tear off the child's cheek.

"I do now, but I really thought I was doing the right thing." Hadley sighed, and swiped the tears off her face. "I hate crying."

"Me too," Lily said.

"Me three," Jason added.

Lily and Hadley's heads swiveled on their necks to look at Jason, who shrugged and took a sip of coffee. "What? You think I don't cry? Everyone does."

Lily's heart expanded in her chest, until she was afraid it was going to burst out and float over her in a pink glow, like in a cartoon. She was dangerously crazy about this man, and the more she got to know him, the harder she was falling for him.

"You seem so…I don't know how to say it," Hadley fluttered her hands as she struggled for the right words. "I guess—macho. I never imagined you cried."

"I do. When we lose an animal. When I lost my dad. Sometimes, when I think about my dad. I mean, I'm not sobbing all the time, but…sure, I cry. I remember when Deidre was surprised to see my dad crying once, he told her to never trust a man who told her he never cried, because he was a liar. It always stuck with me."

"Good advice," Lily nodded in approval.

As Hadley took a sip of hot cocoa, and leaned back in her chair, her furrowed brow told Lily her niece was absorbing Jason's words, and Lily was happy to see it. No matter what Gloria thought of him, Jason was a good influence on Hadley.

The wooden chair next to her scraped against the floor as Jason pulled it out with one booted foot and sat down next to her. "Where's my mom?"

"When I got here, she was on her way out. She let me in, and told me to make myself at home. She asked if I could put on a pot of coffee for you, and showed me where the cocoa was, so I could make a cup for Hadley. She said this was the kind of raw, damp cold that would chill you to the bone."

"She's right; I do feel chilled to the bone," Jason lifted his stoneware mug to her in a toast. "Thanks for making the coffee for me."

"Thanks for the cocoa too," Hadley added. "Lots of marshmallows, just how I like it. Mom doesn't approve of cocoa, so we never had it at home."

Lily wrinkled her nose. "Doesn't approve of cocoa? How is that even a thing?"

Hadley shrugged. "She didn't want me to gain weight."

Never wanting to come between Gloria and her daughter, Lily bit her tongue to keep from saying what she wanted to about her half-sister, and instead said, "You don't have to worry. You're so active—you burn a lot of calories with your sports, and horseback riding, and everything else you do; you need to eat well to fuel your body for all of your activities."

"Your aunt's right. If you're tank's empty, the truck's not going to run."

"Are you comparing me to a truck?" Hadley lifted her chin and regarded Jason down her pert nose.

"Don't get yourself twisted up, kiddo. I don't think you're built like a truck; it was a metaphor, not an observation."

Lily stood up, carried her cup of coffee to the sink, and turned on the tap to wash it. "Speaking of food...we better get a move on, Had. We need to get home and get dinner started. Do you want to join us, Jase?"

He stood and walked next to her, where he bumped her away from the sink, and took the soapy mug from her hand and started washing. "I can take care of these dishes. And, sure, dinner sounds good. I want to go back to my place, take a quick shower, and change my clothes. Then I'll head over to your house if that's okay."

Lily wrinkled her nose, pretended to take a big sniff in his direction, and tried to keep a straight face as she teased, "Please, do take a shower."

Hadley laughed and drained the last of her cocoa as she carried her mug to the sink too. "You're funny, Aunt Lily."

Lily enveloped her niece in a warm embrace. "I love you, Hadley. Never forget that—I'm here with you because I want to be. It's not an obligation, and it's not a duty. I'm here out of love. And I'm happy here with you."

Hadley hugged her back tightly, and her voice was muffled, "I love you too, and I'm glad you're here. I'm going to delete that boarding school application as soon as we get home!"

\*\*\*\*

Jason wrapped Lily in his arms and rested his chin on top of her head, as he leaned against the kitchen door, lingering over their good-nights.

"I wish I could stay like this all night," her voice was a little muffled, where her face was cuddled against his chest.

"The call to your sister is going to suck, huh?"

"Yep." Lily pulled back and squinted at him, before freeing one arm and reaching for her eyeglasses on the table next to the door, where she had placed them before their farewell hug and kiss. "I am not looking forward to telling her Hadley has changed her mind and wants to stay here. Gloria isn't going to be happy, but it has to be done."

"Are you sure you don't want me to stay here for moral support when you call her?"

"No," Lily shook her head and stood on tiptoes to press a kiss to his cheek. "You have an early morning tomorrow. You should get home, so you can get a good night's sleep."

He leaned down and pulled her in for one last kiss. He wasn't good with words, but he put all his emotions and feelings for her into the kiss. It was slow, lingering, with a building heat that made his pulse pound and left Lily a little breathless when they pulled apart. "Call me after you talk to Gloria."

"'Kay," Lily's eyes were unfocused and her breath came in pants, before she inhaled deeply and ran her hands through her short hair. "I don't want to wake you though. I should be fine; we can talk tomorrow."

"Text me, at least, so I know everything went all right."

She smiled at him. "You're a good guy, Jason Braden."

He grinned and winked at her, as he reached behind him to open the door. "Don't let it get out around town. It'll ruin my hard-earned reputation."

\*\*\*\*

Lily shut the door to her bedroom firmly behind her, and pulled her phone out of the back pocket of her jeans. She took a deep breath, several as a matter of fact, in an effort to relax her nerves about the call she needed to make. She sat on the chaise-longue, which was surprisingly comfy, even if it always made her feel a little like she was a working girl in an old-time bordello. At least she would have been a high-class working girl, given what it must've cost her sister. The silk fabric, which matched the bedding, screamed expensive, and probably cost more than she made in a semester at school.

She smiled at the thought, rubbed her damp palms on her jeans, so they wouldn't spoil the expensive upholstery, and pressed the call button on her phone.

"Hello, Lily," her sister's voice came out of the phone.

Show time.

"Hi, Gloria. Is this a good time to talk?"

"As good as any, I suppose." Gloria sounded bored. Lily could practically see her suppressing a yawn, and examining her manicure.

The half-sisters had never been close, and were different enough they rarely called just to chat, the way she did with Roni.

"Is everything all right?" Gloria asked after a brief pause.

"Yes. I'm sorry, I should've said so right off—everything is fine here."

"Good," Gloria's voice was languid. "So what has you calling me so late at night, in your time zone?"

"I wanted to update you on Hadley's thoughts on boarding school."

"Yes, I know she finally saw the wisdom in my idea, and is filling out an application. I'm sure it's a disappointment to you, because you'll have to move out of my lovely home and move back to your dumpy apartment in Baltimore, but you need to—"

"What? Is that really what you think? That my only reason for not wanting Hadley to move to Switzerland was because I wanted to stay in your house?" Lily interrupted. She sat up straight on the chaise, and raked the hand not holding her phone through hair, until it was surely standing up on end. Just in case Gloria's words hadn't been shocking enough to do it for her.

"Of course, darling. You have a pretty cushy deal there."

"I loved my life in Baltimore. I'm happy here in Rivers Bend too, but I'm here for Hadley. Not myself. Hell, I didn't even want to live in this mausoleum! You insisted."

"Whatever. You said you wanted to update me on Hadley, not argue with me."

There was no talking to her sister. Her worldview was so distorted; it was impossible to make her see reason. Lily took a deep breath through her nose and shut her eyes, thinking calming thoughts. Sunsets. Flowers. Puppies. Okay, she was ready to speak without screaming.

"Right. Hadley decided she wants to stay in Rivers Bend after all. She is not going to submit the boarding school application."

"What?" Gloria's voice was shrill and harsh through the phone, and Lily knew her sister had to be alone, because she didn't let people other than Lily or the servants see this side to her. "What did you do to convince her? Lay on the guilt about you having to leave my home? Which is not a mausoleum, by the way, it's the envy of the county."

"That argument only works if I actually want to live in your house, which I don't. You're right about one thing. I want to stay in Rivers Bend, but not in your house. I would move somewhere else if Hadley left. I have a contract at the school through June, and I like it here. I would support Hadley in whichever decision she made, as long as it was what she really wanted to do. She decided boarding school wasn't the right choice for her currently—there was no coercion, one way or the other. I just want what's best for Hadley."

"And I don't? I'm the child's mother, for heaven's

sake, a fact you seem to want to erase. You're trying to take my place in her life, and I want you to know I will not stand for it, Lily." Gloria's voice was so resolute and cold, Lily was amazed icicles weren't forming on the phone.

"You have a lot of misconceptions about me, Gloria. You always have. I am not trying to come between you and your daughter. Not at all. But, I do want what's best for Hadley, and right now it does not coincide with what you want her to do. I love my niece, and I take my guardianship of her very seriously. She wants to stay in Rivers Bend right now. She might not always feel that way, and if she were to decide to move to Switzerland, I will support her as vehemently in that choice. My actions are all about Hadley, and not about you, Gloria. I don't know how to convince you, and I guess it doesn't matter what you think of me—"

"Right now, it's not much." Gloria snorted in an uncharacteristically rude manner.

Lily rolled her eyes. "Right back at ya, sis. But how we feel about each other is beside the point. One thing we both agree on is we love Hadley, right?"

Gloria waited several beats before replying with a curt, "Right."

"Hadley would be unhappy at boarding school in Switzerland right now. She was miserable when it started to become more of a reality. Seriously miserable, and not at all like herself. I think we can also both agree that a heartbroken Hadley is not something either of us want."

"Also true," Gloria still sounded terse, but at least she wasn't angry and insulting anymore.

"Hadley is much happier now that she made her

decision to stay in Rivers Bend, so I would like to suggest, you let her stay here for the rest of this school year. You can revisit the idea with her for another school year at some other time. Maybe over the summer, when you see her. Does that sound like a solution you can live with?"

She heard Gloria exhale in a huff, and there was a long pause. So long, in fact, Lily actually checked the phone to be sure the connection hadn't been lost.

Finally, her sister spoke, "In spite of what you seem to think of me, I want Hadley to be happy, so…fine. I agree to let her remain in Rivers Bend with you through this school year. The doctors want Walter to have some more tests run, and the medical care here is sub-par, so we're coming back to the States in a few weeks. I can speak to my daughter then."

Lily heaved a sigh of mixed relief and trepidation. She was grateful Gloria was backing off for the time being, but it didn't sound like the reprieve would last for long. Maybe Hadley would change her mind, and want to go to boarding school in a year or two. But if she didn't, it seemed as though Lily was in for a prolonged battle with her half-sister, a prospect that did not exactly fill her with glee.

"Fine. Thank you, Gloria. Hadley will be thrilled, and I appreciate it."

"You're welcome. I suppose I should thank you for taking care of my daughter."

Lily smothered a laugh; it was as close to an apology as Gloria would ever get, so she decided to accept the olive branch, such as it was. "I'm happy to do it. I'm enjoying my time with Hadley."

"Really? It's not living in the gorgeous home rent-free?" Gloria sounded honestly shocked.

Lily transferred the phone to her left hand and raised her right one as if taking an oath, even though Gloria couldn't see her. "Swear to God, it is not the reason I'm here, Gloria. I think we just have to come around to the idea you and I will never understand each other."

Chapter 26

"I feel like I'm running my own little bridal sweatshop," Magda shoved her curly blonde hair off her forehead, as she leaned over the kitchen table at the Retreat at Rivers Bend, where she now lived with her fiancé, Jason's brother Jeff.

Tucked into a corner of the Retreat's kitchen, the table had booth seating in an "L" shape on two sides, and ladder-back chairs on the other two sides. Usually, when Lily was here, the housekeeper's mouthwateringly good homemade cookies sat on a plate in the center of the table. Today, a collection of miscellaneous items covered the surface in front of them, where Magda and she sat side-by-side in chairs at the table.

"Thank you so much for helping me assemble these gift bags for the out-of-town wedding guests. I'm going to put them in everyone's room here at the Retreat. I know it looks like chaos, but I have everything organized into piles. Each bag gets one item from each pile. We have a map of the area, a list of things to do around here, restaurants, etc. And some little gifts, snacks, toiletries…that sort of thing. All of a sudden, I feel like the wedding is right around the corner, and I'm terrifyingly behind on everything I need to do, so I really appreciate the help."

Lily bumped Magda's shoulder with her own in a

companionable manner, and reached for the pretty gift bag the bride had selected to hold all the goodies. "No problem. The girls are both at their play rehearsal tonight, so I'm free as a bird. I'm happy to help; I can't believe it's almost your wedding. Time is flying by so fast."

"Tell me about it; Valentine's Day is less than a month away now, and that's the big day! I know it's a little cliché to get married on V-Day, but what the heck, you only get married once, right?"

Her friend blushed, and managed to look pink and pretty when she did so. Lily always felt like a ripe tomato when she blushed.

"Unless you're my half-sister, and then it becomes an annual event."

Magda laughed. "You're sounding extra-special fed up with Glo today, is everything okay? Sam told me Hadley decided not to go to boarding school, and I imagine her decision went over like a lead balloon with her mother."

"Gloria was not pleased, to say the least, but it could've been worse. I think I bore the brunt of her anger, which I'm hoping will spare Hadley some grief. But, I have to admit, Gloria was pretty insulting to me. She suggested...no, that's not right...she literally said I only came to Rivers Bend to mooch off her, and live in her 'fabulous home' rent-free. As if. Do I look like the kind of person who wants to live in a giant, energy-suck of a house like that one, with only one other person? Honestly, the whole town could live in it, and still never see each other."

Magda shook her head, and glanced over at Lily as she reached for a package of granola bars to tuck into the gift bag she held. "No. You don't look like the type of person to want your sister's lifestyle. And I've gotten to know you well enough to know you are not the type of person to sponge off her sister that way. It shows Gloria doesn't appreciate at all the sacrifices you made to uproot yourself and move here to take care of Hadley."

"Exactly!" Lily reached for a map to put in the bag she was filling, but it was at the other end of the table, and she couldn't reach it, so Magda passed it down to her. "Thank you—both for the map, and your kind words. I mean, it's not like it's been awful here. I love Had, and I like my new job, and the town, and, of course—"

"Jason." Magda nodded sagely as she interrupted.

Lily felt her cheeks flame up, and knew she didn't look nearly as lovely as Magda had when she'd blushed so delicately a few minutes earlier. "Right. Jason is part of it. Not that Gloria approves of him either."

Magda waved her hand dismissively, and then grabbed a tiny bottle of shampoo and shoved it into the bag. "Please. You know my feelings on the Jason situation—Gloria is so jealous of your relationship; her hair might turn green."

The housekeeper, Mrs. Wilson, bustled into the kitchen, carrying a platter of cookies. "These were left over after today's group checked out, would you girls like some?"

"We're not exactly girls anymore, Mrs. Wilson," Lily said with a smile.

Mrs. Wilson put the plate on the table between them and made a rude noise. "Please. You will always be girls to me. Wait until you're my age; you'll still be calling Hadley and Sam girls, mark my words. Do either of you want a cup of tea to go with your cookies?"

Magda raised her hand. "I do. Thanks, Mrs. W."

"Me too, but I can help you make it," Lily offered, as she slid her chair back to stand.

The older woman stilled her chair, by placing one hand firmly on the back of it. "You will do no such thing. You're here to help Maggie. I'd be happy to get your tea."

"Thank you." Lily lowered her bottom back onto the seat and got back to work, filling another gift bag.

"You two looked serious when I came in the room. Are you solving the problems of the world in here while you work?"

"We were discussing my sister," Lily said.

"Ah," Mrs. Wilson nodded as she filled the kettle at the sink. "She's a tough one—no offense."

"None taken. And she is. Family can be rough," Lily said.

"Tell me about it," Magda said. "You haven't met my grandmother yet, but she's a real pill."

"Is she coming to the wedding?" Lily asked.

"Believe it or not, yes, she is. I wasn't even sure I wanted to invite her, but Jeff and I talked it through, and she is the only family I have left. I need to make an effort to reconcile with her. She has made some attempts to reach out too, so hopefully, things will go smoothly that weekend."

The kettle began to rattle, and steam came out of its' spout, before the shrill whistle pierced the air in the kitchen. Mrs. Wilson pulled it off the burner, and the harsh sound gradually slowed to a stop. "We'll all help to keep your grandmother busy and happy while she's here for the wedding," Mrs. Wilson said. Although, the determined set of her broad shoulders, and the grim expression on her face didn't exactly say 'happy'. More like…Maggie's grandmother better be happy, or else!

"Thanks, Mrs. W. I think she'll only be here for the actual wedding, which will help ease the tension a bit. I'll be kind of busy that day." Maggie winked and put the gift bag she'd just finished at the end of the table with the others they'd completed.

"You don't need any added stress on your wedding day," Lily said, her tone brooking no argument. "We'll all help with your grandmother. My mom said she actually knows her from Connecticut. They went to the same country club, when my mom was a teenager, so Mom said she can spend some time with her too."

Magda smothered a laugh. "Nothing against your mom, Lily, but she is as different from my grandmother as the sun is from the moon. I would love to be a fly on the wall when they were talking. I can't imagine my grandmother's reaction to your parents' van."

Lily laughed, and even Mrs. Wilson loosened up and smiled at the mental image of Magda's oh-so-formal, old-money granny and her own hippie parents and their psychedelic van. "I'll try to get a picture of them with my phone for you," Lily offered with a grin.

"Seriously, though, I'm thrilled your parents can come. I really loved them when they were here at Christmas. And it's nuts our mothers knew each other, back in the day. Not well, but your mom said they'd gone to some of the same functions, back before they both 'ran away to find their own authentic selves', was how I think your mom described it."

"That sounds like my mom." Lily smiled fondly. "I'm excited to see my folks again too. The timing turned out to be perfect; they've been following that music festival around the southern states, and they're going to be passing through Virginia on their way back to Connecticut the weekend of your wedding. Thanks for letting them camp here again too. I promise to make sure they keep their rig parked somewhere far away, so it doesn't show up in the background of your wedding photos."

Mrs. Wilson put two steaming cups of tea in front of them, "Let me get the milk, sugar, and honey, and you girls can fix these the way you like."

They both thanked her, and Magda got back to the previous topic, "I don't know, Lily, I'm thinking I might ask them if we can pose for a couple of pictures by it. After all, it is your stepfather's artwork on the van, and he's a respected artist."

Lily laughed. "But the trippy solar system on the purple van is not exactly one of his more renowned pieces. Although, it would make for a funny wedding picture." She raised her teacup in a toast. "Here's to making your wedding day a happy one, filled with love and our wacky families."

"It will most definitely be one to remember," Magda clinked her cup to Lily's and looked so happy Lily felt her own spirits lighten just looking at her friend's beaming face.

\*\*\*\*

"Hiya, man. Good to see you!" Jason called out over the cheers of the crowded sports bar, as the Capitals scored another goal. He sat on the stool next to Ty at the bar, and gestured to the bartender. "Sorry I'm late. The vet was checking out one of the horses, and he was running late."

"No problem. I've been watching the game. Caps are up by one."

"Jason Braden, as I live and breathe, I haven't seen you for weeks," the bartender said as he swiped at the bar in front of Jason and put down a cocktail napkin with a flourish. "What can I get for you?"

Jason pointed with his head toward Ty's beer bottle and said, "I'll have one of those."

The bartender popped the top on a bottle and placed it on the bar in front of Jason. "Where have you been, dude? There are rumors some woman took you off the market, but I don't believe them for a minute."

"It's all true, man."

The bartender staggered back and clutched his chest. "Say it isn't so! The mighty Jason Braden has fallen off his throne as the playboy king of Virginia?"

Jason smiled, but rolled his eyes. He jerked his thumb at Ty and said, "Ty is dating someone too, why aren't you busting his chops?"

Ty laughed as the bartender shrugged off Jason's question. "Because it isn't a newsflash Ty is off the market. He's the serious relationship type. Ty's not a man-whore."

"Neither am I!" Jason protested.

"Not anymore," Ty amended to the bartender's amusement.

"You two fight this one out—I've got other customers to tend to," he said as he walked to the other end of the bar.

"Is that really what people think—I'm a man-whore?" Jason asked his old friend.

Ty shrugged. "Some of them, but you can't worry about what other people think; I didn't think of you like that."

"I care about what Lily thinks, and I don't want her out in the world with people saying crap like this to her."

"She knows the real you; she won't listen."

Jason shook his head once and lifted his bottle to his lips. He swallowed and said, "I sure hope not."

Ty squinted at him, and he felt like a bug under a microscope. "You're really worried, aren't you?"

"Things are going good with us, but we've been in our own little bubble world. I know her half-sister doesn't approve of me, but I didn't realize the population at large doesn't either."

Ty put out his hands palms up and said, "Screw the world at large. They don't know you. Lily does."

"How would you feel if people were talking shit about you to Grant?"

"Not great, I guess, but I'd have to trust in him and what we have together."

"Where is he tonight?"

"Thursday is the night his store is open late, so he's at work. What's Lily up to tonight?"

"She's at the Retreat, doing some kind of bridal stuff with Maggie. Stuffing gift bags for the out-of-town guests, or something."

"I'm not saying you were a man-whore before, but I feel like you have made great strides toward a mature relationship, Jase. Before Lily, if a girl you were sleeping with told you she was doing something wedding-related for a friend, all anyone would've seen was ass and elbows as you ran away as fast as you could, before she got any ideas about you and weddings."

"Very funny," Jason rolled his eyes and took a swig of beer.

"Seriously, you never even bring a date to a wedding, because you think weddings put ideas"—he made air quotes—"into your date's head."

"Whatever."

"So, the words 'Lily' and 'wedding' in the same sentence don't send you into a complete and total anxiety attack. In-ter-est-ing." Ty pronounced every syllable of the last word. "Are you ready to settle down with this woman?"

Jason choked on his beer and sputtered. "What? No. I mean maybe…someday, but we're not there yet. Hell, we've only been dating since Thanksgiving! Give me a break. Are you ready to marry Grant? Because you two have been seeing each other around the same amount of time."

"I've thought about it."

"What?" Jason felt as though his eyes were going to bug out of his head. "You have?"

"Sure," Ty nodded. "I knew Grant was the one the first moment I saw him. You were there—you know."

"I know you looked like a total goober; I didn't know you felt like he was the one."

"When you know, you know. You know?"

"Very eloquent. You must dazzle them in the courtroom, counselor." Jason jokingly punched Ty's bicep.

"So, you don't feel the same way about Lily? That she's the one for you?"

Jason's collar suddenly felt two sizes two small. He

tugged at it and drank some beer. Was Lily the one? Was there such a thing as one person for everyone? He'd never really believed in fairy tales.

"Sorry, Jase. I didn't mean to freak you out, I was just asking."

"Freaked out? What makes you think I'm freaked out?" Jason mentally cursed the squeak in his voice, as he asked the question, because it gave away the fact he was, in fact, freaked the hell out by Ty's question. He liked Lily a lot. Cared for her pretty damned deeply, as a matter of fact. But did he see a future with her?

His heart pounded as he realized lately when he imagined his future, Lily was always there by his side.

When the hell had this all happened?

Chapter 27

"The girls are dropped off at their slumber party at Madison's house, so let Magda's farewell to single life party begin!" Lily announced as she entered Bethanne's living room and threw her hands in the air.

"Woohoo!" Heather hollered from across the room, where she balanced a tray of pretty, orange-colored cocktails. "Welcome to the party, Lily—grab yourself a drink and join in the festivities!"

Lily made her way to Heather, but stopped to give the guest of honor a hug.

"Thanks for dropping off Sam at her party for me, Lily. And thanks for coming to help me celebrate. Although, I like to think of it less as a farewell to my single life, and more as a celebration of my new life to come with Jeff."

"That's a good way to look at it," Bethanne said with an approving nod, and sipped her cocktail. "I couldn't wait to marry Cisco."

Lily reached Heather's side, and took one of the glasses off the tray. "What are these?"

"My version of an Aperol Spritz. Prosecco and Aperol, which is an orange-flavored liqueur, topped with some club soda. It's to ease us into the evening's festivities."

"And it's pretty," Lily added, the bubbles tickled her nose as she took a sniff of the aromatic cocktail.

She closed her eyes and enjoyed the spicy, orange scent of the drink, before taking a sip.

"So are you and my other brother going to be next down the aisle?" Heather asked just as Lily drank.

The bubbles burned her throat as she choked on her drink, and it threatened to come out in an epic spit-take. She swallowed. Hard. "What the actual hell, Heather? Don't do that to a woman when she's drinking."

Heather shrugged and looked completely unrepentant. "Sorry. Just asking. It seemed like a logical question."

"And one we were all kinda wondering about, to be honest." Jason's oldest sister Deidre patted Lily's back and reached around her to grab a glass off the tray of cocktails.

Lily's jaw dropped, as she surveyed the room. "Seriously? You all have been thinking about Jason and me getting married?"

"Well, yeah," Bethanne said.

"Me too," Magda sat next to Bethanne on the sofa and nodded in agreement.

"Me three," Jason's mother raised her hand with a sheepish grin on her face.

"*Et tu*, Joyce?" Lily asked.

"Sorry, sweetie, but I've never seen my youngest son act the way he does with you. The thought you might be my daughter-in-law one day soon, has crossed my mind."

"But we've only been seeing each other a couple of months," Lily said as she sank into the chair that was, fortunately, behind her, given that her legs suddenly felt like they were made of overcooked spaghetti.

"Time doesn't matter in affairs of the heart," Mrs.

Wilson, the Retreat's housekeeper who was here as a guest tonight, jutted her bottom lip out and nodded sagely.

"It really doesn't," Magda agreed. "I knew super-fast Jeff was the one for me. Way faster than I even wanted to admit to myself."

Heather patted Lily's shoulder as she walked past to place the tray on the coffee table. "Me too, with Mick. Both times. I think our girl here needs to move from the denial phase to the acceptance phase."

"I'm accepting," Lily said calmly, before leaning forward in the seat and yelling, "I'm accepting of the fact you're all fricking nuts!"

"You mean you two aren't over-the moon crazy about other?" Deidre waved a dismissive hand at Lily. "Please. Give me a break."

Lily took a healthy slug of her drink, and looked at the empty glass in wonder. Where had the whole thing gone? Oh, yeah, she'd been nervously drinking it ever since the topic of conversation turned to her frigging marrying Jason. "Can we please discuss something else?"

"Sure," Heather said with a smile. "Drink up, ladies! We've got to get a move on now…our next stop on the Fun Train awaits. Dinner in Leesburg. And then I hope you've all got your dancing shoes on, because we're clubbing afterwards."

"Some of us are clubbing, and some are going home to sleep," Joyce said firmly.

"No. We're *all* going clubbing, and I for one can't wait!" Mrs. Wilson said as she tipped her glass back and drained the last of her Aperol Spritz. "Y'all heard Heather—let's get the Fun Train rolling!"

****

The next morning, Lily dragged herself into the kitchen in search of the biggest glass she could find to fill with water to guzzle, in an attempt to soothe her parched mouth. Maggie's bachelorette party last night was fun, but she was hurting today. At least Jeff was taking Hadley with Sam to the Braden Farm to go riding. She had a little time on her own, to nurse the pounding headache. She hadn't felt this bad, since after Heather's wedding in Vegas. Apparently, Braden family wedding festivities were things she needed to approach with caution. They might be fun, but the day after was a killer.

She grabbed a glass, which was roughly the height of the Empire State Building, and scrunched up her nose as she blinked in the glare of the reflection of the overhead light on the gleaming stainless steel refrigerator, and tried to figure out how to fit it in the ice dispenser. She finally twisted it into a position that worked, and winced at the clatter of the cubes tumbling into the glass—was the ice machine always this loud? Once the water filled up, she took a long, drink and sighed in relief. Good stuff.

She frowned at the sound of the front door opening and closing. Had Hadley decided to come straight home? If so, why? Hopefully, her niece hadn't hurt herself riding, or gotten sick at the slumber party the night before.

"Had, is that you? Is everything okay? I didn't expect you home for a few hours."

High heels clicked across the marble entryway, and Lily screwed up her mouth. It couldn't be Hadley, as she would be coming home in riding boots.

The kitchen door swung open to reveal one of the last people she felt like facing with this morning's hangover.

"It's me," Gloria announced.

Her half-sister was immaculately dressed, as always, in a winter-white pantsuit, mile-high heels, and a lilac-colored blouse that drew attention to her cat-shaped eyes with their unusual lavender color. Most of the world didn't realize they were from contact lenses, but Lily knew and wondered if Gloria's elderly husband was disappointed the first time he saw her actual hazel eye color.

Gloria put one perfectly manicured hand on her hip. Her nails were painted a pale pink, and done in that long, pointed shape, which was the style at the moment. Lily had the fleeting thought it would be impossible to do anything for yourself with those nails. Guess it wasn't a problem for Glo, who was always willing to let other people do everything for her.

She looked Lily up and down, with an expression one usually reserved for dead animals and garbage. "What are you wearing?"

Lily tugged her gray sweatshirt, emblazoned with the name of the school where she worked, in an attempt to cover her butt in the faded, black leggings she'd thrown on to come downstairs. "I came down to grab a glass of water, I was going back to bed."

Gloria's gaze drifted to the clock on the wall, and she raised her shaped eyebrows. "At eleven o'clock in the morning? Are you hungover? Where is my daughter?"

"Hadley had a slumber party last night, and Jeff Braden brought Sam and her to ride horses after it."

301

"I notice how you're avoiding the other question I asked."

"Fine. Yes, I'm a little hungover. Last night was Magda's bachelorette party, it's not like this an everyday occurrence."

Gloria dropped her bag, which Lily suspected cost more than her teaching job paid in a year, on the marble island. "It better not be, since you are currently my child's guardian."

"I wasn't expecting you this morning." Lily decided a change of subject might be the safest way to keep the peace. "Are you back for your husband's additional medical tests? I hope everything is okay." And she really did. Gloria's husband seemed like a nice man, albeit a few decades older than her sister.

"Some heart irregularities. They are going to do further tests this week."

Gloria sank onto one of the tall stools at the island, and dropped her veneer long enough for Lily to glimpse some true emotion. And what she saw there shocked her. Gloria looked tired and worried. About someone other than herself. Huh.

"Let me make you a cup of tea," she offered.

"That would be lovely, thank you." Gloria sighed.

As Lily gave herself a mental shake, to get rid of the lingering cobwebs on her brain, she pulled the kettle off the stovetop, and filled it at the sink. "I don't mean to pry, but are things serious?"

"Serious enough to make us fly across ten time zones again for more tests." Gloria heaved a sigh, and her face crumpled and showed her actual age. "My darling Walter might have to make some real changes to his lifestyle. He might have to resign his ambassadorship and retire."

Lily put the kettle on the stove, and turned the knob until the soft whoosh indicated the burner had activated. She picked up her glass, and took a long drink. "I'm sorry. I know he enjoys his work, but retirement might be nice."

"We would be able to move back to civilization," Gloria conceded with a small smile, which quickly disappeared as she sighed again. "But without his work, I worry Walter will lose his vitality. However, the doctors think it might be too much for him, at his age, and with his heart issues. We'll have to wait and see what the doctors say after the tests this week at Johns Hopkins."

"That's one of the best hospitals in the world," Lily said. Located near her previous home in Baltimore, she knew people traveled from all over the world for medical treatment at Hopkins.

"It is. I have every confidence in his doctors."

Lily felt a wave of sympathy for her sister, which was unexpected and unusual. She smiled warmly at her and said, "But it's still scary to see a loved one go through all these tests. I'm sorry, Gloria."

"Thank you. It is scary, to see him in a hospital bed. He looks so old and vulnerable, it breaks my heart."

"You really love him?" Lily asked with amazement. Maybe if she was firing on all cylinders this morning, she wouldn't have been so undiplomatic, but she was a little muzzy-headed, and had blurted out her thought before she could stop it.

The kettle whistled, and she pulled it off the stove, and busied herself preparing Gloria's tea.

"Of course I do. I married him, didn't I?" Her sister's voice was once again formal, distant, and a little irritated with her. Looked like any little progress they'd made had been lost with her rash words.

She slid the teacup in front of her sister and said, "I'm sorry. That was really rude; I shouldn't have said it."

Gloria accepted the tea and apology with a slight grimace. "It's all right. Given the way you were raised, I should expect occasional bad manners from you. And I have to admit, just between us, Walter and I grew closer living in that god-forsaken outpost. It bonded us, in a way I haven't experienced with any of my other four husbands."

They both sipped their beverages in silence for a few moments. Gloria spoke first.

"I'm sorry I missed Hadley this morning. When will she be home?"

"Probably not until later this afternoon, but if you want to head over to the Braden's farm, you can see her there."

"Maybe I will. I did want the chance to speak to her in private though. I want to discuss her decision about the school with her."

"Are you going to try to convince her of the error of her ways?" Lily couldn't keep the sarcasm from her voice.

"I do think it's a mistake to pass up the opportunity to attend this school. She'll meet all the right people there, to provide her with the future she deserves."

Lily snorted. "Right. Unlike me with Jason."

"I don't just mean romantically. She'll make contacts there that will stand her in good stead personally and professionally for the rest of her life." Gloria put her teacup down and leaned forward toward Lily. "I know you think I'm ridiculous and old-fashioned, but the world is a difficult place, and I want my daughter to have all the advantages she can get to face it. It seems foolish to me, to pass up any opportunity you have to improve your situation."

"Maybe Hadley doesn't think her situation needs improving."

"You seem to think very little of me, and my feelings for Hadley, but I only do what I do, because I want what's best for her."

Lily had never thought of Gloria's actions in those terms before, and it was a revelation that left her gob smacked. "I never realized you felt that way."

Gloria smoothed her hair and rolled her eyes. "You never realized I love my daughter? Thank you very much. Very flattering, indeed."

"You don't show your true feelings very often—" or ever, but Lily wasn't in the mood to fight with her half-sister today, so she left that part of her thoughts unspoken—"I guess I don't know you all that well, but we've never been close—"

"For me, we were. When our parents were married, I was closer to you than I was to anyone," Gloria interrupted.

"Really?" That was news to Lily, who had always felt a distance from Gloria, which was caused by more than the difference in their ages.

"Of course. When your mother married my father, and had you, I was thrilled to have a baby sister."

"You were?"

Gloria's veneer slipped and she slapped the

countertop so hard the bone china teacup rattled on its saucer. "Yes! Why is this all so shocking to you?"

"Because you never seemed to approve of my mother and me."

"When your mother left my father, she changed. She said it was her true self coming to the surface, but to me she was another person. A stranger. And you got more like her and less like me every time I saw you. Then she met Tommy, and you settled in Westport. You had your new life, and it was so different from mine, and yes, I guess you're right. We grew apart. But, you've always been my baby sister, and you could afford to live a much different lifestyle than you do. I want the best for you."

"And being a teacher and dating Jason Braden doesn't measure up to your standards of what's best."

"No. You're right, they don't, but you seem to be happy." She looked her little sister up and down, and wrinkled her nose in distaste. "Well, not at this particular moment in time. Right now, you look dreadful."

"Thanks."

Gloria rolled her eyes, and lifted her teacup. "But, most of the time you seem happy with your choices, so I suppose I should try to accept them, even if I think they are remarkably short-sighted and foolish."

"Thank you." This time, Lily's gratitude was sincere, it was a major concession from Gloria, even if she did phrase it in the most insulting way possible. Baby steps. She couldn't expect Gloria to become a good person in an instant, like Scrooge at the end of A Christmas Carol. She had to take the small victories as they came, and put in a good word for her niece at the same time, "Do you think you could do the same for Hadley?"

"I'm trying, but she's my daughter, and I want the world for her. Certainly, more than she will find here in Rivers Bend."

"She's happy here, though. At least, she is right now, so could you let her stay here and be happy for the time being? Her feelings could change, and you have enough on your plate right now, without battling with Hadley over this school."

Gloria narrowed her eyes, and frowned at Lily. "And battling with you. You're actually the one I'll be fighting, and Walter's heart troubles have made me realize I don't want to be constantly in combat mode with you, Lily."

"I hate arguing; it goes against the way my parents raised me. They are peaceable people," Lily said.

"You don't even think of our father as your father, do you? You think of Tommy as your father."

Lily shrugged. "Tommy did raise me, and our father had very little to do with me, once my mom left him. But, my point was I hate fighting, and would welcome a truce on this subject."

"Fine, truce. I'll pop over to Braden Farm to see Hadley, but I will not mention the Swiss boarding school." She smiled at Lily, "See how diplomatic I've become since I married an ambassador?"

\*\*\*\*

Lily was getting too old for wild girls nights. It was the middle of the afternoon, and she still didn't have the energy or inclination to do more than sprawl on the sofa in the family room, binge watching a reality show.

She heard the distant thump of the back door, and

her niece's voice called out, "Hi, Aunt Lily. I'm home."

Hadley's voice drew closer as she spoke, and the rumble of Jason's deep voice was right at the doorway to the family room, when he said, "Hey, Lily. I'm here too. I gave Hadley a ride home, thought I'd save you the trip."

"Thank you so much, Jase, I appreciate it."

"And thank you, Aunt Lily."

Her brows drew together, and her smile grew puzzled as she turned from Jason to Hadley. "Thank me for what?"

"Whatever you said to my mom to get her to back off about me moving to Switzerland. She stopped by to see me, and didn't mention it once. It was like a miracle. She said she'd come here first and saw you, so I assumed you had something to do with it."

Jason flopped on the sofa next to her, and gave Lily a quick peck on the cheek.

"I'm not sure I can take all the credit for her change of heart, but I'm glad it's worked out for you, sweetie."

"If I wasn't so sweaty and stinky from riding, I would come over there and hug you, because I'm fairly certain it was you. I'm going to run up and take a shower, and call Madison to tell her the good news. Sam was there, and couldn't believe her ears, when Mom just talked about other stuff like a semi-normal mother." Hadley turned to walk out of the room, and stopped to call over her shoulder, "Mom is sending a car for me in the morning to take me down to D.C. for brunch with Walter and her. Hope that's okay."

"She's your mom, Had, of course it's okay. I'm feeling pretty lazy, so I'm thinking pizza from

Mancini's for dinner tonight. Sound good to you?"

"Sounds great!" Hadley said as she ran up the winding staircase in the front hall.

"Oh, to have that kind of energy still," Lily sighed.

Jason toed off his boots, and stretched out on the chaise of the sectional sofa next to her. "I don't think you can blame your lack of energy on age, so much as tequila. I heard about your wild bachelorette night from Jeff, when he brought Sam over to ride with Hadley this morning. Y'all really painted the town red last night."

She groaned. "Don't mention the 'T' word to me. Mrs. Wilson announced she'd never done tequila shots, and the next thing I knew we were all doing them. That woman is wild when you get her out of the Retreat's kitchen."

"I always suspected she had it in her."

"She does. And then some."

They watched the television in silence for a few moments. Jason frowned at the screen, "Aren't these women supposed to be friends? They're being mighty mean to each other."

"Yeah. My friends and I usually get along a lot better than these ladies."

"Usually?"

Lily squirmed. "Last night, they were all being a little pushy about our relationship."

Jason gestured between them. "Our relationship?"

"Yep. Not to freak you out or anything, but they all have us married off already. I tried to tell them we've only been going out a few months, but they wouldn't back down."

"Ty was the same way, when we went out the other night to watch the hockey game. What is up with everybody poking their noses in our business?"

Lily bumped him with her shoulder. "It's the Rivers Bend way. I should think a native son, like you, would be all too familiar with it. Maybe even participated, a time or two."

"Maybe I have, but I'll tell you what, it's a lot more fun to be the one doing the poking than being the one who gets poked. Why does everyone think they know more about us than we do?"

Lily shrugged. "I don't know."

"I wish everybody would let us live our lives the way we want to, and back the hell off this marriage talk."

"Right?" Lily agreed without hesitation, and they both fell silent again when the commercial stopped and the TV show started up again, with the women bringing up old arguments and fighting them all over again. Her mind wandered from the show, as Lily mulled over Jason's vehemence. Yeah. She agreed, it was too soon to be considering marriage, but she still felt a little insulted when Jason acted like it was the craziest idea he'd ever heard. If she was going to be totally honest, she did sometimes ponder a future with Jason—it wasn't that farfetched. Was it?

Jason put his arm around her, and she curled into his side. They fit together like two puzzle pieces. He felt right.

And warm.

And hard-bodied.

He felt pretty damn good. She pressed a kiss to the firm, well-muscled chest under his soft, flannel shirt, and felt Jason's lips brush against the top of her head. And just like that, the flames between them burst to life, and she was in his arms, pressed beneath him on the chaise, as he kissed the stuffing out of her. His lips were everywhere, her eyes, her nose, her lips. When they moved to her throat, she knew he'd feel her pulse pounding at his touch, and didn't care. But, when his lips moved a little lower to her breasts, and his hand lifted the bottom of her sweatshirt, she put her hand over his. He stilled instantly.

"How long is Hadley going to be in the shower?"

"Not long enough for this to go any further. I'm sorry," Lily answered.

"It's okay. I'm getting to know the drill of dating a woman who's guardian of a child, and spontaneity is not part of the game plan. But, y'know, I kinda like it; the waiting helps build anticipation. Later, though…"

She smiled. "Later, definitely."

He rolled off her, and sat back up against the back of the chaise, keeping his arm around her the way it had been before things got heated. Lily snuggled back in against him, and they went back to watching the show.

Sure. Jason knew the drill, and he said he was okay with it, but it didn't mean he liked it. And maybe his annoyance with people speculating about the two of them getting married, was he didn't see the same future for them Lily did, in her secret heart-of hearts. And didn't that notion just suck eggs?

Chapter 28

"I do not want a bachelor party," Jeff said in a voice that left no room for argument.

Jason was a younger brother though, so he firmly believed there was always room for argument with Jeff. "Magda had one, and by all accounts it was wild. It's only fair you have one too."

"No."

Jeff held open the door to the Nosh Pit, and gestured for Jason to go in ahead of him.

If he thought it would shut Jason up, his brother didn't know him at all. "Why should the women have all the fun? Don't you want to mourn the end of your single days?"

They ordered their lunches from the young girl behind the counter, and waved to their sister, Deidre, who was preparing food in the open kitchen area behind the counter. Jeff pointed to a two-top table in the corner, and they wended their way through the crowded tables to take their seats and wait for their order.

"No, because I'm not mourning the end of my single days. I can't wait to be married to Maggie."

"Fine, then it will be a celebration of your impending marriage."

"If this bachelor party thing is so important to you, then have one when you get married, but I'm not interested."

Jason pounded the table and the glass salt and pepper shakers rattled against each other. "I am not getting married. Why is everyone acting like I'm getting ready to walk down the aisle?"

Jeff shrugged. "Why is everyone trying to force me to have a bachelor party? Same reason—because we live in Rivers Bend, and are surrounded by busy bodies." He grinned and winked, before correcting himself. "I mean, we're surrounded by people who love and care for us, and are interested in our lives and wellbeing."

"Number Twenty-seven is up," the young woman behind the counter called out to the crowd.

"That's us. I'll get it." Jeff's chair scraped against the floor as he pushed it back to stand up to retrieve their order.

His brother might be right, but everyone was a little too interested in his life for his liking. Jason rubbed his temples, and wondered why everybody couldn't mind their own damn business.

Jeff slid the tray on the table, and handed out their lunches.

"Thanks," Jason said as he accepted his Virginia baked ham and Swiss on rye bread. He grabbed his soda off the tray, and hit the table with his straw, to poke it out of its paper wrapper.

Jeff sat back down, took a big bite of his turkey sandwich, and while his mouth was full, Jason said, "Not to beat a dead horse, but I'm pretty sick of people bringing up this whole marriage thing with Lily. She said the other women were bugging her at Maggie's bachelorette party too. Things are good between us right now, why are people interfering?"

Jeff swallowed, and swiped at his mouth with a paper napkin. "It's the first time you've been serious about someone—"

"And that's another thing…everyone keeps saying shit like that to me! Lily and I have only been seeing each other a few months."

"That's a few months longer than you've ever dated anyone else. I can't answer for the whole town, but I know I thought it meant you two were serious. Aren't you?"

"No! Yes…I don't know. Why do I have to define it?" Jason took a bite of his sandwich, and glared across the table at his brother while he chewed.

"Don't shoot the messenger, man. You asked why people are thinking that way, and I answered you. You might want to ask yourself why the question pissed you off so bad."

"I feel rushed. Pressured. Like I'm wearing a necktie that's tied too tight."

"Then I think you should try to ignore everyone as best you can, and move at your own pace."

Jason snorted. "Easier said than done in Rivers Bend. The residents of our fair town are not easily ignored."

Jeff bobbed his head. "Truth. But, if their chatter is coming between you and Lily, and you're both happy where you are, then you have to learn how to ignore the talk. Try to remember it's coming from a good place. You seem happy, and people want that for you."

"I guess," Jason munched a salt and vinegar chip as he thought over his big brother's words.

"Here's your chance to get some practice ignoring the talk," Jeff jerked his head toward the kitchen.

"Deidre's on her way over."

"Hiya, boys! Thanks for coming in for lunch." Their oldest sister pulled up a chair from an empty table, and sat down with them.

"Hi, Dee," Jeff said.

"Hey, sis," Jason said before taking another bite of his sandwich.

"I had a lot of fun with Magda and Lily the other night."

"That's what I hear," Jeff said with a chuckle. "I understand tequila was featured."

Deidre shook her head, and whistled low between her teeth. "That Mrs. Wilson is a wild woman when she's out on the town. The younger women didn't know what hit them. I bet Lily was hurting on Saturday."

"She wasn't good for much," Jason acknowledged with a laugh.

"I really like her, Jase. Don't blow it."

"Thank you for the vote of confidence, Deidre."

"I'm sorry, Jason, I didn't mean to insult you, but you don't have a lot of experience with relationships. With women—lots. With a serious relationship with a woman like Lily—zilch. And if you want to get to where Jeff and Maggie are now—"

"Who says I want to be there?" Jason interrupted with an angry wave of his hands.

Deidre held hers up in mock surrender. "Ease off there, baby brother."

"I'm sorry. Sore subject with me."

"Clearly. Look, if you don't want a serious relationship with Lily, I only hope you're being clear with her. She was a little skittish when the subject came up on Friday night too, so hopefully you're both on the same page, but just in case, it's always better to err on the side of being transparent. Let her know you only want fun and games."

"Who said I only want fun and games?" Jason asked, every bit as heatedly as when he'd denied he was serious about Lily.

Deidre shook her head at Jason, and stood up "You get mad when I say you're serious with Lily, and you get mad when I say you're not. I'm going back to the kitchen. Everything in there is easier to understand than you. See y'all at brunch at Mom's on Sunday."

"Sounds good," Jeff said.

"Sorry, Dee. See you Sunday."

As Deidre shook her head and walked back to the Nosh Pit kitchen, Jason sucked up the last of his soda noisily through the straw. When he finished, he slammed the glass on the table. "See what I mean? Everyone keeps prying into my feelings."

"Maybe because your feelings seem to be all over the place. I think—"

Jason made a rude noise and scowled, but Jeff was not deterred.

"I think you're scared by the depth of what you're feeling for Lily, and are lashing out at the rest of us. Just my opinion. Take it how you like."

Jason crumpled up his napkin and tossed it on his now-empty plate. Jeff's words hit a little too close to home for comfort. What he felt for Lily was new to him, and he didn't know what to do with it, but the pressure to get hitched from everyone in town was not helping him process things.

"You might have a point about me needing to learn how to ignore people interfering. I'm going to start by ignoring you."

Jeff just laughed as Jason stood up and carried his empty plate to back to the counter.

\*\*\*\*

"That was an amazing dinner. Thank you," Lily smiled over at Jason from the passenger seat of his truck as they pulled up to his place.

"You're welcome. I'm glad it was okay; I've never been to that restaurant before."

"I went for brunch once, when Roni visited that weekend, but I'd never been for dinner before. It was delicious! And very romantic...you're a man of hidden depths, Jason Braden."

Even illuminated by the dim dashboard lights, she could see Jason's cheeks grow ruddy at the compliment. "I don't know about that."

He stopped the truck next to the renovated barn, which held their offices on the first floor, and his apartment on the second. Hadley had another sleepover—tonight at Sam's house—so, Lily was able to spend the whole night here with Jason. It was a treat for them. Maybe the fact that these times were rare, due to her guardianship of her niece, made them more special. Fingers crossed it was the way Jason looked at it, but Lily feared it wasn't, and he saw the limitations on their alone time as more of a nuisance. She took a deep breath through her nose and released it slowly, as anxiety built at the notion. She drew on what her parents had always taught her. She had to live in the moment, and not worry about the future or the past, as the present was all that was guaranteed. And she had to admit the present moment was pretty darned good. Jason had gotten out of the truck while she did her breathing thing, and now opened the door, and lifted her in his arms, bridal style, out of the truck.

"What are you doing?" she asked through startled laughter.

"Carrying you upstairs."

He jostled her a little as he tried to climb the stairs to his door without putting her down.

"You can't carry me all the way upstairs this way."

"You're right," Jason said, and suddenly the world turned upside down, as he shifted her over his shoulder in a fireman's carry. "This will be easier."

She could hear Jason's dog barking a greeting behind the door at the top of the stairs, but could only see Jason's ass as they made their way upward. Not a bad view for living in the moment, but dinner wasn't setting well with this upside down bounce up the stairs. Lily heaved a sigh of relief, when they reached the top, and Jason stood her on her feet, and the world was right side up once again.

He opened the door to his apartment, and the dog barked a happy greeting, wagging as he pressed against Lily's legs.

She patted Dingo on the head. "Who's a good boy?"

Jason waggled his eyebrows. "Not me. Haven't you heard?"

Lily rolled her eyes. "Trust me; I've heard all the rumors, Loverboy, but I think your prowess is exaggerated."

"Oh yeah?"

"Yeah. Maybe you better prove to me the stories are true."

Dingo whimpered, and Jason grimaced. "Hold that

thought, Moonbeam. I've gotta take my boy out, but I'll be back to defend my honor."

"Don't you mean 'dishonor'?" Lily asked with a giggle.

He patted his leg, to indicate the dog should follow, and said over his shoulder as he went downstairs, "You tell me later."

Lily's heart sped up, and she fanned her face when she heard the door shut behind the man and dog. Jason's cockiness got her motor going like nothing else could. It used to get her on nerves before they were dating, but now she knew he could back up his words with smoking hot actions, his self-confidence did it for her in a big way.

The door opened, and Dingo's claws clicked up the stairs. When he spotted Lily, he ran to her with his tail wagging madly. Jason followed, and the distinct glint in his eyes, and slow smile spreading across his face, told Lily he was just as happy to see her as the dog was. Maybe he was one of those guys who had trouble showing his feelings with words. Maybe like Dingo, Jason showed her with his actions how much she meant to him. His actions were nothing to sneeze at—the man had moves—but, Lily couldn't help but wish he could tell her what she meant to him with words too.

Jason reached her and pulled her into his arms. He slid his hands down to cup her ass, lowered his face to hers, and captured her lips in a kiss that had her world spinning like it had when she was upside down before.

Okay. Maybe words were over-rated.

\*\*\*\*

"This place is a mausoleum." Lily's stepfather, Tommy, observed as he stood outside Gloria's house a few days later.

"It's not our taste, but I wouldn't say it's a mausoleum." Her mom tried to be more diplomatic, but the way her face was scrunched up in distaste gave away her true feelings.

"Please," Tommy tsked his tongue. "It's like the Taj Mahal meets Tara from Gone with the Wind."

"Maybe, but I'm trying to focus on positivity. Gloria was kind to ease up on her previous position, and let us stay here this time. It will be nice to be closer to Lily and Hadley."

"Really, you guys can stay in the house. You don't have to sleep in the camper," Lily said.

"No need. We're happy in our camper," Tommy said with a grin. "But your mom is right; I like being here with you, instead of across town."

"And I will take advantage of using your shower, if you don't mind. The one in the camper is a little cramped," her mom said.

"Especially for two, if you know what I mean." Tommy bumped his wife's shoulder with his.

Lily covered her ears with her hands. "Too much information about my parents."

The backdoor flew open and Hadley ran down the stairs, "I thought I heard y'all pull up—why didn't anyone call me?"

"We were on our way inside to see you," Lily said with a fond smile at her niece, who seemed so much more like a happy kid than she had when Lily arrived in Rivers Bend last spring. Back then, Hadley had been more like a world-weary forty-year old socialite.

Hadley tugged Tommy by the hand. "We've been working on charcoal drawings in art class. C'mon to the craft room and see what I've been working on—I've been dying to show them to you!"

"The craft room?" Tommy mouthed at Lily and Jane as he entered the house behind Hadley.

"There's a room for every conceivable activity in this house," Lily said with a grimace. "Let's get out of this February chill, and I'll make you a cup of tea."

Jane put her arm around her daughter, and hugged her to her side. "That sounds lovely, Lily. I'm so happy to see you again."

Once in the kitchen, Lily moved to the stove to put the kettle on, and Jane shrugged out of her coat, and hung it on one of the hooks next to the back door.

"It's great to have you here, Mom."

Jane's brow furrowed and she frowned as she asked, "Is everything all right here? You look happy on the surface, but I sense a disturbance in your aura."

"I'm happy." Lily finished filling the kettle with water and turned off the tap. She put the shiny, aluminum kettle on a burner, and added, "Mostly."

"Tell me about the non-mostly part. I thought everything was better with the Hadley/Gloria situation."

"It is. Gloria will always be…y'know…Gloria, but her husband's health scare seems to have made her marginally more human."

"The universe can work in mysterious ways; it brought her to this point of illumination."

Lily chuckled. "She's still Gloria, I wouldn't say she's exactly illuminated, but she's a little softer around the edges."

"Is it Jason? Is everything all right with you two?"

Lily raised one shoulder, and then turned her back on her mother's all-seeing eyes. She busied herself taking teacups down from the shelf, and putting tea bags in them. "Things are pretty good with us."

"But…" Jane drew out the word, and waved a hand for Lily to continue.

"But, we haven't said the 'L' word to each other yet. I feel it for him, and I think he feels it for me, but he hasn't said it out loud."

"Have you said it out loud to him?"

"No," Lily admitted.

"Why not? It's not the dark ages, sweetie, the woman can say it first now."

"I know, but you've always taught me love should be freely given, and if I tell Jason I love him, he'll feel pressured to say it back, even if he's not feeling it. I don't want to make my love for him be some kind of burden to him."

"Love is never a burden."

The kettle whistled, and Lily pulled it off the burner and poured it into the cups. The steam rose up to give her a little spontaneous facial, and helped to cover up how hot, red, and uncomfortable this conversation with her mother was making her feel.

"I sense you two are soul-mates, Lily. Your declaration of love won't be a pressure. It will be a gift."

Lily slid the teacup and a honey pot across the island to her mother. Picking up her own cup, she walked around the island and sat next to her mom, and said with a snort of disbelief, "That's me. A gift."

"You are. You've always been a treasure to me."

Tears burned at Lily's eyes. She shoved her glasses up her nose, and blinked away the tears. "Thanks, Mommy."

"I'm sure you are a treasure to Jason too. But you know best, and you shouldn't feel pressured to say it either. When the time is right, all the signs will come together in perfect confluence, and you'll be in harmony. Never fear."

Lily stirred a spoonful of honey into her tea, and blew on it before she took a sip. Sometimes it really rocked to have an aging hippie for a mother, and this was one of those times.

Hadley burst into the room, her face aglow with happiness, "Tommy thinks I have a talent for drawing!"

"That's great, Had."

Tommy entered behind Hadley. "She really does. We're going to work together a bit while we're here in town."

"Marvelous," Jane clapped her hands together and beamed at Lily. "See how the universe puts everything in alignment at precisely the right time? Isn't it beautiful?"

"It is, Mom."

Lily hoped her mother was right, and it would be beautiful for Jason and her too when the moment came to declare her love, and that it wouldn't trigger the beginning of the end of their relationship instead.

## Chapter 29

Lily's phone buzzed, and she reached across the vast mahogany desk to see who it was. Gloria. Huh. Her sister was supposed to be traveling back to the small former Soviet republic, where Walter was the U.S. ambassador. She tapped the phone to answer.

"Hi, Gloria. Is everything all right? I wasn't expecting to hear from you today. Aren't you traveling?"

"I am. We have a layover in London, so I wanted to try to reach you. Is Hadley there?"

Lily wrinkled her nose. If Gloria wanted to talk to Hadley, why didn't she call her daughter directly? "No. I'm sorry; she's not. My folks are in town—thank you again for letting them stay on your grounds—and she wanted to take them to see her ride."

"I thought your mother and stepfather don't approve of domesticated animals?" Gloria's voice dripped with disdain.

"The Braden's farm seems to be bringing them around to the idea. They see how much the animals are cared for and loved there, and it's changing their minds."

"How wonderful of them to stagger out of their cave and join the rest of us in the twenty-first century."

Good thing they weren't on a video call, since Gloria's rudeness about her parents had Lily shaking her fist at the phone on the desk. She managed to keep her voice level though. Hadley called it her 'teacher voice', the one she used when the students were acting up, and she was trying to keep calm and in control of the situation. "I'll let Hadley know you called—"

"I called to speak with you. Not Hadley," Gloria interrupted her.

"Oh. What's up?"

"We spoke with Walter's doctors before we left the States. They think his ambassadorship is too stressful for his heart right now. They recommend, at least a temporary, retirement."

"I'm so sorry, Gloria. I know you were both proud and pleased with his appointment to the position."

She could hear the sigh Gloria heaved through the phone. "We were, but this might be nice too. We're going to be moving back to my house in Rivers Bend, at least for the time being. Walter also has properties in Maine and South Carolina, where we will want to spend time."

"That sounds very nice," Lily said, but wondered what this meant for Hadley, her, and her guardianship of her niece.

"I think it will be. Walter went to buy something to read on the plane, so I can speak honestly; I'm going to miss being an ambassador's wife, just the teensiest bit."

"When will you be back in the States?"

"We need to wrap things up there when we get back, and wait for the temporary replacement to arrive, so Walter can hand over the reins. Then we'll be back, so you'll be free to leave Rivers Bend."

"My contract runs through the school year, so I'll stay in town at least through June. But, I think I'll stay on here after that; I like it here. But don't worry, I'll get my own place and be out of your hair."

The relief in Gloria's voice was evident. "Wonderful!" Her half-sister must've realized that wasn't the most appropriate response, and quickly covered, "I meant it's wonderful you like Rivers Bend so much you want to stay. Not that it's wonderful you'll be moving out of my house, although you had mentioned before you would..." Gloria's voice trailed off and left the sentence hanging.

Lily rolled her eyes so hard, she was afraid they were going to pop out of her head and roll across the desk. "No worries, I'll find my own place as soon as possible."

"It's actually helpful to me you want to stay in town. That way, you can help with Hadley when Walter and I want to travel, or visit one of our other homes."

"Of course. I love Hadley, and am always happy to spend time with her. Do you want to tell her all of this yourself?"

"No—no reason to wait. You can tell her when she gets home. How long are your parents staying?"

"Through the weekend, they've been invited to Jeff and Magda's wedding on Saturday."

"That's right. They're getting married on Valentine's Day. How ticky-tacky."

And Gloria was back in her usual form, ladies and gentlemen...let's give her a hand to welcome her back. "I think it's sweet and romantic."

"You would. Are you going with Jason?"

"Yes and no. He's in the wedding party, so he'll be occupied for a lot of the wedding activities. I'm going to attend the wedding with Hadley and my folks, and meet up with Jason at the reception."

She could hear a muffled announcement on a loudspeaker in the background at the airport, and Gloria said, "They're calling our flight for boarding; I need to find Walter. I'll be in touch. Bye now."

"Bye," Lily said, but it was to dead air, as Gloria had disconnected the call as soon as she was done speaking.

****

"Thanks," Lily accepted the towel Ty handed her, as they dried off after their Thursday afternoon swimming workout in the school's pool. She towel-dried her hair—one advantage to this short style was that it was low maintenance.

"So, you need to move out of Gloria's place?" Ty asked.

"I do, why?"

"Are you moving in with Jason?"

"What? No! It's too soon for that step."

Ty's face reddened. "I don't know it's too soon. Grant and I have been together around the same length of time, and we're...um...moving in together."

"You are? That's great! It's right for you two, but I think it's probably moving a little too fast for Jason. Before me, I don't know if he ever had more than two dates in a row with a woman. We've got to move with baby steps; I don't want to spook him like one of his horses."

Ty threw back his head and laughed. He put his towel around his neck. "You're a wise woman, Lily Davis."

She bowed. "Thank you very much. I know when to pick my battles—Gloria is my sister after all; it taught me that particular lesson early in life."

"Where are you going to live?"

She shrugged, and propped her foot up on the bleachers around the swimming pool to dry off her legs. "I don't know, but I don't think staying with Gloria will be a good option for very long, so hopefully I'll find something soon, maybe even before she gets back to Rivers Bend, so I can move out as she's moving back in."

"Grant is going to move into my place, so his apartment over the Nosh Pit will be available. It's small—"

"It's perfect!" Lily exclaimed.

"—and perfect, evidently." Ty smiled.

"Do you think it will be all right with his landlord?"

"The landlords are Hank and Deidre, whom I suspect are your future in-laws, so I think it's safe to say there won't be a problem there."

"Stop with the in-law talk! I'm happy you and Grant are moving right along with your relationship, but Jason and I aren't there yet, so please stop talking that way."

Ty raised his eyebrows. "Doesn't look like Jason is the only one to be spooked by relationship talk."

Lily busied herself drying off her already dry legs to avoid eye contact. "Maybe he's not."

"No pressure from me." Ty held up his hands.

"Sorry for the over-reaction, but it seems like Jeff and Magda's wedding has everyone in this town in hyper-wedding mode. They can't wait for the next one, and they seem to really, really want it to be Jason and my wedding. Hey! Maybe you and Grant could get married, and take the heat off us."

"Because that's the right reason to enter into marriage—to take the heat off your commitment-phobic friends."

Lily held her towel taut and released one end to flick Ty with it.

He dodged the blow and grinned. "Sorry. Couldn't resist. So what does Gloria's change in situation mean for Hadley?"

"She asked if I could continue to help with Hadley when they want to travel to one of their other homes, since I'll be staying in Rivers Bend. I guess what it really means is Gloria is having her cake and eating it too, but it's okay. I'm happy to spend time with Hadley."

"She's turning out to be a good kid, thanks to her aunt's influence."

Lily blushed and shrugged off the compliment.

"It's true!" Ty protested. "No mention of shipping her off to the Swiss boarding school?"

"Nope. That seems to be off the table for the moment. Thank God."

"I guess I'm off the clock as your attorney then?"

"Looks like, but thank you for all your guidance. I really appreciate it."

"I'm happy things have worked out so well for you. I'm meeting Grant for dinner now, I'll ask him if his place is available and let you know."

"I guess I owe you for this too—I was afraid when Gloria and Walter moved back into her house I'd be sleeping in my office at school and showering in the locker room in the gym."

Chapter 30

Jason straightened the bow tie of Francisco's tuxedo, and leaned back to squint at his handiwork. "It's straight now. You're all set."

"Thank you for the help, *meu amigo*, I've never been good with these ties." Cisco jiggled his leg and checked his watch for the one-hundredth time that afternoon. "Almost show time."

Jeff stretched his long legs out in front of him, and leaned back in the chair where he sat in the groom's waiting room at the church. He appeared to be a man without a care in the world.

"It's your wedding day, man. How can you be so calm?" Jason asked.

Jeff shrugged. "Because I know I'm doing the right thing. Magda is the perfect woman for me. There's no reason to worry."

Jason shook his head once in wonder. "How can you be so sure?"

"Are you trying to make me nervous? If so, it's not working." Jeff wagged his index finger at Jason. "But see, this is why Cisco is my best man and not you."

Jason shoved his older brother's crossed feet with his own. "I'm not trying to make you nervous. I honestly want to understand."

"I don't know how to explain it. I look at Maggie and...I know."

"Know? Know what?"

"That she's the one."

Cisco fidgeted with his boutonniere, and Jason went to his rescue once again. As he adjusted the pin placement, he asked his friend, "Was it like that for you with Bethanne?"

"It was. Well, not at first. I mean, I knew I was attracted to her, but one day, I looked at her across the table—we were having lunch—she was telling me a story about the library, and she laughed. In that instant I knew, without a doubt in my mind, she was the woman for me," Cisco said.

"Huh."

"You don't feel that way with Lily?" Jeff asked.

Jason frowned and shook his head. "I know I have different feelings for her than I did for anyone I've ever dated before, but I haven't had that lightning bolt moment y'all are talking about having with Maggie and Bethanne. Maybe she's not the one."

Jeff's eyes twinkled with deviltry. "Or maybe there's something wrong with you?"

"You can always count on your brother to be a freaking idiot. Even on his wedding day." Jason rolled his eyes.

Jeff threw back his head and laughed.

The minister stuck his head in the room. "Gentlemen, the bride has arrived. Are you ready?"

"Yep." Jeff stood up and said without hesitation.

Jason restrained his brother with a gentle touch to his arm. "Are you sure? Because, if you're not, it's one of the duties of the groomsman to offer you a ride to the border."

"What border? Maryland? We're in Virginia."

"Whatever, man, you know what I mean."

Jeff clasped Jason's shoulder and smiled. "I do, little brother, and I appreciate the offer, but I've never been more ready for anything in my life than I am to go into that church and become Maggie's husband."

\*\*\*\*

Jason entered the church from the side entrance, and stood at the altar behind his brother and Cisco, to await the bride's arrival.

The organist struck a dramatic chord to indicate it was time for the ceremony to begin, and started to play the Wedding March. Jason smiled and looked to the back of the church.

His niece, Sam, came down the aisle first. A little faster than the music, in her eagerness for the ceremony to begin. He knew she couldn't wait for Maggie to officially be her stepmother, and she looked adorable in her version of the bridesmaids' dresses, clutching her bouquet of pink roses.

Heather followed, and then Bethanne. He saw Cisco visibly relax next to him, when his wife appeared and smiled directly at him the whole time she came down the aisle. He glanced at his sister Heather, and saw her smiling at her husband, Mick, who looked at her as if she were the only person in the room.

And then Magda came down the aisle in her poufy, white cloud of a wedding dress, on his brother-in-law Hank's arm. She glanced around the people assembled in the pews, but once her eyes landed on Jeff, her gaze didn't waver from his brother's.

As the ceremony began, he looked into the crowd in the church for Lily. He spotted her in the second row, on the bride's side, between her parents and Hadley.

She must've sensed his attention, because she turned her head to look his way and smiled.

As Jeff and Maggie pledged their vows to each other, he couldn't take his eyes off Lily. She looked beautiful in her blue velvet dress with a lacy shawl-thing around her shoulders. She pushed her funky eyeglasses up on her nose, and seemed to blush under his intense gaze.

All of a sudden, it was like everything in the world clicked into place.

The words Jeff and Maggie said to commit their lives to each other, took on a new meaning to Jason. He'd been to plenty of weddings in his time, but had never really considered what it meant when the bride and groom pledged 'to have and to hold' before. As he looked at Lily—he understood the words for the first time.

He wanted to stand in front of their families and friends one day, and pledge to honor her with all that he had and all that he was.

He loved her.

****

The bridal party had yet to arrive at the Retreat's ballroom to begin the reception, but the party was in full swing without them. Cocktail hour had begun, and Lily held a Manhattan in one hand, and a cheese puff on a tiny napkin in the other.

Ty and Grant held hands and laughed at something her father said. Lily listened with half an ear. She hadn't been able to think about anything except Jason since she'd left the church. He had stared at her in such an intense way during the ceremony. What did it mean?

The band finished the song they were playing, and

the lead singer announced into his microphone, "Ladies and gentleman, please welcome for the first time as husband and wife—Jefferson and Magda Braden!"

Lily joined in the cheering crowd, as Jeff and Maggie entered holding hands and looking like the happiest people in the world. Maggie hoisted her bouquet of red roses in the air.

The rest of the wedding party entered behind them, and Lily saw Jason. He was the only other person in the room not looking at the bride and groom. His head pivoted around, until his gaze lighted on her. His shoulders visibly relaxed and a wide smile spread across his face. She lifted her cocktail glass in his direction, and smiled back, as he took to the dance floor with his sister, Heather, for the first dance.

When it was over, he leaned down to whisper something to his sister, who smiled at whatever he said to her. He stood up, looked straight at Lily, and made his way over like a guided missile toward its target.

"You look beautiful," he said when he reached her side.

"You too," she stammered, a little unnerved by his intensity. Jason was normally nothing if not laidback, and she didn't know what to make of his demeanor.

He took the cocktail, and cheese puff out of her hands, and put them on a nearby table. "Can we talk for a minute? Outside?"

Had the wedding ceremony freaked out her commitment-phobic boyfriend? Was he going to dump her at the reception?

"Okay," she answered, as he took her now free hand, and tugged her through the crowd.

He didn't stop until they were alone on the front

porch of the Retreat. Lily shivered in the night air, and pulled her lacy pashmina a little tighter around her.

"Sorry to drag you out into the cold, but I didn't want an audience for what I'm going to say."

Oh, God. Jason was dumping her. At his brother's wedding reception, no less. This had to be a new low in the annals of getting dumped.

"Can we get this over with?" Lily's teeth chattered a little, more from nerves than cold.

"Yes. I'd like that too," Jason said and mopped at his forehead, as if he were hot, in spite of the nip in the February air.

"Jason, say what you have to say."

"I love you, Lily."

*Wait...What?*

"You love me?"

"I do. With all my heart."

Lily had been so certain Jason was going to break up with her, this sudden turn of events threw her for a serious loop, and her mind spun and no words came out of her mouth.

Jason fidgeted with his bow tie. "I think this is the point where you tell me you feel the same way about me. Or don't...no pressure..."

His words jolted Lily back to the here and now. "I do. I love you too, Jason. So very much."

He whooped and pulled her into his arms. "It hit me like a lightning bolt during the ceremony tonight. I love you, Lily Davis. You are the one woman in the world for me."

"I thought you brought me out here to break up with me."

Jason's eyes bugged out of his head. "No way.

335

Now I've found you, I'm never letting you go. You're stuck with me."

Lily laughed. "Who would've guessed a one-night stand in Vegas would lead us to our soul mates?"

Jason laughed, and lifted her off her feet and twirled her around. "We should've known you wouldn't follow a conventional path. You're an individual—you do things your own way. I love that about you. Hell, I love everything about you. I'm so glad you decided to stay in Rivers Bend."

Lily's unconventional parents and upbringing had always left her feeling a little bit like a round peg in a square hole—like she didn't fit in anywhere. But here, in this town, with this amazing man, she fit. And her heart raced with happiness at the realization.

"Aren't you going to kiss me?" she asked with a laugh.

"You better believe I'm going to kiss you. Every chance I get for the rest of our lives."

And Jason put words to action, and suddenly Lily wasn't cold anymore. She was warm…hot, even.

She was loved.

She was home.

## A word from the author...

My career has been a winding road. I worked in the business world for years, got my MLS and worked in a school library, and am now living my dream as an author. I love to read and write contemporary and fantasy romance.

I live in Maryland with my husband, who is my real-life romance hero. We both enjoy traveling to visit our far-flung family and friends, and spending time on the beach with an umbrella drink and a good book.

Thank you for purchasing
this publication of The Wild Rose Press, Inc.

For questions or more information
contact us at
info@thewildrosepress.com.

The Wild Rose Press, Inc.
www.thewildrosepress.com

To visit with authors of
The Wild Rose Press, Inc.
join our yahoo loop at
http://groups.yahoo.com/group/thewildrosepress/